PRAISE FOR THE WORK OF GEMMA O'CONNOR

'Constantly enjoyable'
The Times

'Full of the tensions of oppressed emotions . . .
A welcome twist on the genre'
Sunday Times

'Grimly convincing . . . Compulsively readable'
Daily Telegraph

'A real writer . . . in the great tradition of Irish
storytellers'
BBC Kaleidoscope

'Eminently readable'
Independent

'Gripping . . . The reader becomes increasingly
entangled'
Irish Independent

TIME TO REMEMBER

Gemma O'Connor

McArthur & Company
Toronto

A TIME TO REMEMBER
McArthur & Company

First Canadian edition

Copyright © 1998 by Gemma O'Connor

Set in 11pt Sabon by
County Typesetters, Margate, Kent

Canadian Cataloguing in Publication Data

O'Connor, Gemma
Time to remember

ISBN 1-55278-077-5

I. Title.

PR6065.C66T55 1999   823'.914   C99-931430-0

McArthur & Company
322 King Street West, Suite 402
Toronto, ON, M5V 1J2

10 9 8 7 6 5 4 3 2 1
Printed in Canada

McArthur & Company
Toronto

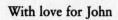

With love for John

In memory
of children killed in wars not of their making,
for ideas they did not understand.

Lay your sleeping head, my love,
Human on my faithless arm;
Time and fevers burn away
Individual beauty from
Thoughtful children, and the grave
Proves the child ephemeral:
But in my arms till break of day
Let the living creature lie,
Mortal, guilty, but to me
The entirely beautiful.

W. H. Auden

The Beginning

During the Second World War

CHAPTER ONE

When I remember that time or think of that place, I see blue butterflies – or were they moths? – rising in clouds in the shimmering heat as we followed each other through the high grass by the river-bank. I see their tiny, delicate, veined wings and I stretch out my hand to touch the glistening velvet. Yet, as my fingers reach out, they disappear, fluttering away in a random jumble of dazed blueness.

The afternoon seems to stretch to infinity. Do I imagine we could hear the sawing of the cicadas that day? Probably not, for it was early June, so I know that my memory has gathered all the days of that summer, and every summer before it, into one single scene. And though I am part of it, I am also a spectator, floating above, looking down. Since, in my recollection, I also see the church spire, I know I am on the far bank of the river. Safe, so I know I must have run away. Which is, after all, what I have always done, or have done since. Forever a spectator, even of my own life.

It was hot that day and the air was still, when Marie-Eulalie led us out of the shade of the trees into the meadow by the river. I see us now in my mind's eye, across the years, as we must have looked to anyone watching from the opposite bank; playing follow-my-leader. First the tiny blonde curly-haired child. She wears a little blue and white candy-striped summer dress with short puffed sleeves whose tight cuffs bite into the rosy flesh of her plump arms. It is tied at the back in a bow which, I seem to remember, is half undone. Could it have remained in that state of half-undoneness all afternoon? The dress is short but her bare legs are hidden by the tall grass, so tall that sometimes the little girl disappears from sight. She is followed by Guy, then Fanny, Edmond, Angel, me and, last of all, Roger, who is the tallest.

We are grumbling at Angel because of Marie-Eulalie. From the start we boys insist the child is too young, that she is a nuisance, that she should be left at home. But Angel says she's promised their mother she'd take care of her little sister, that if she comes with us the child must also. We continue arguing until at last Angel caves in and promises that she will deliver the little girl to their aunt, long before we reach the river-bank. Half an hour, she tells us, is all it will take to tire her out. Then we will ask their aunt, as we pass her house, to let Marie-Eulalie play with her little cousins for the rest of the afternoon.

But when we call, the aunt is not at home. So we play follow-my-leader. The game Angel has dreamed up as a ploy to humour Marie-Eulalie, to cajole her into keeping up when threats fail. We march on towards the river. By then, we have forgotten our irritation and the child is included. She twirls around in delighted triumph and begins to sing. Laughing, the rest of us join in.

What is that song? Sometimes I think I hear echoes of the words, but in the same instant they drift away. I believe, superstitiously, that somehow, if I ever catch the childish phrases, I will have the key to the tragedy. But that is merely obfuscation; other questions also plague me. Did what happened hinge on the decision to let the little one tag along? If she had not been there we could all, somehow, have crossed the river by the tree swing and been away before the trouble started. Even Fanny, who didn't like the rope but was the best swimmer of us all, might have been persuaded to swim across. Or had we boys suggested crossing that way to get rid of the girls once and for all? Were we just being thoughtless? Showing off? Forgetting, in our swagger, that there was no way Marie-Eulalie could ever manage it. Even riding piggyback.

I see the rope hanging from the tall lime tree, swinging to and fro. The boys leaping from it to the opposite bank. I see Angel suddenly lose hold of the rope. We stand aghast, but in a second she comes laughing out of the water. Then everything goes blank. I peer into the far distance, willing myself into the past, into the long cool green space between the lime tree and the bridge. I listen for the sounds but hear only silence. Until I see the great ball of dust come rolling towards me. And the noise, the noise. But I can never see the children.

I start again, endlessly, over and over. I go back to the beginning. Angel is standing outside her house, holding Marie-Eulalie by the hand. I am sitting on the wall, talking to her, trying to charm her with my ponderous wit. In the distance I see Guy

15

and the rest of the gang come whistling towards us along the road . . .

Clouds of pale blue butterflies rise as we walk along. Marie-Eulalie marches in front waving a stick to clear the insects, which then swarm above our heads. Here and there along our path is a scattering of red poppies. The blue butterflies, the red poppies and Fanny's yellow dress. Then the golden-haired child disappears and only the stirring of the grass marks her passage as the bigger children follow after her. I remember thinking that the blue butterflies exactly matched the colour of the child's dress.

Strange, but apart from Marie-Eulalie and Fanny, I cannot remember what the others wore, except that I had borrowed an old white shirt of my father's. It is as if I made a snapshot in my head of the line of seven, child to youth, rising in height so perfectly. The sun, the palomino grass and the pale blue butterflies. Perhaps they *were* moths? I cannot tell. Nor can I tell why I see that scene from afar, for I was there too. I am there still.

The Beginning of the End

CHAPTER TWO

Recognition, when it came, came peculiarly and unexpectedly, when the events of that terrible day had at last begun to fade from my mind. I had finally allowed myself to fall in love and, absurd though it was at my advanced age, it was also utterly delightful. Amy was recently widowed when we met through the machinations of mutual friends. She was ten or more years younger than I but we soon found that we had much in common. For two blessed years we were utterly happy and then, as suddenly as I found her, I lost her. Or perhaps it would be more true to say that I withdrew from her, back to my preoccupation with the past. At the time I was enraged that she called it obsession; for me it was not a choice, rather something I had to do. I know now that she was right.

I remember each detail of those last days we spent together. How could I not? For I never saw her again. One moment she was there, affectionate, companionable; the next she had gone. She walked away and disappeared for ever, after our first and only row. She said she would not compete where she could not hope to win. I am almost driven insane when I think of what might have been, had I not broken the habit of a lifetime.

I rarely attend international conferences since I am neither particularly enchanted with air travel nor the discomfort of staying in overheated hotels, trying to make myself understood in languages I do not speak, eating ersatz food I abhor. I content myself with contributing research papers, encouraging my students to take the podium while I remain in my laboratory, getting on with my work. There are, of course, occasional exceptions. One such was an invitation I received some years ago, to give a keynote lecture at an important symposium in Japan. This I considered an honour as well as international recognition of my work. Nonetheless, that might have been insufficient to tempt me, but when I realized the conference was to be held in Kyoto, a city Amy particularly longed to visit, I agreed. There was also the matter of a couple of first-class return air tickets, which swung the balance. Venal perhaps, but I make no apologies. Twelve hours sardined into an aircraft is no joke, specially with my cardiovascular problems. Immobility and dehydration can seriously damage your health.

My original plan was to attend the conference on the first couple of days only, give my talk and see a few people in the same line of research. Afterwards Amy and I would do a little sightseeing and fly home. But it turned out to be an enormous international gathering of many disciplines, and I found myself more involved and excited than I expected. What I didn't bargain for was that one lecture would change my life; radically and utterly.

On the second evening, a friend from the Netherlands happened to mention that a group in

Oxford was doing some excellent work on the musculo-skeletal system which was reasonably close to my own research. As luck would have it, the leader of this team was scheduled to give a talk, late the following afternoon. Since Amy and I had arranged a visit to the Sacred Spring Garden of Shinsen-en next day, which I was reluctant to cancel, I said I would try to make it if I got back in time. In many ways I wish I had stayed longer in that beautiful, reflective place, but alas I did not. Instead I left my companion to return to the hotel with the rest of the tour, and took a taxi back to the conference hall.

I arrived only a minute or two before the lecture was scheduled to start. In the half-light the auditorium looked vast. Rows of seats, each with a folding writing-flap attached to the arm, horse-shoed a low rostrum. As I entered, a stooped figure mounted the steps to the podium. He was a fidgety individual who fumbled nervously with his notes while he gathered his thoughts. He cleared his throat three or four times and was about to start when he looked up and blinked rapidly against the strong glare of the spotlight which was trained on his face. 'Can you dim that a little?' he asked irritably. Then: 'Is the projector loaded?' From somewhere at the back of the hall a dis-embodied voice answered in the affirmative and immediately the light transferred to the screen behind the speaker, leaving him in half-shadow.

Still he couldn't seem to get started, but con-tinued fiddling with his papers until a crouching figure scurried up from the front row and switched on the lectern reading-light. Effusive thanks from the speaker were interrupted by a member of the audience who asked impatiently if they could begin. Immediately a slide bearing the name of both lecturer and lecture flashed onto the screen.

I had just entered the hall and was standing behind the back row of seats, from where I watched the foreplay with only half an eye. There was an unusually large audience. As soon as I adjusted to the dim light of the auditorium, I looked around for a seat and eventually found one of the very few empty places at the end of the second row from the rear. Crouching, I made my way past the plethora of wires and cables which snaked off in all directions from the powerhouse at the back of the hall. As I fumbled with the armrest, my neighbour turned to me irritably, but apart from several loud shushes, mercifully restrained himself from comment.

Thus I missed the speaker's opening remarks which must have been amusing, since laughter and applause rippled through the room. Though we were in Japan, the lecture was in English, the lingua franca of the scientific world. The lecturer spoke formally and grammatically though he had a strong accent. Strange that I am aware of this in others, since I am told that I too speak my adopted tongue with a strong accent. I cannot hear it in myself and am always surprised when it is remarked upon. To my own ears I sound authentic, indistinguishable from my friends.

Although the subject of the lecture wasn't precisely in my own area of interest it was near enough, and I soon became absorbed. But it went on far too long. The day was hot and the lecture hall, allegedly air-conditioned, was not, and rapidly became stuffy. Within minutes, my impatient neighbour on my left was snoring gently and I have to confess that my own thoughts were beginning to wander.

I do not know at what stage I began to concentrate on the speaker rather than on what he was saying. The rake of the floor was such that I had the illusion that I was above him looking down, and, as in a theatre, I was audience to his actor. He made a dull enough spectacle. Though he had an occasional amusing turn of phrase, his delivery was poor; he seemed more concerned with accuracy than with performance. He seldom looked up and when he did, it was to blink like a blind man. But his illustrations were extremely innovative. It was, in fact, the first occasion I had seen a computer animation of the human locomotor system, and though the technique was simple, perhaps even primitive, it was advanced for the time. To underscore his lecture he superimposed these computer images over slides of well-known paintings. I was enchanted.

I remember with infinite precision the moment when my mind began to spin, spin, spin back to the past. It was as if we were the only two people in the world; that speaker and I. He, with the huge screen behind his head, on which was projected a cleverly faded copy of Fragonard's 'The Swing' as background to a computer animation of a walking figure, so that the smiling girl in the painting

23

and the simulated stick-figure moved back and forth, creating the illusion that both were in motion.

Now, at last, he had my full attention. I was totally mesmerized, not just by the elegant explanation of the function – and interaction – of muscle and ligament, but by the beautiful girl on the swing. I have no idea how the animation was achieved, or even if I imagined it, but the swing seemed to move. Back and forth, back and forth, like a metronome it went. I was vaguely aware of a short burst of spontaneous applause.

But my thoughts were elsewhere. Fully alert now, I stared down at the lecturer and, strangely, at that exact moment he raised his head and seemed to look straight at me. Was it another illusion? His pale eyes stared blindly into the light and I began to tumble backwards in time. The red-gold hair had turned white, but I recognized the face. I leaned forward and must have given an involuntary cry of surprise because he raised his hand to shade his eyes and tried to see where the sound had come from. By now my neighbour had roused himself and began to remonstrate with me again. I brushed him irritably aside and sat back.

My mind had cleared. I did not miss a single other word and by the time the lecture ended I had been won over – in a manner of speaking – to his point of view. I was determined to shift the emphasis of my own line of research. As soon as the applause had died away and the lights came up, I slipped quietly away and began to make discreet enquiries about the speaker, and, more particularly, his field of research.

But that lecture had stimulated more than my professional interest, it had, alas for my personal life, reawakened my own peculiar fixation. For several days I kept it to myself, but on our return flight I described the incident to my love and thus made the second greatest mistake of my life. The day after we got home, Amy left me.

Oxford

1995

CHAPTER THREE

As research funds contracted, the fight for what little there was became ever more aggressive, bitter, then, finally, desperate. There were too many people chasing the same little pot of gold. *Little* was the keyword, since there simply wasn't enough to go around. As independent financial support dried up, university research teams began to contract, then disband. At first Oxford survived, barely, on its centuries-old prestige and endowment, but eventually it too began to feel the pinch.

It was at this point that Professor Paul Forge, who had never before run short of support for his excellent team, suddenly found that they were without the wherewithal to continue for more than a few months. The new National Lottery was universally blamed for squeezing out voluntary donations to the many charitable foundations which had hitherto helped support many small research teams, but now found their own income dwindling. Up until then there had always been some other funding organization or charity to tap, whereas now, all at once it seemed, each dried up. At first Forge was not unduly worried, but, as his applications for grants continued to be turned down, his alarm grew. Uncertainty about his approach turned to self-doubt and he began to lose confidence in his ability as a researcher, as well as fund-raiser. This very quickly seemed to spread to other areas of his life and even his scholarship.

As depression settled over him like thick grey cloud, Paul Forge began to consider retirement. For him this was a novel, if depressing, admission, for he had always hoped to die in harness. Being long widowed, his work and his students were his life and his joy. Now the foundations of his very being quivered beneath him. Worse, he held himself responsible for those of his team whose academic futures were so entirely linked to what they might achieve in those few short years under his guidance.

Guidance was as strong a description as he ever allowed, since he often claimed, a little pompously it must be admitted, that many of his students were brighter than he. This might have been because he would never accept a research candidate unless he or she could demonstrate liveliness of mind, interest and commitment, as well as brains. He never thought of himself as their superior; he was adamant that the young taught him along with themselves, stimulated, stretched him; that he was no more nor less than the conductor of his small orchestra.

Now a bleak, unfunded future stretched before him. True, he could, at a pinch, continue alone but where would be the fun in that? Who then would share his excitement in each tiny step forward? With no-one to take over the reins, to continue the work to which he had devoted his life, retirement began to look like his only real option. He hated the very sound of the word but suddenly there seemed to be no alternative. This was especially daunting because, like many men of his age, he was slowly waking up to the fact that he had precious few interests besides his work.

Then, one sleepless night, he began to get a glimmer of the shape of events. Earlier that day, he'd had an e-mail from one of his ex-students who worked in an American university. Perhaps he had been too depressed and preoccupied when he read it because, irritated by the boy's breezy greeting and few lines of personal gossip, he had overlooked the urgency of the final short paragraph. But now, as he tossed and turned in bed, it popped straight back into his head and would not be shifted. After a few minutes he sat up resignedly, switched on the bedside light and jotted some names on a scrap of paper. Then he stared and stared.

Paul Forge lay back and closed his eyes for a good five minutes before he hauled himself stiffly out of bed and slipped across the cold landing and downstairs to his study. After he found his glasses, he logged onto his computer and reread the previous day's e-mail.

A paper given by George Swinton is claiming your results (ref Swinton/Brüch/Hiller & Molloy, April '97). Much discussion afterwards but never a mention of the Oxford contribution. My own protest made little impact, the speaker sidetracked me so elegantly I didn't realize until too late that I was dismissed out of hand. Any suggestions?

Notice the work has been funded by one of the ECSC (European Committees for Scientific Cooperation). Suggest search ref files on Hiller/ Stevens/Brüch; Brüch/Mackechnie/Hiller; Morland/ Dalbert/Hiller; Hiller/Bach/Lopez. More later . . .

Forge stared at the screen and cursed himself for utter stupidity as he began to make connections which had not occurred to him before. Slowly and painstakingly, he linked the e-mail information with other, apparently unrelated, incidents until the full impact of its references hit him. He paced the room furiously muttering to himself, until suddenly inspired he opened the file of his most recent grant application and read through the names of the funding-committee members. He sat back and, having reflected for a few minutes, logged onto another file, then another, trawling back through the past five years' applications to several different agencies. The sheer amount of work involved in each lengthy submission appalled him anew. Bad enough when weeks, or sometimes months, of work proved successful; but a thorough-going, heartbreaking, waste of time when it did not. Up to now he'd always consoled himself with the thought that at least the preparation of these papers provided him with a carefully annotated reference of both his accumulated results and his projected research for several years into the future. This, he usually argued with himself, was the saving grace if the applications themselves were unsuccessful, for then he had a comprehensive summary of work done and a well-defined and -described way forward. But now he was enraged by the realization that he had, it seemed, also provided this detailed approach for anyone unscrupulous enough to take advantage of his – or her – position on the funding committee. It had simply never before dawned on him that anyone would stoop so low as to plagiarize his ideas before he could publish his work. But now, it seemed, someone most assuredly had.

He threw two columns up on the screen and, one by one, set successful against unsuccessful grant applications for the previous five years. Working faster now, he located each unsuccessful submission of the three-year period before that, which brought him back to 1986–7. As far as he could recollect, it was around this time that the rot had first set in. Perhaps even earlier if there was, as he had suspicions there might be, a systematic effort to do him down. Destroy his life's work. The very thought put him into a state of shock.

Why? Why? Why? What possible motive could there be? His was a fairly esoteric field, hardly one open to major commercial exploitation. Had he been involved in genetic research where the stakes were enormous, attempts at piracy would not be surprising. But his obscure little contribution? Was there something he had missed? He racked his brains but nothing particular came to mind. It was all so preposterous yet so very personal that he began to sweat with anxiety. He felt as if he were slowly opening a tightly folded paper puzzle, each square of which both revealed and destroyed some intimate part of his working life. By the end he would be erased. He closed his eyes wearily and told himself he was being paranoid, that he was inventing a plot from his own, personal disappointments. Yet when he opened the files again and read what was on the screen, the story hadn't changed. The facts were there, staring him in the face. What most astonished him was that he simply hadn't noticed that from the late Eighties the milch cows had begun to dry up, remorselessly, one after another. Now the question which most concerned him was, what had happened then to trigger the decline?

There were sixteen documents which he now copied and dragged into a new file. He stared at the screen, appalled, as he slowly scrolled through the couple of hundred pages, pausing here or there to jot little notes on a pad beside his computer. He repeated this several times, checking and rechecking until his vision became too blurred to continue. He leaned back, passed his hand over his aching eyes, then shuffled off to the kitchen to make himself a cup of coffee.

He would retire. Throw in the sponge. Give up the unequal struggle. Run and hide. After all, there was no need to strive on, he was already beyond the age at which most men willingly give up. His stay of execution had already run out. First they had pensioned him off, but, in tribute to his distinguished career, had allowed him to retain his lab as long as funds and an endless stream of research candidates were forthcoming. Soon the powers that be would, belatedly, realize that his time had come. Of course they didn't know what he himself had almost forgotten. The tiny readjustment of the facts. The neat subtraction of a couple of years when he first presented himself for interview at the university. The lost years he could not bring himself to think about. Could not, would not. Even now. He tightened the belt of his dressing-gown irritably.

Dawn broke as he waited for the kettle to boil. Though it was not yet five o'clock, the summer sun rose majestically, its rose-red light transforming the shabby kitchen furniture with its warm glow. He sat moodily by the window as he sipped the strong black coffee, all the while tapping his fingernails on the chipped white paint of the sill. Outside, the birds were in full voice. His eyes ran pleasurably over his garden, snipping at a shrub here, planting a contrasting colour there; shaping, adjusting, improving. Was it at its best in June? he wondered. Or March, or September? He could not tell: as each season yielded the changes planned in his head, he was constantly surprised and delighted with the accuracy of his vision. He smiled ruefully. Could he content himself with these small acres? Well, just under half an acre to be precise. Would cultivating – recultivating – this already almost perfect space be enough to exhaust his active life? In his mind he tore up the curvaceous lawn and sank a long rectangular pond. Lines of hidden fountains on either side formed perfect transparent parabolae, in imitation of the water garden of the Alhambra. He rearranged his spectacular collection of lilies, dropping clumps here, then there.

'It would keep me amused for only a few

months,' he mocked himself aloud. He guessed that the pleasure he derived from gardening lay partly in the fact that there was never quite enough time. That thieving sly hours from his work added a tiny, pleasurable *frisson* of guilt without which his interest would quickly pall. He drained the last of his coffee and opened the back door to admit his ginger tom. Vivaldi, meowing with triumph, deposited a portion of what looked suspiciously like a baby blackbird on his master's slipper and sat preening himself, waiting to be congratulated. Forge fussed over the cat for a few minutes, poured him some milk, and, while Vivaldi was otherwise occupied, slyly disposed of the mortal remains. Then he went back to his computer.

When he sat down and began to move the mouse over its little rubber pad there was an air of reluctance about his sluggish movements. He seemed as if he were no longer interested in the search or as if he didn't want to admit that he already knew *what* was going on, though as yet he had no idea *why*. He called up a list of charitable foundations onto the screen and isolated those which had funded him in the past, then a second list of those which had turned him down. He placed them side by side in two neat columns, then under each one he listed the names of its committee members. And there it was, right in front of him on the screen. Two names danced out of the list of the seven agencies which had most recently refused to support his work. W.S. Brüch and Felix J. Hiller. He chewed his lip for a long time while he tried to recall what he knew of either man.

Hadn't Brüch been a student of Hiller's in the University of Chicago? But Hiller had moved several times – according to his published work – to Stockholm, Basle and was now in Brussels. So far as Forge could recall he had never met Hiller, face to face. But Brüch was another matter – he had most definitely met him. When was it? Ah, yes, at a meeting in Rome, sometime in the early Eighties. He remembered Brüch vividly, now. He fidgeted uncomfortably as he recalled that pushy individual. Thin, intense, seemingly desperate to make an impact on the great Professor Forge. His ideas facile, if forcefully argued. It had been so easy to put him down. Paul regretted it immediately, as he always did when he allowed his sardonic wit to get the better of him. He had penned a few lines of, well, not exactly apology, then promptly forgotten the incident. Was it so easy to make lasting enemies? Not for a moment had he registered that the young man was a student of Hiller's, though, even had he done so, he would not have seen it as particularly significant.

The position of Brüch's name on their published papers confirmed his junior status. And he was on only two of the committees, whereas Hiller was on several. So the odds were that the enemy was the ubiquitous Hiller. 'Who is this man?' Forge asked himself angrily. 'Why is he doing this?' It seemed outlandish to think that Hiller could be so driven by professional jealousy as to usurp other people's ideas. Or was it just his, Forge's? And if so, why?

He bit his upper lip and stared at the screen. Then with great deliberation he searched his archive for a list of published papers on and around his group's research. It was about two hours later when he logged off his machine and took his chilled and tense body for a long reflective soak in the bath. He sat on the side of the huge old tub, trying to blank out his thoughts while he waited for it to fill. He noticed idly that the coppery green drip-stains beneath the old brass taps had swelled out to meet in the middle. When he looked around the rest of the room he wondered why he'd let the place become so shabby. His once-weekly help had long since given up the unequal struggle. She was almost as depressed as he was himself and nowadays didn't so much clean as shift the dust from one surface to another. On the pretext of 'not wanting to disturb your papers, sir,' she had let the rot take hold. Or perhaps it was simply the house getting them both down?

When at last the tank emptied and the scalding water had almost reached the rim of the bath, Forge eased himself gingerly into it and unreined his most venomous thoughts. It was pointless not to admit that Hiller had been systematically stealing and exploiting his and his students' ideas. How had he failed to grasp that war had been declared? Sly scheming bastard, getting his minions to do his dirty work. Why had he not noticed how the Hiller group had persisted in edging into his subject even before they started to plagiarize his work? What was worse, Hiller had been much more successful at getting recognition for the ideas – Forge's ideas – thereby making himself *the* power in the subject, at the same time as he was neatly sidelining Forge. And, to add insult to injury, Hiller had also been co-opted onto at least four of the most affluent and influential committees doling out European research funds. Each of these, by turning down Forge's applications, had, over the past couple of years, accelerated the sharp decline in his group's income. Bad enough by itself but, at the same time, Hiller and Brüch, having plundered his ideas, had somehow been successful where he had not. Then they'd walked away with all the loot.

Professor Paul Forge FRS lay back in his scalding bath and closed his eyes while he desperately tried to work out how best to sort out the mess and reclaim his work.

OXFORD

Two years later: June 1997

CHAPTER FOUR

It was early June and normal summer weather was about to be resumed; overnight the temperature had dropped almost ten degrees. Outside the small café a couple of dispirited waiters washed down dark blue plastic tables and chairs and arranged them in two neat rows, three or four chairs per table, by the plate-glass windows. As if on cue, after six stifling days, the early-morning sky threatened rain and a nasty, malicious little wind blew along the street as if to rouse the town. It was twenty minutes to seven and the city rush hour had not yet begun, though a steady dribble of regulars had already started arriving for their first hit of coffee of the day.

The Café Madeleine, situated in a tiny fourteenth-century courtyard off the High Street, adjacent to-the covered market, was known to serve the best and most authentic coffee in Oxford. It was also the most successful small café in the city centre, renowned for its excellent and reasonably-priced meals. Lunch was most popular, though there was also a devoted following for early evening, pre-theatre supper. But for the discerning, breakfast was in a class of its own. Since the café opened its doors at six thirty sharp each morning, besides being without parallel, it was without competition for early birds, of whom, it must be said, the town boasted few. But those few were utterly faithful.

At that hour, before the tables were dressed in their gaily-coloured cloths, the place most resembled a French *bar/tabac*, an impression enhanced by the waiters' navy and white Breton shirts. Customers, looking morning-stunned, sat at tables or stood at the bar, making only the most desultory murmured conversation. Eyes flickered towards the television set above the hissing espresso machine. The barman, Jack, who stood – or rather perched – on a duckboard behind the counter, dominated the scene and appeared unnaturally tall until a glance at the relative length of short arm to broad shoulder suggested otherwise. Now and then he shot a greeting – in French, naturally, since Oxford took itself seriously and he was not one to spoil illusions – at some favoured client, in a style which owed much to the influence of the late great Général de Gaulle. Ironical, since he was London born and bred. At regular intervals he turned to bark a command into a hatch behind him, and in response a pair of reddened, disembodied hands pushed forward a tray of gleaming white cups and saucers and an occasional basket of mouth-watering breakfast breads.

The scene was unremarkable, ordinary. The bar had cleared and the remaining early customers who sat at tables, singly or in pairs, were almost invariably silent. Some idly watched the silent TV screen over the bar or read the newspapers. One or two just sat gazing into their coffee-cups as if the dark liquid might reveal the secrets of the universe, or at least provide strength to face the day ahead. Right at the back, in a dark corner, a solitary woman sat quietly dunking a croissant into her coffee in a serious and concentrated, even obsessive way. Nobody paid much attention to her, for she had long since become part of the morning routine; dunking with one hand and with the other restlessly tap-tapping on the tabletop.

She was an elderly bag lady who came in each morning for her free breakfast. She had done this from a few weeks after the café first opened, by which time the pattern of its early-morning clientele was established. The owner found her sitting on the doorstep at six o'clock one wintry morning. Ever since then, without fail, and at precisely the same hour, she returned, but always waited politely until invited inside. She kept to a rigid routine, stayed for precisely three-quarters of an hour and then disappeared among the first wave of customers. It wasn't clear which of the staff had nicknamed her Madeleine. It was not her name, but since she never spoke, she didn't correct them. Soon, as business picked up, they began to regard her as their lucky mascot. Her manner was reserved; her silence lent her a strange air of mystery. She made them feel charitable, kind. Madeleine the Mystery Woman.

The boss called her Lady M. What most intrigued him was the way she appeared to rise above her hobo appearance. This indication of hidden power didn't so much unsettle him as make him accept her on her own terms – though what those terms might be, was more difficult to pinpoint. She took her free breakfast with grace, always waiting until it was proffered, then invariably accepting with a vague, fleeting smile and a gracious inclination of her head. Everything about her was frail and pale, even her wispy faded hair which looked unhealthy rather than historically unkempt. Though her clothes were stained and tattered, they were once, undoubtedly, good clothes. From the first, the waiters concluded she'd come down in the world, or else experienced some terrible trauma, and was, therefore, worthy of their tolerance. No trouble to anyone, they said, except perhaps to herself. Or harm. It was only her vacant expression which disturbed a little, and the exact, unchanging ritual of her behaviour. Day in day out, she sat as if waiting for the grim reaper himself, eyes fluttering restlessly between the counter and the door and her fingers tap-tapping their incessant rhythm.

That particular June morning followed the same pattern as on every other weekday. As the early customers dribbled in, the TV news bulletin changed to a (still silent) weather forecast. With a shouted word over his shoulder the barman set several new scoops of coffee into the machine and rubbed the mirrored surface with a soiled white rag. He steamed a new jug of milk and turned to greet a couple of elderly dons as they shambled up to the counter.

'Ah *Professeurs*, cutting it close,' he joked, as he pushed forward two large cups of black coffee.

The younger of the two, who was called Fibich, was a balding, heavy-set, cheerful-looking man, dressed in a rumpled buff-coloured linen jacket. He heaved himself onto a bar stool and carelessly tossed his panama hat onto the counter. As his backside crinolined around the blue leather seat, he hooked one stout foot onto the steel bar separating its spindly chrome legs. The other, older man remained standing until Fibich was properly settled, then fastidiously took the next stool but one. He had white-grey hair and eyebrows and a pasty complexion. Of medium height and weight, his clothes were nondescript: a somewhat faded, navy blue suit, overwashed white shirt and plain dark red tie.

Though the barman greeted them in French, he had always assumed them to be Middle European since both men spoke with heavy accents. He privately called them the Einsteins since the day he'd asked the morose one, Professor Forge, what his subject was, and in reply was given half an hour's seminar, not one word of which he'd understood. Except that it had something to do with scientific or medical research. Not wanting to release another unstemmable flow, he had never risked the same question again.

'*Merci, Jacques*,' the fat man wheezed, then turned in surprise as a hand slapped his shoulder. 'Ah Mowbray, this is an unexpected pleasure. Are you usually abroad so early?' he asked, looking distinctly put out.

'Indeed not, but I've to catch an early train to London. And you tell me', nodding at Forge, 'that they do an excellent breakfast here,' he boomed heartily, perching on the empty stool between them.

Fibich signalled the barman. 'Jack, a coffee for our late bursar, Mr Mowbray,' he said.

'Late? Come, come, Fibich, I'm not quite dead yet, merely retired,' Mowbray interjected jocularly, then smiled expansively at the waiter. 'A couple of croissants, please.'

Everett Mowbray was a little older, though better preserved, than either academic. Taller too, and formally dressed in a dark blue, fine pinstripe, suit and regimental tie, he had the bearing of a military man, which indeed he had been, before taking up his college post. This was not so radical a move as might be supposed. One of the running jokes in Oxford was that it was impossible to become a college bursar unless you were, at the very least, either an ex-brigadier or ex-admiral. In fact Mowbray, distinguished though he was rumoured to be, had not risen above the rank of major. But in his particular line of service, to which he never referred, few rose even that high.

Jack watched with amused interest as the newcomer tried to engage Forge in conversation. But it was uphill work and he soon gave up. For some reason, Mowbray seemed curiously ill at ease. He kept checking his watch and glancing about as if he were expecting someone, though Jack wondered if it were simply embarrassment at barging in on an established routine. What really intrigued him was that, for some reason, the ex-bursar's unexpected appearance in the café had knocked the other two men completely off form. After greeting Mowbray, Fibich, who usually talked non-stop, buried himself in his newspaper, leaving poor Forge to the social niceties. After a particularly awkward silence, Jack leaned forward and murmured something to Fibich who glanced at Mowbray uncertainly before conferring earnestly with the waiter. Mowbray gulped down his coffee and croissants and announced loudly that he had to go. 'Excellent breakfast, Professor Forge,' he said and put his hand on Forge's shoulder. 'Thank you for recommending it.' As he stood searching his pockets for change he glanced at the racing page over Fibich's shoulder and ran his finger down the day's runners. With an impish grin, he trumpeted: 'Inspired Investment, third race. Put your shirt on it.' He picked up his bill and tossed a fiver and some change on the counter.

'What was that?' Fibich grunted irritably. 'I didn't catch it.' He continued perusing the racing page while Forge glared at Mowbray with something like distaste. Fibich looked up, met Jack's eyes and shrugged. 'Oh, I think we'll stick to our own choice, right, my friend?' He filled in a betting slip and passed it over the counter. 'Avenging Angel, in the four forty. Ten pounds to win, Jack. OK?' He turned to Forge. 'What about you, my friend? Are you going to try your luck today?'

'I have no luck any more,' Forge murmured morosely.

'Well, goodbye, gentlemen.' Mowbray patted Forge on the shoulder, turned on his heel and strode across to the lavatory which was at the back of the room, near old Madeleine's table. He paused by her table on the way out and looked down at her with surprise, or perhaps contempt. He murmured something but the bag lady ignored him totally. The tiny encounter was lost on all but Jack, and it confirmed his impression of the arrogance of the man. He almost cheered when Madeleine deliberately turned her back on Mowbray and sat staring, vacantly, into the courtyard. After a slight hesitation Mowbray headed for the door. Meantime, the barman picked up the coins, threw them in the till and called goodbye.

A customer who had apparently just arrived stood quietly away from the open door to let Mowbray pass. Jack watched with amusement as they did a little avoiding quickstep before the bursar stood back apologetically. He said something to the newcomer, who turned slowly and looked across at the bar. Jack assumed he was the person Mowbray had been waiting for, since both men then left the café together. It seemed somewhat odd, therefore, that Mowbray strode ahead once they got outside. Bombastic sod, Jack thought. He picked up a dish-towel and began to polish some glasses.

Anton Fibich turned to his companion. 'Wasn't that the chap who caused such a fuss last night?'

'What chap?' Forge sounded as if he were miles away.

'The chap who left with Mowbray.'

Forge slowly drained his coffee-cup. 'I didn't notice anyone with Mowbray.' He pointedly ignored the reference to the evening before, when there had been an ugly little scene which had almost ruined – perhaps did ruin – his retirement party.

'Oh, I'm er, I meant . . .' Fibich muttered awkwardly, becoming flustered. Paul Forge's expression remained blank, but poor Fibich couldn't let it go. 'He seemed very interested in you . . .' He stopped, suddenly and vividly recalling the awkward incident of the evening before, and cast wildly around for inspiration. 'You know, I don't care for that Mowbray. Too friendly. And such a busybody.'

'Indeed,' Forge murmured faintly, then roused himself. 'He's probably interested in your gambling syndicate,' he suggested.

'Really? How do you make that out?' Fibich asked defensively.

Forge shrugged. 'Just that he cannot resist the sly innuendo, I notice. Inspired Investment indeed! But don't worry, my friend, it is no longer any of his business.' Forge sounded a little more cheerful. In his private view, dear old Fibich was even more of a conspiracy theorist than himself. Mowbray had stepped on his toes too often. Until his arrival, Fibich had guided some of the college's more successful investments. It was generally admitted among the fellows that he had a certain unorthodox flair on the stock market. Privately, Forge was more of the opinion that the college might have reason to be grateful to the equine world. But that had all stopped once Mowbray became bursar and uncovered Anton's addiction to horse-racing. The little betting side-play earlier had been a trifle awkward, specially in view of Mowbray's part in it.

'Was that the same chap who turned up at your party last night?' Fibich adroitly diverted attention from any discussion of his pastime. He was far more interested in getting to the bottom of the ker-fuffle of the night before. His companion had been extremely distressed about it. Indeed, he still looked hurt and upset. Fibich was therefore sur-prised that Paul clammed up and wouldn't discuss it.

'Who?' Forge looked perplexed. 'Anton, old friend, I do not know what you are talking about. What chap?'

'He's gone,' Fibich said. 'He was standing by the door staring at you. Us. Then he left with our mutual friend.' He wriggled awkwardly on the stool.

For no discernible reason a hush fell on the café and, for a moment, the only sound, save the light clink of crockery, was Madeleine's tapping, louder than usual and more frenzied. Forge swivelled slowly around and glanced across at her and, as she became aware of his scrutiny, she stopped altogether and stared back at him.

Forge turned to his companion. 'What about a stroll around the town?' he asked. His expression was preoccupied, and his voice full of emotion. 'There's something I'd like to discuss with you. I'd value your counsel.'

Ah, thought Fibich, now I shall hear all about it. He glanced at his watch. 'I have an appointment in half an hour, so let us go at once,' he urged.

'Mowbray quite spoiled my breakfast. Perhaps a stroll will restore our spirits. I always like Oxford in the early morning.'

Jack nodded towards the window. 'Before the town is overrun by visitors, eh? Very wise. But it's not a very good day, looks like rain.'

'I have an umbrella in my college room,' Fibich announced and eased himself off the stool. 'Why don't I go ahead and fetch it and meet you at the gate to Christ Church meadow?' Forge murmured that there was no need, while Fibich placed his dingy old panama on his head and slapped the counter. 'It won't take five minutes. Goodbye Jack. Don't forget to place my bet. I'll be in tomorrow to collect my winnings.' Fibich grinned.

'You wish. That old nag will fall at the first fence.'

'So now you think my tips are not reliable, huh? Tut, tut, tut.' He waggled a plump finger. 'Have we not had our winners?' The two academics gathered themselves and ambled towards the door. 'No delay, Jack, my friend. Do it early, while the price is good, eh?'

'At once, Prof,' the barman called after him and laughed. 'Good luck, gentlemen,' he muttered, as he made his way to a pay phone on a shelf close to where old Madeleine sat. He made a brief call to his wife and on his way back to the bar stopped to greet her. As usual, she didn't reply. Jack was idly rolling Fibich's betting slip between his palms and, when she pushed her coffee-cup towards him, he inadvertently dropped the scrap of paper on the table and didn't notice her hand snake out to pick it up. 'Like another cup?' he asked. The old woman looked up at him and he was upset to notice tears in her eyes. 'What is it?' he asked. 'What's wrong?' She stared at him blankly, carefully gathered up the breadcrumbs on her coat front and put them daintily in her mouth. Then she picked up her shopping bags and shuffled off to the wash-room. Jack carried the empty cup to the bar. After a few minutes Madeleine reappeared and as she passed the phone she searched it furtively for returned coins. This was also part of her daily ritual, except that this time, having found none, she angrily stuffed the rolled-up betting slip into the slot.

Meanwhile it had begun to rain. Great lolloping drops splashed lazily on to the newly-washed tables. A couple of waiters were smoking outside the doorway as the two academics passed. 'Rain,' one said disgustedly to the other. 'The minute we put the damn tables out.' The two men hastened to the shelter of the stone archway where Fibich again suggested going ahead for an umbrella, but Forge had already begun his saga and was reluctant to be deflected. They stood talking under the arch until the rain eased, then turned into the High Street. Fibich was torn; anxious to hurry away but equally anxious to help his depressed friend. In fact it was impossible to get away since Forge kept a firm grip on his arm and, without preamble, launched into an overexcited account of the evening before.

They continued together towards the zebra

crossing on the next block, about a hundred yards further down the street. But by the time they reached it both were talking so hard, and at once, that they forgot to press the button to cross. Professor Forge looked flushed and unusually agitated. He kept making extravagant points on his fingers while his whole body twitched with barely suppressed anger. Fibich kept trying to pull away but each time his companion detained him with another outburst.

It was still only a few minutes after seven and the traffic was beginning to grow in volume, though it was still fairly light. Since the shops were firmly shut, there were, as yet, few pedestrians. Again the sky darkened perceptibly and threatened more rain. The two men now stood close to each other with their heads bent, Forge still talking, shouting almost, Fibich listening, an expression of outrage on his face. When he managed to get a word in edgeways, he announced that he would have to go ahead after all or he would miss his appointment. By now it was evident that they must abandon all idea of a walk, with or without an umbrella. Fibich suggested his friend take a bus home with a promise to meet him at college for lunch. But Forge wasn't listening; he continued talking.

After another couple of minutes, Fibich finally managed to get away. Without waiting for the light to change, he charged across the street and veered off into Magpie Lane, a short distance to the left of the crossing. Forge, apparently unaware of his friend's departure, remained *in situ*, but his whole demeanour had subtly changed. His shoulders sagged and he shook his head as if in disbelief.

A solitary man, of much the same build and style as Forge, limped to the crossing on the other side and also stood waiting for the signal to change. A light sprinkling of rain started as he pressed the button on the beacon irritably, several times, glanced at the red light and wiped his face with his hand. He seemed unable to keep still. He kept brushing back his straggling grey hair or flicking imaginary flecks of dandruff from his hunched shoulders. Then, noticing that his shoe-lace was undone, he stooped stiffly to retie it, thus missing the signal to cross until almost too late. He started forward without looking up, then hurriedly pulled back to the pavement to avoid collision with Forge. Both men had their heads down, apparently so self-engrossed that they collided and tripped over each other. For an instant they became hopelessly entangled, then, with a cry of outrage, a hand was raised and one man staggered, and fell against the kerbstone.

A truck thundered by and then another. When the crossing cleared, the man remained lying just beside the pavement. He slowly curled up and lay still. Across the street, sitting on a step at the lower entrance to the covered market, old Madeleine looked on.

Retrospective

CHAPTER FIVE

A long coarse rope hung from a huge lime tree on the river-bank. It had been there as long as I could remember, though nobody could say who had first put it in place. I think – but who can be sure just what is remembered or what is told? – I think I recall my father pointing it out to me the first time my mother brought us to visit my aunt and grandparents. But now it seems a little unlikely, because, as I picture it, I appear to be sitting in my baby pushchair. It is grey and low-slung, with curved springs on either side, which makes it wobble and rock very satisfactorily. My mother walks alongside, wearing shining white ankle socks with her clumsy high heels. She has one hand on the handle but it is my father who pushes me. That's the unlikely part. My Papa was not a man to push a child's perambulator. At least, not until my stepsister was born, after he returned from the war. His war and mine. Then he, newly gentle and depressed, would walk her around for hours, as if he could not bear to let her out of his sight. That was how things were, for those who survived. But that came much later.

Every summer, I went to stay with my grandparents. As soon as I could swim, and even before, a group of us children would make for what we called the rope-tree, where the bigger boys would show off. It was just part of the summer holidays, part of the ritual of those seemingly endless hot, sunny days. And because it took courage, it became an essential ritual of belonging to the gang.

The rope had a hard rough knot at the end from which strands of loose hemp escaped, which after a time became as smooth as silk. Like a horse's tail. We would grab hold of the rope above the knot, pull it backwards as far as we could, take a flying leap over the middle of the river and bomb into the water. It was a favourite game for us boys though not for the girls who, with the exception of Angel, were far too timid to have a go. This, of course, made us feel gratifyingly superior. I can't now recall which of us discovered that, if we got our speed just right, we could, after three or four oscillations, land neatly on the opposite bank of the river.

Usually it was late June or early July by the time we considered the water warm enough for swimming, but that summer there was a brief hot spell around the end of May which seemed, in my memory at least, to continue for the few weeks until I ran away.

The great rope-tree is our goal that Saturday morning. Roger calls for me, as arranged, at about ten. We sit at the kitchen table while my aunt packs my lunch of bread and cheese. The smell of the bread is just too tempting. We grab the first two slices and stuff them in our mouths before she has time to protest. But when we make to grab some more she raises the knife and brings the flat of it lightly down on the back of my hand. 'Don't you know there's a war on?' she protests, laughing. 'Leave some for somebody else.' Then, still smiling, she shoos us out of the house. At this point Roger must have gone off somewhere because he falls out of the picture, briefly.

My aunt wasn't pretty or clever like my mother, but she was much more comfortable to be with. Solid, dependable, dutiful. And good-natured. She had coped with her elderly parents for years and when I was dumped on her, for the duration of the war, she made no complaint – or at least not to me. Though perhaps she did to my mother, her sister, because they were always testy with each other and, as time went on, my mother came to visit less and less.

It must have been around eleven o'clock that morning by the time we set out on the three-or-four-kilometre walk to the river. We pick up the others, in turn, from the scattered little hamlets on the outskirts of the town. Angel and Marie-Eulalie first. That's when Edmond appears and immediately begins the argument with Angel which rumbles on for the next hour or so. Marie-Eulalie is, he insists, much too young for such an expedition. But as usual Angel, having made up her mind, is not about to be deflected.

Oddly, I cannot now remember which route we took after we assembled. Was it through the little town – really little more than a village – or the back way, past the mill and through the fields? Sometimes I try desperately to trace that journey from the beginning. I see Roger standing at the kitchen table and my aunt slicing the crusty warm loaf I'd just collected from the baker. I see us wandering past our friends' houses but I do not see them emerge. Nor do I have any memory of how our number grew to seven, or in what order. What I see next is the line of us children walking by the river-bank: Marie-Eulalie, Fanny, Angel, Edmond, Guy, me, and Roger, bringing up the rear. I am fifteen.

I don't think we originally intended to swim, for it was too early in the summer and the river was still high from the spring rains. Yet, somewhere along the way, it must have been decided that we will cross to the opposite bank to eat our lunch, where it is more sheltered and therefore warmer. I can't recall who suggests it. I only know that it has a much better picnic spot as well as a safe, stony place for the younger children to swim from – if they have a mind.

It must have been well past noon when we reach the rope-tree. By now our adventurous plan is that we'll swing across the river on the rope. It all seems perfectly possible until we get there and look at what suddenly seems a very broad expanse of water. After some argy-bargy, Roger, braver and older than the rest of us, goes first. He loops the rope around one hand, grips it firmly with the other, backs away as far as he can, takes a running leap and swings high into the air. He very nearly makes it on the first arc. When he comes careering back, Guy and I give him a great shove which carries him safely across, second time around. He punches the air triumphantly and shouts at us to join him as Edmond catches hold of the rope. We have to push him four or five times before he finally makes it. Just as I begin to wonder who will push the last of us across, specially the younger children, Angel decides she wants to have a go. As she tucks her skirt into her drawers, I am surprised to notice how tall she has grown from the year before; her legs are long and slender.

Edmond's eyes meet mine. He looks as embarrassed as I feel, but we both turn away without saying anything. Strange, how grateful I still feel that we don't begin to titter nor make smutty remarks to cover our shyness. As Angel hitches herself up on the rope, Marie-Eulalie howls that she won't be able to manage. I say recklessly that I will take her on my back and am relieved when she shouts she doesn't want to cross that way, that she's too afraid. As Fanny starts to berate her, Angel swings past, but she barely makes it to the middle of the river. On her return, I give her too violent a push which sends her flying. She loses hold of the rope and splashes heavily into the water. The girls scream. Edmond is about to dive in after her when her head pops up. She is laughing. She swims back and we haul her up onto the bank. She looks like a drowned rat as she jumps up and down, but she is still laughing. Then, as we all join in, she dances crazily around and around, the water sloshing out of her black canvas shoes. We are entranced by her antics. She looks so strange and, with her plastered-down cropped hair, oddly grown-up. She stretches up her arms and calls out to Roger, 'Wait for us. We'll take the little one and go back and cross by the bridge.'

Fanny looks relieved, and is all for setting off at once. 'I'll take the sandwiches,' she says, snatching up our discarded lunch bags. 'Then you guys won't be able to eat them all. You'll just have to wait for us.' Edmond nudges me. 'Give us a shove,' he says, taking hold of the rope. 'I'm not going the long way round. You can if you like.' He swings to and fro three or four times before he manages to land on the other side. I stand there indecisively, on the point of saying that I will accompany the girls, when Angel catches me on the raw. 'And what about you, oh brave one?' she challenges. Fanny titters when Angel says: 'Shall I push you? Or perhaps you want to come with us girls?' I know she wants me to go with her, but I am too perverse to agree.

She is still in her wet clothes and her teeth are chattering. I take off my shirt and hand it to her silently. She takes it gratefully, goes behind a bush and after a minute or two emerges wearing it. She looks so beautiful. The shirt is one of my father's, so long that it comes down, modestly, well below her knees. I watch as she wrings out her sodden dress and drawers. She does it slowly, each simple action deliberate, languid, and, though she does not appear to be aware that she is being watched, I know she is taunting me with her new, untried power and that it excites her almost as much as it excites me. I think that is why I don't follow her to the bridge, but decide to cross by the rope. Or maybe it's just a silly way to try to impress her.

When she sees me turn away she thrusts her wet clothes into my arms and bossily instructs me to look after them. I watch as the two older girls take little Marie-Eulalie by the hand but, instead of setting off, the three of them stand waiting to see what I will do.

Though I desperately want to go with them, I turn away, sulkily, feeling rejected. And frustrated because I know the boys will tease me unmercifully if I go with Angel. In any case, it isn't all that far to the bridge, no more than a fifteen-minute walk, perhaps twenty for someone as small as Marie-Eulalie. I make a ball of the wet dress and drawers, tie it tightly by the sleeves and throw it across the river to Edmond. Then, full of bravado, I grab hold of the rope, take a flying leap into the air and by some miracle make it to the opposite side first time.

Barely. Roger catches hold of me as I land and we both roll over and over. When we stand up, we see the girls set off through the long grass, Angel bringing up the rear. I squeeze more water from her clothes and hang them on a branch to dry.

Angel looks back and notices what I've done and calls her thanks. My heart turns over; she looks so absurdly pretty in that too-big shirt. I wave and she does another little dance, just a few steps, twirling around with her arms in the air before running off to catch the others. So carefree and gay. And oh, so alluring. The thin cotton of the shirt clings to her damp body, revealing her maturing figure. And my own interest in it. I stuff my trembling hands into the pockets of my baggy shorts to hide my confusion, but I cannot hide my flushed face. When I turn to my companions they are rolling around on the grass, pointing at me and howling with laughter, but Edmond's eyes follow mine and I can see that he is just as affected as I.

I suppose that was my first experience of lust, yet it seemed then, or maybe it was only afterward, that I revised my reaction – that I had suddenly perceived Angel as a beautiful girl and not an old pal, and that I was halfway to falling in love with her. That moment froze in my memory as we watched the girls walk away through the high grass – Marie-Eulalie leading, in her blue candy-striped dress, Fanny in bright yellow and Angel in white, bringing up the rear. As they move along, the little clouds of blue butterflies fly out of the grass and cluster, magically, around their heads.

Oxford

June 1997

CHAPTER SIX

The man lay still, face down, on the pedestrian crossing, with one foot resting on the kerbstone. He looked oddly compact, neat, as if in falling he had tried to emulate the position of a sleeping child. His body was curled up with his arms beneath him. Cars, parked overnight, still lined the street on either side of the crossing, so that even had there been any passers-by, the injured man would not have been easily noticed.

The High Street, despite its name, is not the main shopping street in Oxford. It runs from the central crossroads, Carfax, for about three-quarters of a mile east to Magdalen (pronounced Maudlin) Bridge. Besides the Examination Schools and the university Church of St Mary the Virgin, seven colleges have frontages on the High: Lincoln, Brasenose, All Souls, Oriel, University, The Queens and Magdalen, which only leaves space for a scattering of retail premises in between these ancient buildings. But at either end of the street there are short uninterrupted rows of shops on either side. The more vigorous of these is at Carfax where there are several clothes boutiques, antique and gift shops as well as the usual banks, insurance companies and restaurants. Few opened before nine, some even delayed until nine thirty or ten, when the school run and the dash both for the

London commuter trains and the city offices were over.

Running from Carfax, on the north side of the street, four stone archways punctuated the row of shops. The first opened into the little courtyard in front of the Café Madeleine, while the other three provided entrance to the avenues of the medieval covered market. Unlike the café, the market gates did not open until eight o'clock. Daily deliveries had to be made at the back entrances, off Market Street. Because of traffic congestion, no buses stopped at the top end of the High, on either side. The nearest bus-stops were around the corner, either in the Cornmarket to one side; or on St Aldates's, outside the Town Hall, on the other. For all those reasons, but also because it was too early for all but the most ardent tourist, there were very few passers-by that morning. Nobody saw the prostrate man for almost five minutes.

It was a harried car-driver, fuming behind a stalled truck, who, at precisely seven sixteen, first noticed him, and even then it took a few seconds for his plight to register. She was on her way to the station and, because she'd overslept, was already in fear of missing her train. Her immediate reaction was that he was a drunk, sleeping it off until it struck her that he was far too well-dressed. She closed her eyes and hoped that, if she sat tight, he would get to his feet and stagger off. When he didn't move, she mentally threw up her hands in despair and abandoned hope of catching her normal train at seven twenty-one. She glanced at her watch and made a quick calculation. If she caught

70

the seven fifty, she might just about make her first meeting. But whatever happened, she mustn't miss that, because the train after it wasn't until past eight. She checked ahead for a space to park while she eased open her seat-belt. The truck in front juddered and slowly moved off. Swearing silently, she pulled over to the pavement and jumped out. She was almost knocked sideways by the slipstream of another truck as it thundered by.

She thought she heard a faint moan as she bent over the man. She laid her hand gently on the back of his head and looked around for someone to call an ambulance, but there was nobody about. Oddly, just then, there was also a slight hiatus in the traffic. A few cars screeched by but didn't stop. Then, as she fumbled with the man's collar, a quiet voice asked: 'May I help?'

'He was just lying here. He must have had a heart attack or something,' she answered, and looked up. An elderly, grey-haired man, of much the same build and dress as the man on the road, knelt down beside her and felt the victim's neck for a pulse. After a moment or two he drew in his breath and sat back on his heels. 'I think you may be right.' His voice was so low she could hardly make out the words. She wondered distractedly if the two men were related, or if they looked alike. But she couldn't see the prostrate man's face, since he was lying face down. In any case the newcomer kept his hand on his head.

The woman fumbled in her bag and became flustered. 'Damn, I must have left my phone at home. I wonder is there anywhere open? We'd better call an ambulance.' She looked around nervously, but the newcomer was already pulling a mobile phone from his pocket. 'I've got one here.' As he held it up she let out a gasp of relief. 'Look,' she said quickly, seizing her opportunity, 'can you cope? I have a desperately important meeting . . .'

'Don't worry,' he cut her short. 'It's all right, go ahead.' Relieved, she stood up and continued to burble on nervously about her fear of missing her train. She was ashamed to notice that, once set on a course, how difficult it was to be deflected. All she could think of was that she'd left her mobile at home and couldn't make those calls she intended on the train. She was so preoccupied that it took a second or two for her to realize that the man was smiling up at her, encouraging her to go. She had a vague impression of thick, ill-fitting spectacles and huge, unfocused blue eyes. He had a kind face. She wasn't at all surprised when he said: 'I'm a doctor. I'll stay. You carry on.'

He dialled his pin number and, as he waited for a network, said: 'His pulse is rather uneven.' He spoke vaguely, not quite looking at her. 'As you say, it may be his heart. Don't worry, I can wait,' he added, more loudly. 'I'm in no hurry, help will come along soon enough.' As she hurried away, she could hear the beep, beep, beep, as he dialled the three emergency digits. She looked back as she got into the car and saw that he was speaking into the phone. By then, a couple of pedestrians had appeared at the crossing. She switched on her ignition and headed for the station at full speed. It was twenty-three minutes to eight. She might just

72

about make it if there were no more hold-ups.

Had she stayed another three or four minutes, she would have witnessed the arrival of a young policewoman, and might have concluded that the emergency services were remarkably prompt in answering the call. But she would have been wrong.

CHAPTER SEVEN

The young policewoman, pedalling furiously up the High Street on her way to St Aldates police station, knew nothing whatsoever about the incident on the crossing. She had other things on her mind. By the time she came upon the scene she was already in obvious distress. Her shirt was torn at the collar and a thin line of blood trickled down her face. She had such a splitting headache, it felt as if her head would burst open. Although confused, she knew who she was and where she worked. The only thing was, she was uncertain whether she was coming or going.

Her memory of what had happened to her was unclear, except that one moment she'd been speeding down the steep incline of Morrell Avenue, and the next she was lying flat on her face. She thought she'd simply lost her balance or that something had got caught in the spokes of her bicycle wheel, until she realized her radio phone was gone and wondered if she'd been mugged. After lying in a stunned heap for a couple of minutes, she had somehow managed to find her hat and climb back on the bike, but it took considerably more effort of will to force her wobbling legs to push the pedals. It was at that point that she lost her sense of reality and went into a blind panic. All she could think of was that she had to get to the police station, which was strange because, while it was a good mile away, she was no more than a couple of hundred yards from home.

Yet she didn't go back, instead she put down her head and concentrated on getting to the station. At some point, she must have bitten the inside of her lip which was bleeding into her mouth and making her feel sick. But bad though the loss of the radio and her injuries were, they were nothing compared to the total, crippling humiliation she knew would envelop her when she turned up at the station to explain this latest catastrophe. 'It isn't fair, I'll be late again,' she muttered over and over, 'it isn't fair.' She had simply no idea how she was going to explain herself. It didn't occur to her that, in her present state, she mightn't need to.

She didn't notice the little group at the zebra crossing until she was almost on top of them, and so barely saved herself from colliding with them. As she fell sideways off her bike, all she could think of was how stupid she must look. She swallowed hard, then, slowly and with grave deliberation, parked the bike against the beacon post, using the time to try to collect herself. Faced with what looked like an emergency, her training began to take over and she went onto automatic pilot. She pulled her hat forward, gingerly, in an effort to hide the gash, and dabbed her eyes and lip with a crumpled tissue. Then she straightened herself painfully and went to offer her assistance.

An elderly man was kneeling just beside the kerb, holding a prostrate man's head in his lap and murmuring gently to him. Both were grey-haired and sombrely dressed. A couple of pedestrians stood on the road trying to shield them from the passing traffic. WPC Juliet Furbo cleared her throat. 'What's happened here?' she heard herself ask. Her voice sounded strange, sleepy. She cleared her throat and repeated the question.

'Nothing much, my friend took a bit of a turn,' the kneeling man replied complacently, continuing to stroke the stricken man's head. 'He's got a heart condition. He'll be fine in a few minutes. See? Glyceryl trinitrate.' He held up a small respiratory-puffer by way of explanation. Juliet, who didn't understand what he was talking about, brushed her hand across her damp forehead and tried to concentrate.

'Not an accident then?' she asked croakily, as relief flooded over her.

'No. He just keeled over, fainted.' The grey-haired man seemed remarkably unconcerned as he looked up at her. His extraordinary blue eyes seemed to laser into her drowsy brain, making her feel dizzy. She felt a trickle of blood run down the side of her face. 'It happens from time to time,' the man continued. 'He just fell down.' His voice was low and indistinct but strangely authoritative.

Thank goodness it's not an accident, she thought. Or worse. She tried vainly to gather her thoughts, trying to remember procedure. 'Has anyone called an ambulance?' she asked at last.

'Yes, of course,' he said. 'A passing motorist did. What about you . . . ?' He left the thought hanging in the air.

'I'm fine. When was that?'

'When was what?'

'The ambulance call,' she said wearily. Her eyelids kept drooping. She wished she could snuggle down beside the man on the road, and have her aching head stroked.

'Seven or eight minutes ago.'

So long? She glanced around but could see no sign of an ambulance. Surely it should be here by now? The hospital was only a mile or so back up the road, and as far as she could remember no ambulance had passed her on her way up the High. Though she couldn't be sure, since the haze in her head wouldn't clear. She wished she could think straight. I can't cope with this, she thought, as her head continued to swim. She blinked hard and tried to control her breathing. The bystanders drifted away, singly, covertly. They shouldn't have gone, she thought, in case . . . What? She didn't seem to have an answer to that one, or be able to think what to do next.

'Is he alive?' she asked and knelt down clumsily and touched the unconscious man's neck with her shaking hand. She thought she could feel a pulse, but her own heart was pounding so hard she couldn't be sure. The other man seemed certain, though. 'Of course he's alive,' he said impatiently and glared at her. 'The pulse is getting stronger. He'll survive. What about you?'

'I'm fine. Can you wait here?' Juliet said and got to her feet awkwardly as a woman pedestrian stopped to gawp. 'Someone called emergency, did you say?'

'Yes, I've already told you so.' He sounded

irritated. The man on the ground began to stir. 'A woman motorist promised to call in at the station on her way past. She was trying to catch a train. There wasn't anywhere open . . .'

'The Madeleine Café is open,' the newcomer said, and pointed to the top archway on the opposite side of the street.

'Oh yes, so it is,' Juliet murmured. She tried to keep hold of her thoughts but they kept slipping away. What train? What station? Ah, maybe the old bloke meant the police station. So where *were* the police? She looked down at the blue-eyed man who simply stared straight back at her, hypnotically. 'Perhaps you should . . . ?' he started. Juliet grasped the suggestion with relief. 'Right. I'll go and check. Sort it out,' she mumbled. 'Will you be OK for a few minutes? Is he OK?' she heard herself babble and pretended not to notice the man exchange a despairing glance with the woman.

'I told you he'll be fine, he's coming round. Don't worry, I'm sure the ambulance will be along any minute now, though perhaps it's as well to check. You might be able to hurry it up . . . ?'

'Yes, I better . . . You stay here till I get back, will you?' She crossed the street without looking either to right or left and barely missed being mowed down, first by a car then by a nipper bus. As soon as she left, the woman bystander murmured an apology and headed off.

Meantime, Juliet lurched through the archway into the little courtyard. A young waiter who was slouched against the café window, smoking, straightened up at her approach. When she asked if she could use the phone, he jerked his thumb over his shoulder. 'Yeah, but the boss is using it, try the one at the back.' She stared at him blankly as if she hadn't heard a word. As she pushed open the door, he asked her if she was feeling OK and tried to take hold of her arm.

'Get off. What's it to you?' she asked aggressively and pushed him away.

'Be like that.' He shrugged and took a long drag on his cigarette. 'Your face is covered in blood, that's all,' he shouted after her. 'Your old man thump you then?' he muttered provocatively but she was already out of earshot. He eased himself upright, stamped out his fag-end and followed her inside.

She glanced around frantically. There were about a dozen customers in the café. A few of the tables were occupied, and three people were perched at the bar. There was a man already using the counter phone. When Juliet prodded him in the back, he shrugged her off impatiently without turning around. The barman pointed to a second phone on a shelf on the back wall of the café. She edged herself around the tables, grabbed the receiver, dialled 999 and spoke to the operator. The waiter, who had followed her in, joined Jack behind the bar and whispered something in his ear before disappearing into the kitchen. Jack busily polished glasses and watched the young police-woman cradle the phone and redial. As she did so, she idly tugged at a scrap of pink paper which was stuck in the coin slot. She held it up to the light, then, as she began to speak, slipped it absently into her pocket.

The customers at the surrounding tables grew silent and eyed her with interest, if not suspicion. And some alarm when she began to shout. 'No, I'm not dreaming . . . Ten or fifteen minutes ago. You're making a mistake. Not George Street, the High, I said. By the zebra crossing. At it, then. Well then, you . . . No, I did . . .' she shouted and slammed down the receiver. She looked around wildly, suddenly clamped her hand over her mouth, then dashed into the Ladies.

When she emerged less than two minutes later, she had washed away the blood but her face was as white as a sheet. She swayed rather than walked to the door. Jack nipped around the bar and pulled it open for her. She gave him a dazed smile. 'Thank you,' she said. He took her firmly by the elbow when she tried to march across the little courtyard. 'You need to see a doctor, at once,' he urged. 'Get that ugly wound dressed. Come back inside, I'll call an ambulance.'

'No need,' she said hoarsely. 'I already did.' And suddenly tears began to stream down her cheeks and her body became racked with great gasping sobs.

'Hush now, you'll be all right.' She's coming out of shock, he thought and tightened his hold of her arm. He spoke soothingly, as to a child. 'Come back inside. Jack will take care of you. Sit down while you're waiting. Have a hot drink. You look like you need one.' Juliet shook herself free and pushed him away. 'Not for me,' she gasped impatiently. 'I told you, there's been an accident. Outside on the street. By the crossing. Ooh.' She stumbled and pitched forward. Jack grabbed her again and held her upright. 'I'll come with you,' he said firmly. He half walked, half dragged her into the street.

In the few minutes which had elapsed the traffic had noticeably increased. Now there was a steady, unbroken flow in both directions. Juliet, flailing about, broke free and staggered the short distance to the crossing with Jack following hard on her heels. She stopped short at the edge of the pavement and looked across, her mouth opening in disbelief.

The crossing was absolutely empty. Both the victim and the man she'd asked to guard him were gone.

CHAPTER EIGHT

'They're gone,' Juliet said blankly and left Jack standing. Without any regard for the traffic she darted out on the road. Cars screeched to a halt. 'They're gone,' she shouted again but her words were drowned in a cacophony of car horns as startled drivers slammed on their brakes. Juliet gestured at them angrily and stumbled to the opposite pavement where she stood with her hands clamped to her ears, turning frantically this way and that. Her mouth opened wide in a silent scream. They were gone. There was nothing; no-one. She bent down and touched her head to her knees. Behind her the traffic roared past. I'm dreaming, she thought, as the blood began to seep from under her helmet. My God, I'm going mad, I've dreamt the whole damn thing. What the hell's going on?

As she straightened up she registered an ambulance siren. It came screaming up the High Street towards her. Juliet jumped up and down, waving furiously. But instead of stopping, the ambulance passed by and turned into the Cornmarket. She could see its blue light over the tops of the cars. 'Stop! Stop!' she shouted. Her arms fell limply to her sides. Why didn't it stop? she thought dazedly. She turned to a couple of pedestrians waiting for the signal to cross. 'Have you seen a man?' she cried. They looked at her blankly, as if they were embarrassed by her. Or for her. She saw their eyes slide from her bloody face to her torn shirt. 'He was lying here, two men . . . the ambulance should have . . .' Her voice trailed off. They shook their heads.

The signal changed and she limply followed the pedestrians over the crossing, silently admonishing herself for not getting the ambulance registration. She didn't yet grasp the peculiarity of the situation or wonder if it were just a figment of her disturbed imagination. All she could think of was that she must, somehow, follow that ambulance, find those men. Yet she was hardly able to move; her feet, like her head, felt leaden. She was rubbing her face with the back of her hand, wondering what she should do, when a squad car came racing around Carfax from the direction of St Aldates, its siren screaming. It screeched to a halt, near the entrance to the Madeleine, to avoid Jack who jumped off the pavement to flag it down. He went forward to meet the two police officers who got out. They spoke briefly, then one of them turned around and hailed her.

'Oh, help, oh God, oh damn,' Juliet swore, as she recognized the younger of the two men. 'What the hell is he doing here?' As she started towards them she bashed into an old woman who stumbled out of the market entrance and grabbed hold of Juliet's arm. Her face was working furiously. 'What?' Juliet asked. The woman pulled at her arm and mumbled something under her breath, too faint for Juliet to catch. Yet somehow, almost unnoticed, the unarticulated sounds lodged some-where deep in her memory. Not so much words, more a rhythm, a mantra. As Juliet leaned closer, the woman brushed her aside and half walked, half ran up to the crossroads. At the time it didn't strike Juliet as strange that the seedy old woman didn't smell. But then, at the time, she had hardly registered anything at all. Apparently.

She went slowly towards her two colleagues who were still talking to the waiter. One was Inspector Peter Dallimore, who, for some reason, had appointed himself her mentor, which infuri-ated her, though she respected and even quite liked him. But it was the second man who really gave her palpitations. Constable Steve Winter fancied himself irresistible to women. He was also a complete smart-ass, fond of scoring points. Particularly off her. As usual, she had played straight into his hands. She steeled herself as he came hurrying to meet her, but all he did was clamp his arm around her shoulders and walk her firmly to the car.

'And what happened to you?' he asked lightly.

'I was mugged, I think,' she muttered and looked away. 'But never mind about me. We have to follow the ambulance,' she protested shrilly, still trying to get her head straight.

'Mugged, eh?' His tone was over-casual. 'Where? Here?'

'No.' She brushed his questions aside. 'We have to follow it.' She became quite agitated.

'You don't mean the bloody fool who nearly ran us down as we came around Carfax?'

She could tell he was humouring her. He helped her into the back seat of the squad car and sat in beside her. Too close. When she tried to clamber out over him, he became impatient and asked if she'd lost her mind. She began to babble incoherently that the body – suddenly it had become a body – had been hijacked and that she must find out where it had gone. In her agitation she scratched at the wound on her forehead which began to bleed profusely again.

Her companion held her down and demanded to know what on earth was going on, though his language was more explicit. To her mortification, she began to sob both with delayed shock and with fury at how she'd made a complete pig's ear of everything. Dallimore was still talking to the waiter. Before Winter realized what she was doing, Juliet leaned over the front seat, grabbed the handset and shrilled out instructions for a tracer to be put on the ambulance. Steve Winter took the handset from her. 'Don't be an idiot, it's not switched on,' he said irritably. 'Cool it, Julie. For Christ's sake calm down.'

'Juliet,' she corrected through clenched teeth, as Inspector Dallimore got back into the car. The two men's eyes met in the rear-view mirror. Dallimore pulled in the clutch and eased the car out into the traffic, then switched on the siren and increased his speed. 'You can tell us all about it on the way to the hospital,' he said soothingly, over his shoulder.

High above the city, a photographer slowly climbed down from atop a giant crane on the

Lincoln College site between the High and Bear Lane. He had three or four cameras hanging from his neck and a pleased expression on his face. And at least a half-dozen rolls of great shots in his pocket.

CHAPTER NINE

The casualty department was unusually busy and the waiting area was crowded and chaotic. There were children everywhere, in various states of disrepair. Unlike Juliet, who was utterly dazed, they were exhaustingly busy; screaming and jostling, and generally raging about. Two tiny children, one with a bandage around its head and the other with a heroically snotty nose, were fighting furiously over a filthy teddy bear. Juliet, sitting glumly between her policeman minders, wondered vaguely whether they'd deposit or catch more germs from its squishy surface. An eternal lending library of microbes; a bacteriologist's nightmare.

She already felt in a considerably worse state than when she had arrived five minutes before. She also felt completely trapped. Had she been alone she'd have got out fast, turned on her heel and run, but her minders would have none of it, and, anyway, by now her legs were much too weak. Here she was and here they seemed determined to keep her. She kept worrying about the old man with the blue eyes and wondering why she couldn't remember what the dead man looked like. *Was* he dead? There was a pulse, wasn't there? Or had she imagined it? *Not dead but sleepeth*. She closed her eyes wearily.

After a few minutes Inspector Dallimore stood

up and muttered that he was off 'to do some checking up'. PC Winter moved closer and held her hand. She was surprised, shocked even, because she didn't like him one bit, but at the same time, infuriatingly, she wanted the broad comforting hand enveloping hers. He tried to get her to talk, tell him about the mugger who had split her head open. He would keep calling her *Julie*, which she hated. Or *love*, which was even worse. She bit her lip to stop herself screaming.

Inspector Dallimore came back after about ten minutes holding a polystyrene cup of evil-smelling tea which he pushed into her hand. 'Drink that,' he instructed gruffly. 'The doctor will be with you in a few minutes.' She held out her hand and eyed the tea with distaste. It had milk in it which she loathed, with a greasy scum working its way across the surface. Dallimore sat down heavily beside her. When Juliet moved closer to him to avoid contact with Winter, he absently patted her knee. She knew he meant nothing by it except to console her, but she wished he wouldn't, wished both of them would stop treating her like an imbecile child. Wished they'd keep their hands off her. She hated being mauled. She moved her leg and he immediately got the message. He coloured slightly and folded his arms across his chest.

'I wish I knew what happened,' she said miserably to make amends, and knew at once she should have kept quiet. Even before he started talking she knew they didn't believe her story. Either one. It was all a ploy. Dallimore was just pretending interest to get her to talk about her injuries. She sipped the over-sweet tea and gagged. I've tasted this before, she thought, and the room slowly began to revolve.

'You all right?' The words seemed to come from a great distance. 'Yes,' she said after a long time. 'I wish I knew. That's all.'

And, because he assumed she was referring to the morning's incidents, Dallimore, as if to humour her, said calmly: 'Well then, let's work it out.' His eyes warned PC Winter to hold his tongue. 'You got mugged and your radio nicked? On your way *to* work? That right? About six thirty?' He waited. 'I don't know what time it was,' she mumbled. 'I can't remember. It's all a blank.' Her stomach was churning so badly she couldn't think straight.

'Well, let's not worry about that,' he said smoothly. 'You didn't see your assailant?' A question, not a statement. He sounded distinctly unconvinced. Pretending she didn't notice the look the men exchanged, she nodded miserably. 'We'll leave that for the moment, then, shall we? – and try to sort out what happened on the High?' Dallimore continued heartily as if he were at last getting to the important thing. But, like a bad actor, he overdid it. Blustering, cajoling. It was easy to see that he thought she'd made the story up. She tried, unsuccessfully, to tune him out, all the time wanting him to shut up, leave her alone, go away.

'Now Julie, to be honest, you're not making a lot of sense. Not surprising, with that gash. Want to tell me about it?' He smiled at her encouragingly and, when she didn't respond, Winter weighed in and took up where Dallimore left off. His patronizing tone set her teeth on edge.

'So, the story goes something like this: you were cycling up the High when you came upon the, er, incident. That right? Which nobody else around at the time seems to be able to substantiate. But never mind. *You* saw a man lying injured on the pedestrian crossing with another chap trying to give him artificial respiration? Right? Oh, I see. Just holding his head? He tells you that the police and ambulance have already been called by a passing motorist. When you see no sign of a response, no squad car arriving, or ambulance, you *leave the scene* to check with the emergency services and find that they were never called. So you put in an SOS for the bloke on the crossing and ask them to send an ambulance straight away? That right?' Juliet chewed her nails and kept her eyes down. She didn't answer but it didn't matter; Winter was well into it. 'After that, you call St Aldates yourself and the desk inspector says we weren't alerted either. No good Samaritan dropped in on her way to the station. The lady motorist, always assuming there was one, vanished into thin air, without leaving her calling-card. And when you get back to the crossing, the alleged victim has also vanished. Plus the witness, of course. But then you notice an ambulance turning into the Cornmarket and instead of assuming that they've come to the rescue, you think . . . What did you think, Julie?' he asked softly and patted her hand again. 'Because, to be honest, that's what really intrigues me.'

She snatched her hand away. 'I don't know,' she

mumbled. 'I just felt . . . the man was gone . . . I thought he must be in the ambulance, but . . .' she stopped uncertainly and looked from one man to the other. 'But he couldn't be, could he? The ambulance passed me when I was on the crossing,' she finished slowly. 'It didn't stop. So the man was already gone.'

Steve Winter broke the silence. 'If there was ever a man,' he said, not quite under his breath.

'What?'

'Shut up Winter.' The inspector pursed his lips and delivered the *coup de grâce*. 'Julie, don't you see? If someone had been injured he would have been admitted here.' He enunciated each syllable, as to a slow-witted child. 'This is the on-call casualty department, for the city. But just to be on the safe side, I checked with the emergency people again. The ambulance you saw turning into the Cornmarket was on its way to George Street. The fact is, Julie, not a single casualty service in any hospital in the county has admitted a man, dead or alive, within the last three hours. Women yes, kids too, *but no men*. Got that? So what we have is, no body, no injured party, no witness and no sign of any disturbance. I'm afraid I cancelled your 999 call since nobody from the café, the only place that was open at the time, seems to have seen a thing. All they saw was you, acting very confu . . . er . . . distressed.' He paused. 'Look love, you have a bloody great hole in your forehead. And like everyone else, you're the one I'm concerned about.' He eyed her solemnly. 'I'd say you're suffering from concussion. So, what I suggest is this, while you're having your head seen to, we'll make our way to headquarters and try to sort the whole story. Then I'll come back and tell you. OK? How does that strike you?'

From his conciliatory tone Juliet knew he was simply trying to calm her down and that he had absolutely no intention of doing anything of the sort. Not only did he not believe her story, he thought she was simply trying to deflect his attention from her injuries. Which was, in a sense, true. Except she hadn't imagined the men on the crossing. Or had she? By now her head was throbbing so hard she neither knew nor cared. Luckily, she was spared any further comment because at that moment a nurse approached and the two men got to their feet. Dallimore looked down at Juliet. 'After you've had that wound seen to, wait here. One of us will come back and drive you home,' he said firmly. Juliet looked away. 'Do you hear me, Julie?' He raised his voice.

'It's all right, I can get home myself, I'll call . . .' Juliet began to protest.

'Your boyfriend?' PC Winter interrupted innocently. His eyes narrowed. She forced herself not to react but she felt like spitting at him.

'No, no . . . he's . . .' Juliet's voice rose anxiously. 'Oh bugger off and leave me alone,' she shouted, losing patience. 'I can look after myself.'

The nurse took her by the arm. 'Julie, isn't it?'

'No,' Juliet said through clenched teeth as her head began to spin again. 'No, it is not. My name is Juliet.'

'Juliet, then,' said the nurse imperturbably. 'Tell

you what, why don't we ring the station when you're ready?' she suggested chattily. 'It's going to take a little while to X-ray your head and dress it. That's a nasty cut.' She smiled at the two men. 'I'd say a couple of hours, at least,' she said quietly. 'She needs a bit of a lie-down. And some sick leave, I shouldn't wonder,' she added brightly as she led Juliet away.

The two officers picked up their caps and strolled to the entrance. 'That nurse was pretty quick off the mark. I take it you filled her in, sir?' Winter murmured admiringly.

'I did, and the doctor as well. They'll admit her, keep her in for a few days,' Dallimore said grimly.

'But you said we'd drive her home.'

'Never mind that, I was simply trying to calm her down. I knew she'd go ballistic if *we* suggested she should stay.'

'Give us time to sort that bastard out. Otherwise he's going to kill her.'

'Really? And how do you propose we do that, Constable? She'll never make a charge.' He pursed his lips and gave Winter a very sharp look. 'Tell me, Winter,' he said, over-casually, 'just what is it between you and WPC Furbo?'

'Nothing, sir.' The embarrassed constable ground his teeth remembering an incident at a drunken party when the boyfriend had thumped him one. 'Stuck-up bitch,' he murmured, not quite under his breath.

'I see.' Dallimore gave a snort of derision, then added seriously: 'Tell me, just how much of that rigmarole do you believe?'

'None of it. Though the mugging was a new twist.' Winter was relieved to be let off the hook.

'I wasn't thinking of that so much – for the moment anyway – it was the other business.'

'Weird, wasn't it? She wasn't in control, was she? I wondered if she crashed into someone, knocked them down or something? And was afraid to say,' Winter suggested.

'Mmm . . . That's what I thought, but maybe she was simply trying to divert attention from the mugging, if that's what it was. Didn't she say she was reporting *for* duty?'

'Yes, sir, she did. But she wasn't, was she? I was going off as she came on duty yesterday evening. I saw her driving that snazzy little MX5 of hers into the car park. She should have finished at six this morning.'

'That's what Harry said. He checked the roster. That missing radio phone also bugs me. Something strange there. But what? Only makes sense if it was a mugger,' he said, half to himself. 'I suppose he might have tried to make it look like that?'

'Or she did? She didn't report it when she called in, did she?'

'Nope. Harry said not a dicky-bird.'

'So, you think she's protecting someone?'

'I wonder? You?'

'Bet my shirt it was the boyfriend. Bit of a thug from what I've seen,' he said and could have bitten his tongue off. But Dallimore contented himself with giving the younger man an old-fashioned look. He'd no doubt what was eating Winter. The station grapevine was quite efficient. Juliet Furbo was a very attractive girl and, from what he'd heard lately, he assumed she hadn't succumbed to Winter's rather crude blandishments. Now, that would be folly, he thought, as the two men got into the car.

The temperature had risen. They kept the doors open to let a draught of air through the car, which had been sitting in the sun and was like an oven. Winter turned the fans on full blast and called in their position but they didn't drive away.

'That may be it,' Inspector Dallimore said, though he sounded less certain than Winter. 'Or else he followed her. I bet she was just running away, looking for help but afraid to ask.'

'By the way, sir,' Winter interrupted. 'It's only just occurred to me. She wasn't wearing her baton, was she? That was missing as well.'

'Was it now?' They exchanged glances. Dallimore said: 'Steve, why don't you get through to that café and ask the waiter if he's heard anything further, will you? Jack he was called, if I remember correctly.'

Jack had been pretty busy. He'd checked with every shopkeeper on the block, he said, including the bloke who opened the market gates, but couldn't find anyone to back Juliet's story. Absolutely no-one had seen anything. Winter thanked him and cut the connection. For a moment neither man spoke, but it was plain that Dallimore was coming around to Winter's conclusion.

'I don't understand why some women put up with it,' PC Winter suddenly exploded. But he sounded as though he was suppressing what he really thought: *some women ask for it.*

The inspector made a despairing gesture: eyes closed, hand held outwards. 'I don't think most of them understand that either. If they did, there probably wouldn't be a problem, would there?' He sounded exasperated, upset. He pushed his hair back from his forehead. 'Know anything of WPC Furbo's history, do you?' he asked quietly. Winter shrugged but didn't reply.

'Then don't wade into deep water till you know what's lurking there,' the inspector said tartly. 'She's been through a lot. She shouldn't really be in the police force at all,' he added, half to himself as the nurse came trotting out of the casualty department. She stuck her head into the car. 'We managed to find her a bed, Inspector. We'll keep her in for a couple of days at least. I'll let you know when she's being discharged.'

'Thanks very much,' he said. He got out of the car. 'How bad is it?'

'She's certainly got concussion and that wound will have to be stitched, it's quite deep. No fracture though. The doctor thinks she may have been hit with something like a cricket bat. A fairly hefty blow.'

The inspector looked down at her. 'Not a cricket bat. I think we know what hit her,' he said grimly.

'She's very confused, agitated,' the nurse continued as if he hadn't interrupted. 'She's also got a broken rib. She's in a bad way, poor girl. Needs a proper rest. What happened to her? She won't say.'

'What do you think, Sister?'

'If she wasn't a policewoman, I'd say domestic.' She rubbed her hand up and down her cheek. 'Just the way she's acting. I noticed she was terrified when you said you'd drive her home.'

'Even policewomen sometimes have domestic problems,' Dallimore said ironically and held out his hand. 'Thanks for playing along, Sister. You've been a great help. Given us something to go on.' He stood by the car until she disappeared through the hospital entrance, then he climbed back in.

'Know where she lives?' he asked as they banged the doors shut.

'Yep.' Winter turned the key in the ignition and revved up the engine. 'That new development near the top of Divinity Road and Morrell Avenue. What's it called? Poncy bloody name,' he said, rolling his eyes.

'Little Oxford?' Dallimore said drily. 'Right then. Let's go and make discreet enquiries about her radio phone. And the stick.'

'And while we're about it, we might even nail the bastard,' Winter said. He sounded as though he was spoiling for a fight.

CHAPTER TEN

The hospital ward never achieved complete darkness. Even in the dead of night, when the lights were doused, reflected light came in from the nurse's station or from the grounds outside, specially on those nights when the nearby football stadium was floodlit. For eighteen hours Juliet drifted in and out of deep, obliterating, drugged sleep, not quite knowing where she was or why. A notice on the door forbade visitors unless cleared by the nurse on duty. Inspector Dallimore had been quite specific: the boyfriend was not to be admitted.

She was tucked away in a small amenity room off the acute ward on the fifth floor where there was little likelihood of her being found. But she didn't seem to realize that. During her brief moments of consciousness, between the injections prescribed to keep her sedated, she became hyper-agitated and anxious. When this happened, Nurse Rose Mackay sat beside the bed, held her hand and tried to discover just what had caused her injuries. But even in her drowsy, weakened state, Juliet gave nothing away.

Nurse Mackay thought it extremely odd that she didn't want to talk, not even as she began to recover. Unusual. It seemed such an exaggerated response, somehow. True, the head injury was nasty and the rib painful, but neither was life-threatening nor particularly serious. The girl had walked into hospital and before too long she would walk out again. In casualty, as soon as she realized her police colleagues were gone, she'd argued strenuously to be allowed home, yet, once the decision to admit her had been taken, she caved in and became quite docile. Nor did she bother to hide her relief, but allowed herself to be swept along without complaint and in complete silence. This greatly intrigued Rose Mackay, because in her long experience the more minor the injury the more dramatic the reaction. Most people couldn't wait to over-embellish but Juliet Furbo was as silent as a nun.

She wrapped the blood-pressure cuff around the girl's arm, pumped it up and watched the red liquid slowly run down the gauge. Juliet kept her eyes shut. She doesn't look much like a nun, Rose thought. The colouring was too vibrant, somehow. Crinkly dark auburn hair tumbled across the pillow and framed the thin, strained face. Long nose, perhaps a shade over-long, her mouth too wide, her teeth, if white, uneven. A flawed beauty. The pale skin was heavily freckled, almost laughably so, even the lips, which gave her a tomboyish look, even in repose. But the purplish shadows around the eyes aged the face prematurely and somehow the combination of these and the freckles gave the features a pitiful vulnerability. She had rather beautiful greenish-grey eyes, Rose had noticed, on the few occasions they were open. Surprisingly for a policewoman, she was neither tall – probably no more than five six or seven – nor strong-looking. About average weight, slim rather than thin. She had small broad capable hands, the nails bitten to the quick. But by far the most striking thing about her was her exaggerated response to even the most minor kindness. She was obviously someone who wanted, maybe even demanded, to be cared for.

Needy, and therefore probably unreliable, Nurse Mackay concluded briskly, as she slipped the thermometer into Juliet's mouth and lifted her limp wrist. She counted the beat against her watch and, as she bent over to push a strand of hair off the girl's damp forehead, she heard her whisper, 'I've smelt that before.'

Rose leaned closer to catch the words. 'What have you smelt before, Juliet?'

'Perfume . . . your perfume.' The words were clogged, indistinct. Beads of sweat stood out on her forehead. Rose sat on the side of the bed and gently stroked her hair.

'It's eau-de-cologne. Can you hear me, Juliet? Do you like it?'

'Mmmm. 4711. Nancy wore it.'

'What's 4711? Juliet?'

'The perfume. That's what she called it. I smelt it again . . . today, I think. Yesterday? I . . .' She drifted off. Rose hesitated, wondering if she should encourage the girl to talk. She sponged her face gently while she slept. Time enough, she thought, for her to face reality. The sedation was already being reduced and within a day or so she would be discharged. Whatever she was bottling up would be still there to confront her. Rose Mackay hoped that somewhere there was a friend to help. She was surprised that no-one had made enquiries about her – none save the police inspector. She tiptoed out and closed the door.

Juliet lay still, somewhere between sleeping and waking. Her eyes felt as though they were glued shut, yet blurred images continuously drifted past. She was lying on the road. There were grey blobs of chewing-gum melted into the road surface where her cheek was resting. There were thousands of tiny pebbles embedded in the tarmac, like bits of glass in the lead of a stained-glass window. The spittle coming out of her mouth tasted strange: fleshy and sweet. She vaguely heard a roar from behind as she struggled to her feet. She was on the ground again.

Now her head was resting on the handlebars. She desperately wanted to sleep. She screwed her eyes shut yet she could see everything, the colours were so vivid. The shouting stopped. She felt herself try to push the pedals. Round and round. It was so hard to keep going. Her legs were like lead. St Clement's rolled slowly past, the roundabout at The Plain, then Magdalen bridge. The sun glinted on the golden stone of the tower . . . but the ground was wet. Not at the bridge, further up on the High. A spattering of raindrops, big and round as fried eggs.

Blood dripping into her eyes. Wiping it on her sleeve so she didn't see the man lying on the crossing. His face was hidden, the other man had his hand on it. She put her head down to the man on the road. Wanting to sleep again; lay her head on his chest. Wanting the other man to stroke her temples, stroke the headache away. The smell is there too. 4711. On their clothes? Watery, pale blue eyes looked up at her. The same smell. Nancy's eyes were also blue but they looked down, down, down . . .

Darkness. I stretch out my hand and twitch the curtain. There are stars in the black winter sky. My mother switches on the pink bedside lamp and in the dim light she is pale and beautiful. The light makes a halo of her golden hair. She is bright, bright. 'Guess what?' she cries, picking up my sweater from the bed. 'Surprise, surprise. Dad's coming too. He's taken the day off. So we're going to leave early and make a great day of it. Avoid the traffic.' I groan and snuggle into the pillow. 'And when we finish the Christmas shopping we'll have lunch in Bewley's and go to the pictures. Come on sleepyhead, it'll be a great jaunt,' she laughs and pulls back the covers. 'We don't often have a day out all together.'

She sits down at the end of the bed and tickles my feet. Downstairs, I hear my father and brother moving, the clink of cups and saucers. My dad is always up at the crack of dawn. He makes the first pot of tea every morning and brings it to my mother in bed. When he's at home. I crawl down the bed to her and we pull the duvet over our shoulders. She cuddles me in her arms and tells me to stop messing and get up.

My brother appears at the door. 'Get up,' he says in his croaky voice. 'Dad's waiting, he's made the breakfast. Mum? Why isn't she dressed?' He's five years older than me and won't let me forget it. He's so bossy, thinks he's terribly grown-up. With the light from the landing behind him I notice how tall he's grown. Only fourteen and almost as tall as our dad.

He stretches out his hand to switch on my bedroom light. 'Do you want me to bring you up a cup of tea, Mum?' he asks. 'It's all right, darlin',' my mother says. 'Don't bother, we'll have it downstairs. Down in a minute.'

I start to put on my jeans. Mum helps me dress, like I was a child. I stretch up my arms for my sweater. The room is cold, I want her to hold me. 'I can't find my shoes,' I say stupidly. 'It's OK, darling, just put on your socks.' She gives me a little hug. 'There now.' She holds up my scruffy old lace-ups. 'You can put on these horrible old clodhoppers when we get downstairs,' she says. But I know she'll 'lose' them and make me wear my stupid patent shoes instead which I hate because they blister my heels. So I grab my old shoes and insist on putting them on right away. She holds up her hands. 'I give up, as long as you don't wear that old duffel coat.' I have my hand on the coat which was slung over the foot of the bed. 'Leave it,' she laughs. 'Your lovely red one is down in the hall. Wear that. You look great in it. For me, OK?' She grins at me when I say I will. Reluctantly. I leave my old duffel where it is. 'Good,' Mum says. 'Hurry up now, we can't keep your daddy waiting any longer. Don't forget to brush your teeth. Five minutes, OK? Then we're off.' She sounds so excited, impatient to get going.

She leaves my bedroom door wide open. I hear her going down the stairs while I tie my hair in a bunch. I can hear their voices on my way to the bathroom. My dad is standing in the hall putting on his coat as I come downstairs. He chucks me under the chin and shakes his head. 'What are we going to do with you, little sleepyhead?' He smiles and follows me into the kitchen and while I eat my cereal, we all talk at once about what shops we'll go to. We're delighted with ourselves, laughing and happy.

My dad tidies away. He's always like that; everything has to go exactly in its place. The rest of us get our coats and hats. He says it's really cold, that we'll need gloves. I can't bear the red coat. I hate it. We're just going out the door when I say I need to go to the loo again. They all roll their eyes and say they'll wait in the car – that they'll put the heater on full and warm it up for me. I dash upstairs again. 'Hurry up slowcoach,' they shout after me.

I don't know why I hate the red coat so much except that it was a cast-off from one of my cousins. I throw it on my bedroom floor, put on the old duffel and stuff my gloves into the pockets. I hear the hall-door opening. I delay for another second or two, knowing that if I leave it long enough, Mum won't have the heart to send me back to change. 'Wait for me, I'm coming, I'm coming,' I yell as I run downstairs.

There is a terrible bang. The hall door bursts wide open and I am thrown backwards. I see the road exploding with huge, huge flames roaring up into the sky. I open my mouth to scream but no sound comes. My hands stretch out. The car, our car, is burning. Where are they? I can't see them for the fire. 'Mum. Dad. MICH A E L . . . MAA MMM EEEE.'

My knees give way and I pitch forward and fall down. Everything is so hot. The whole road is blazing, smoke everywhere. I am lying beside the open door. I drag myself up by the handle and begin to run towards the fire. But then there's another bang and I'm flying in the air. I can't open my eyes. There is a terrible roaring noise. Another explosion. I scream and scream and scream.

I am frozen, face down on the ground. I cannot look. I claw through the broken glass, and slowly open my eyes. My mother is spread-eagled a little way from me. My brother is draped like an old coat over the garden wall. But no Dad. There's blood everywhere. People shouting, running. Sirens. Don't look. Don't look. I fall, fall, fall . . . My mother is whimpering but I cannot see her face for the blood. I scream for my dad and snuggle down beside her. I can still hear the whimpering. There is warm blood frothing all down her front but she doesn't stir. Her hair is wet. I cannot find her face.

There are voices all around, hands pulling at me. I push them away. More wailing sirens. I close my eyes and lie still. My face is wet. A voice calls out, 'Police,' and a woman's voice says, 'The little girl's alive.' Hands grip me and everything goes black. I don't know where I am. A soft, far-away *voice urges me to wake up. A woman's scent. I open my eyes and see Nancy's kind face. She is crying. Tears are running down her cheeks. She doesn't say my name.*

Retrospective

CHAPTER ELEVEN

As soon as the girls are out of sight, Roger begins
to berate us for letting them take the sandwiches.
He is already looking bored. I tell him to shut up,
take off my shorts and plunge into the cold water.
The others immediately join me. We lark about
until we become chilled, then we lie down in the
sun to dry off. I don't remember that we discussed
it, but I think we are all affected by the emergence
of Angel as an object of desire. I guess that, privately, each of us had wanted to accompany her,
practise a gallantry which we only allow ourselves
when we are alone, or with a girl.

After we dress, Guy pulls a small tin box out of
his pocket and begins to split open a dozen or so
fag-ends. He makes a neat little pile of the accumulated strands of tobacco. After another
search he finds a half empty packet of cigarette
papers and an old lighter. He carefully divides the
meagre hoard of tobacco in three and makes us
each an ultra-thin roll-up. We light them up
eagerly and have four or five deeply satisfying
drags at the stale tobacco.

But somehow all the fun has gone out of the
day. When, after half an hour or so, there is still no
sign of the girls, Roger starts to make noises about
going home. 'Are you coming?' he asks me casually. When I shake my head he smiles at me

pityingly. 'You poor sap,' he says. 'Don't make yourself so obvious.' He winks but I look away sulkily. After another few minutes he says he can't wait any longer, and mutters something about his mother needing help in the fields. I don't believe him, I know that it's only his usual excuse for disappearing. Something he does, often for days at a time. I can sense in him an excitement which I'd noticed before, though he never shares the reason for it. He doesn't have to. I know full well where he is going. I've followed him several times over the past couple of months.

The first time I shadowed him on one of his adventures, he'd gone all the way to the other side of the next town and linked up with two older boys and a man I didn't know. I followed them until they disappeared down the railway embankment. I was afraid to get close enough to see what they were doing, but it wasn't difficult to guess. That night I lay in the grass hiding for almost two hours before they reappeared. I nearly missed them because their hands and faces were blackened. Next time I followed Roger right to the meeting-place, which seemed to be run by an Englishman, so that I knew where I could go if in the future I ever needed help. It didn't occur to me then, though I would learn soon enough, that the secret groups moved around all the time, never staying long in one place. Occupied France wasn't always safe, even for Frenchmen. Now, as I watch Roger amble off, I marvel at how skilfully he has managed to free himself from the rest of us. He is barely eighteen months older than me but he seems so very grown-up, already involved in adult things.

As soon as Roger leaves, Guy and Edmond begin to grumble about feeling hungry. One of them, I think it was Guy, suggests we go back into the town to see if we can cadge lunch from his grandmother. I say I'll hang on. I don't want to walk through the streets without my shirt. When I propose strolling towards the bridge, they say they aren't going to go traipsing after the girls whom they now accuse of running off with the food. They tell me I'm a soppy fool for waiting. They shuffle away and I watch them scramble up the bank and cross the road. Shortly afterwards they climb over the low stone wall which encircles the village. Then they, too, disappear from my sight. I am less patient than I pretend. I am also in something of a pickle: I don't feel like leaving the wet clothes hanging on the branch, nor do I want to walk to the bridge without my shirt. I am less self-conscious about nakedness than about the virulent acne on my shoulders. So I wait.

I lay in the sun, beneath a cloudless sky, and wished I was old enough to stop waiting for my life to start, terrified that the war will be over before I can begin fighting. I was impatient to get stuck in, cover myself in glory; the one seemed a simple corollary of the other. Sitting it out seemed utterly pointless. So often when I came into a room unexpectedly, or upon a group of adults in the village, they would stop talking and start gabbling the rubbish they reserved for children they considered too young to defend their country. I was sick of it all. Sick of being hidden with my country relatives for five long years, while my mother enjoyed the excitement of the city. My father, who had been gone since the first year of the war, was a prisoner somewhere in eastern Europe. I had wild schemes for rescuing him. I wanted to set him free so we would fight side by side. I was bored to death of being a charity case.

I must have slept for a time because the sky had clouded over when I opened my eyes. I remember feeling slightly disorientated, startled by the thought that something is wrong. I lazily stretch out my hand to Angel's dress and, stroking it, find to my surprise that it is dry. I shake myself awake and stand up. In the distance the church clock strikes two. I wait. Sure enough, after a couple of minutes' pause, it rings twice again. Two o'clock, then. Almost an hour has passed since I crossed the river but there is still no sign of the girls. Perhaps they've got fed up and gone home? I can't bring myself to believe that Angel – she'd become *my Angel* in my fevered mind – would leave me stranded without my shirt. Nor do I believe she'd run off without her clothes. Her dress maybe, but her drawers? No fear. Her mother would give her a good clip about the ear. And the rest of us as well, given half a chance. No, Angel would definitely not go home in my shirt. I plonk down on the grass again.

For a long moment – do I imagine it? – everything is still, silent, heavy. Full of foreboding. Then slowly, from a great distance, I hear a long low rumble. At first I mistake it for the start of a thunderstorm. Away to the south-west a huge cloud of dust rises into the clear air. By now I am standing up, straining to see the bridge though I know it is too far away for me to see it properly. The feeling that something is seriously awry grows in me, yet I know that Angel is sensible and careful and that neither Fanny nor Marie-Eulalie would do anything without her say-so. Why then the fear? The urge to do something?

It takes me several moments to galvanize myself into action. I pull Angel's dry clothes off the branch, roll the drawers inside the dress and tuck them neatly into my waistband. Then, as quickly as my trembling hands can manage, I begin to climb up into a tall beech tree a few yards further along the bank. I take it slowly, hauling myself from branch to branch until, at about fifteen feet from the ground, I can see the bridge. The leaves are fresh and plentiful and hide me well. In colour they are halfway between the pale green and the copper they will become later. Their perfume almost overwhelms me.

Strange that I have never again encountered that particular scent. I peer through the leaves, straining my eyes, and there, not far from the bridge but, astonishingly, still on the opposite bank, I suddenly see Fanny dragging Marie-Eulalie across the meadow towards the tobacco field. I recognize the girls by the colour of their dresses: yellow and pale blue, like the butterflies. As the little one stumbles, I see Fanny drag her to her feet and try to lift her. Marie-Eulalie is kicking violently. They look so comic that, I'm ashamed to say, I begin to laugh.

Not that I can hear myself. By now the noise from the main road is thunderous.

Because my view is impeded by the stand of tall lime and beech on the opposite bank, I still cannot make out what is happening on the main road beyond the bridge. Then when I look for the girls again they have disappeared. I assume, wrongly, that they are playing some childish game, trying to avoid going to their catechism lesson which, I only now remember, is being held in the church that afternoon, in preparation for Marie-Eulalie's first communion the following week. Hadn't we been reminded to get her back in time, as we set off?

I look back at the bridge. Now I can see a small group of people standing on the road beside it, on the village side. They have their backs to the church. I can't make out whether they are men or women, only that they seem to be pointing or waving at something on the other side of the bridge on the main road. They fall back as the first of a huge convoy burst out of the dust – jeeps, half-trucks, tanks, motor cycles – and head straight for the town. The noise is deafening even from where I sit, safe in my tree. It takes only a few minutes to pass, four or five at most. But, for many, those minutes turn out to be eternity.

Then out of the corner of my eye I see a flash of white on my side of the river between me and the bridge. Angel? She stands up, facing the river, and waves her arms in the air. The long white shirt flaps around her. She takes a few steps one way, then the other. Why is she running back towards the bridge? Straight at a soldier who stands beyond her. He slowly raises his rifle. My mouth opens to shout her name but no sound comes. A shot rings out. I watch her float up into the air, arms outstretched, my father's shirt billowing around her. Time stops. Then she topples sideways, rolling over and over as she falls, down, down, until she lies in a crumpled little heap in the green, green grass.

The soldier lowers his rifle and walks slowly towards my hiding-place. I watch transfixed as a second, much taller, comes to join him from the shadow of the trees. They walk slowly, turning this way and that. They raise their legs high out of the long grass, first one then the other, their bent knees reaching halfway up their chests. Like lead soldiers. Each holds his rifle at the ready, in front of his chest. Their helmets are low on their faces. It takes only seconds for me to realize that they are looking for something or someone. I scan the ground beneath my tree to make sure that we've left nothing behind and shrink well back out of sight.

Oxford

June 1997

CHAPTER TWELVE

The door opened slowly with just the tiniest creak of warning. Juliet, immediately alert, lay still, feigning sleep, listening. Not the nurse's light step. A man's, but hesitant. She slowly expelled her pent-up breath as she opened her eyes a slit and covertly studied Peter Dallimore. Because she was lying down he appeared much taller than his six feet. His was a kindly rather than handsome face, with sad brown eyes and thinning hair plastered over his bald dome. Ageing suited the rugged features – as if he'd somehow grown into them, getting better-looking as he got older. He'd probably looked rather gawky, even ugly, as a young man. But not now. He looked – she searched for a word and surprised herself with *contented*. Even in repose the smile-wrinkles around his eyes and mouth remained etched into the weathered skin, giving him a good-natured look. Avuncular. A face you could trust. Maybe. If she was a trusting sort of person, which she wasn't. She opened her eyes. 'Inspector,' she said. He picked up a chair, tiptoed clumsily to the bed and stood indecisively for a few moments before handing her a small bunch of grapes. 'It's what my old mum always told me to bring to hospitals,' he said, making an awkward stab at drollery. 'But, somehow, I usually end up eating them myself,' he grinned.

'Help yourself, Inspe—'

'Try Pete,' he said.

'Only if you try Juliet.'

He looked mystified. 'Isn't that what I always call you?'

She shrugged. 'Probably, I'm being ridiculous. Thanks for looking after me on Tuesday,' she added stiffly.

He shifted uncomfortably in his chair, absently pulled a couple of grapes off the bunch and popped them in his mouth while he sorted out what to say. He liked the girl but never felt at ease with her or confident of taking the right approach. She somehow always gave the impression of being poised, ready to bolt. Quick to take offence. Or maybe it was a class thing. 'Nothing turned up on that accident you mentioned. On the High,' he said pointedly.

'No.' She avoided his eye. 'I didn't think it would.'

'I checked,' he protested, rather feebly, 'of course.'

'Of course.' She waited politely, knowing he wouldn't be here just to tell her that. Her body tensed against what might be coming.

'We did try,' he repeated more vehemently. 'But honestly, love, you were in a shocking state. Don't you think you might have been . . . erm . . .'

'Hallucinating?' She was beginning to wonder herself. Specially now that the High Street incident was being pushed aside by other, more personal anxieties.

'Now then, do you want the good news or the bad news first?'

She swallowed hard. 'The good, please,' she whispered.

'It wasn't Freddie,' he said and watched her pale face flush with relief. *Not this time*, he felt like adding, but held back for the time being.

'How do you know?' she asked softly. Not *why did you think it was Freddie?* or *I never said it was Freddie*, he noticed. So the speculation at the station was spot on; the boyfriend, partner or whatever he was, *had* been beating her up. Dallimore was struck, as he always was, and saddened, by how easily people gave themselves away.

'We checked his digs in Manchester *and* his place of work,' he replied dryly. 'He played poker with his flatmates until four, but somehow managed to show up for work at six. Likes the high life, your Freddie, doesn't he? Quite the life and soul. Though I believe he was having a quiet kip when our lads turned up at the airport to check he hadn't gone walkabout.'

'How did you find out where he worked?'

'Eh, er,' he cleared his throat. 'It's my job, actually.' He pulled a droll face. 'I *am* a policeman, remember.' He grinned. 'Your next-door neighbour is a proper fund of knowledge, isn't she? Good-looking gal.' He pursed his lips.

'Cindy Breckford?' Juliet attempted to smile back. 'Oh, yes. She keeps her ear to the ground. She's *very* fond of Freddie. Not too fond of me though, since I charged her husband with drunken

driving. But Freddie talked to her a lot, I believe.'
Her expression blanked.

'So she said. Drops her a card now and then as
well. But she hadn't his address, you'll be pleased
to hear. We found that in your address book.'

'You found my things?' She sounded annoyed,
rather than pleased.

'Some. Which brings me to the bad news,' he
said and waited for her to respond, help him
out. But she said nothing, didn't appear much
interested. He wondered if it was because she, too,
had believed it was her partner who'd mugged her.
As she slowly assimilated her mistake, he saw that
her expression of relief was being replaced by
something else: fear. He had a very good idea of
exactly why. As long as she thought it was her
bloke she didn't worry that it might be someone
else, someone much, much more threatening. He
waited, expecting her to quiz him very carefully
now. Instead, she just looked through him as if her
thoughts were miles away.

He hesitated and hoped he was making the right
guess. 'Julie, listen to me. I reckon it was kids who
broke into the house. Same crowd that's been ter-
rorizing the whole of east Oxford for the past
couple of months. You know what they were up to
as well as I do. Looking for the price of a quick
fix.' He hesitated before taking the plunge. '*They
were not professionals*. Are you hearing me?
That's what you're afraid of, isn't it? That—'

'Yes,' she said and broke down.

'We found your car,' he said eventually.

She sat up too suddenly and made herself dizzy.

Her ribs hurt like hell. 'Where?' She swallowed hard.

'At the Thornhill Park and Ride. Turned up at about three this morning.' He gnawed on his lower lip. 'Burn-out, I'm afraid. Your bag was in the garden,' he said. 'Everything was gone except the address book and an empty wallet. Your baton was beside it. Full of prints,' he said with grim satisfaction but didn't add: *and your blood.*

'The radio?' she asked in a small voice.

'No.'

'Oh.' She waited, fearing what he would say next.

'You must have disturbed them. So they whacked you over the head with your own baton. Bastards.' He paused and she could almost see the words ballooning over his head: *you are supposed to leave your stick and radio at the station.*

'I'm sorry about the radio. I should have—'

'No,' he interrupted. 'Nicking the radio was a stroke of luck, *for us.* If they've hung on to it *and used it*, that is. Unfortunately we wasted time rounding up Freddie Kimber, but Winter is on the trail and you know what a terrier he is. They're not going to get away with this. But we'll need your help, Julie.' *Juliet. My name is Juliet.*

'It would help', he said softly, 'if you could tell me what you remember. Why did you think it was, er, Freddie?'

She stiffened defensively before she caught the drift of his question, then closed her eyes, the better to concentrate. 'It *was* a he, I'm pretty sure of that. Mind you, it's only an impression. I didn't actually see anybody. I think I had my key in the door when whoever it was jumped me.' She paused and drew in her breath. 'My bag must have been on my shoulder . . .'

'Remember what time it was?' he asked casually. Juliet shook her head, which made it ache even more. She held her hands to her temples.

'Working back from when we, er, met you on the High, it would have been around six thirty?'

'Oh, was it? How can you tell?'

'I can't, not really, but you were coming off duty – don't you remember?'

'I thought I was going on. Ah . . .' Her face cleared. 'So that's why I was holding my baton and radio under my arm. I must have forgotten to leave them in my locker. One minute I was pushing the door open, next I was flat on my face.'

'What about the bike? How did you manage to get hold of it?'

'I've no idea. I must have grabbed it from the side passage, that's where I usually leave it – against the side wall of the house.'

'That tallies. It's where we found your bag. What else can you remember?' he asked gently. Juliet bit her lip. 'Honestly, Inspector, Pete, the whole sequence of events is confused. I remember thinking I had to get help but I couldn't find the radio. So I suppose I ran for the bike. I must have blacked out and fallen on the road at some point. After that the only thing I could think of was that I had to get to the station. That I was late or something . . .' She hunched her shoulders and snapped open her eyes. 'It's all such a blur.' She put her

124

hand to her mouth and began to chew on her thumbnail. 'Next thing I remember was Steve pushing me into the squad car,' she lied and looked away.

'We were on our way to your address, as a matter of fact,' he said. 'The desk sergeant thought that was where you were phoning from.'

'I phoned? I don't remember calling the station.' She chewed on her fingernails, absently. 'I thought . . . I called for an ambulance? For the accident.'

'You did, but you also rang the station. Didn't make much sense, so we thought we'd go take a look.' He made a face and popped another grape in his mouth.

'The house was trashed, I'm afraid,' he continued after a brief pause. 'Vicious bloody crew. Fucking vandals,' he spat, in a rare burst. Usually he was rather prissy about his language. 'We won't be able to tell what's missing until you check it out. But if you had any electronic stuff, it's all gone. I'm sorry, love, I hope you're fully insured?'

She didn't answer. Her expression was preoccupied, her fingers played restlessly on her lower lip.

'Let's try and list what might be missing,' he coaxed. He took a notebook from his pocket and held his pen poised over a blank page. 'What about credit cards? We should stop them . . .?'

'Just a Switch. Oh hell, I better ring the bank.'

'Don't worry, I got our accounts people to do that.' He jotted something down. 'No credit cards?' He kept his tone neutral.

'No,' she said mutinously.

He jerked back his head and raised his eyebrows. 'None?'

'There were a couple in my wallet but they were already cancelled,' she muttered and took a deep breath.

'That's a bit of luck,' he said dryly.

'No electronic stuff either,' she said, ignoring his last remark. 'It's all gone. There was nothing of value left in the house.' She blushed. It wasn't true, but she didn't want to admit that she had a hunch Freddie had tried some sort of insurance scam which had gone disastrously wrong. She wouldn't shop him to Dallimore but she was damned if she was going to make life easy for him.

'Cash?'

She shrugged, gnawed nervously at her fingernails but said nothing.

'Anything in the bag?'

'About fifty quid. I'm strictly cash economy these days.' She tried to hide the humiliation with irony.

Dallimore let it pass for the moment. 'Fifty quid would be hardly any use to them, you know that. And no electronic stuff either? Unusual.' His tone was acid. Juliet avoided his eye. 'That's probably why they trashed the place. Kimber was out of a job for a while, wasn't he? Were you financing the poker?'

She gave in suddenly. 'For a while. I stopped.' Must have been using her credit cards, Dallimore concluded. What a little shit the man was.

'That when he began beating you up?' he asked gently, catching her off guard. She turned her face away. 'Juliet?' He got her name right for once. 'Did you talk to anyone? Get any help?'

She shook her head, as the tears began to flow. 'Couldn't.'

'We could have helped. I could have helped, Julie, I *would* have helped. Surely you know that?'

'Couldn't. It was too complicated. I can't talk about it. Sorry.'

'You should not have let him get away with it,' he insisted. 'These things have to be sorted.'

'He wasn't always like that.' She started to defend him but stopped when Dallimore gestured impatiently with his hand. He held back for her to continue, which she did after a moment or two, woodenly uncovering the end of a relationship. She looked stunned. 'He didn't mean to, not really. He's an only child, he found it hard to share, couldn't get used to being . . . Didn't like it, said I invaded his space. He just couldn't stand accounting for his time, his absences. The way I complained about his spending. That's what used to set him off. He used to go wild. The last time, I think he really frightened himself.' She shrugged hopelessly. 'I just couldn't take it any more. I threatened him,' she said grimly, 'with the, er, police.'

Dallimore raised his eyebrows. 'Did you? Really?' he asked and waited. She gave him a watery smile.

'The house is being sold to pay off the debts. There won't be much left,' she said bitterly. 'In the middle of it all he lost his job in London. He hated me being in the force,' she added almost as an afterthought. 'Poor Freddie.'

127

'Poor?' Dallimore exploded. 'Get a grip, Julie. How long were you two together?'

'Six years,' she muttered defensively. 'I threw him out, you know. Finally.'

'The house the last straw?'

'Yes. It woke us both up, I think. I didn't realize for ages how much . . . he owed. We've had it five years so it's worth a fair bit. He just threw it away,' she said absently, thinking how the decline of the relationship had less to do with debt than . . . What? She couldn't bear to think of the past few months. Or the bile he'd come out with. It was all so complicated, baffling. The accusations he'd hurled at her, the jealousies, after he found her snogging some bloke at a party. She'd been so drunk, she couldn't remember his name. 'You can't resist, can you? Everyone has to love Juliet. You're a leech, you know that?'

What about you? What about the violence? she wanted to shout but was terrified at the thought of being pushed out, being alone. Deep down, a still small voice protested: isn't that what you expected, arranged?

'No, no! I love you, Freddie . . . I can't stand the . . .' She was going to add 'insecurity', but he wouldn't let her finish.

'You don't love me, you just want . . . Oh, fuck knows what you want. Everything, you want everything. You have to have it all, but you give nothing. You haven't a clue, have you?'

Home truths at last. Juliet closed her eyes at the memory of her pain and bewilderment and the death of his affection for her. The death of her faith in him. Yet they had loved each other once. Well, *hadn't they*? He was so strong when she met him, so beautiful. So popular. Everyone's best chum. They were never alone. She never had to feel afraid.

Dallimore watched her during that long silence, sensing that he was gaining her confidence at last. Or perhaps it was only that she was weary of keeping her misery to herself?

'The shame is the worst, you know,' she said softly. 'The humiliation. It distorts everything, you can't think straight.' She rubbed her eyes dry and gave him a pathetic little smile. 'You keep asking yourself why. Why me? What did I do to deserve it?'

'You've been very patient, Inspector . . . Pete,' she said at last. 'I'm sorry for giving you the run-round. I'm glad it wasn't Freddie.' She bit back the fear that plagued her. Did I do this to him? Did I really leech on him? *Will anyone ever want me again?*

'We guessed it was going on. He shouldn't have got away with it.' The words were mild but he looked angry.

'I threw him out', she mumbled, 'a couple of months ago. He was really upset.'

'Upset?' he snorted. 'Pity about that. You did the right thing. It isn't as if you were married. And even if you were, you didn't have to put up with it. The man's a brute. It would have got worse, you know. But I don't have to tell you that. Can't but notice that once it starts it never ends. It's not something I understand very well, domestic.' As indeed he did not, being an unusually kind and uxorious man. 'You should have brought charges,' he added.

'No. You know I couldn't?' she pleaded. 'It's not just . . . Look sir, I've got something to tell you . . .'

'Mmm?'

'I've decided to leave the force,' she said abruptly.

'Oh? When?'

'As soon as possible. I've made up my mind. I'll send in my resignation in a day or so. I should have done it long ago. I can't go back, I've lost my nerve. I've got enough leave owing to cover my notice – that and sick leave.'

She was surprised and slightly disappointed that he didn't try to dissuade her, except to say: 'I'm sorry about that. You're good, you know. Could be very good.'

'Nice try, but you're an awful liar.' She gave him a half-hearted smile. 'And you've covered up for me far too often. You know perfectly well I've spent most of the past couple of years in a total funk. I just can't hack it any more. It's just about the most unsuitable job I could have.'

'Not all the time. We all have our individual strengths,' he replied, rather ponderously. 'People find it easy to talk to you. I'm not the only one to notice. I'm sorry you won't be back. You're very good with the victims. Outstanding, in fact.'

Takes one to know one. She kept the thought to herself. 'Thanks Peter, I value that,' she said politely. 'But I was never right for the job. I couldn't face it any more. And, admit it, you're as relieved as I am.'

'*You? In the police? You're completely out of your mind,*' Freddie had jeered when she announced she'd been accepted as a trainee. 'You'd be useless, for God's sake. You're a brain-box, not a Rambo. They wouldn't know what to do with you.' That wasn't really what he meant; Frederick Stockly Kimber just felt the police force was beneath her. And him. Her job embarrassed him, socially. He couldn't understand why she wouldn't go back to college and finish her degree. She realized, of course, that he wouldn't have been able to stomach her getting a better degree than his miserable third, either. So whatever she did was bound to be wrong.

She didn't share her terrors with him, then or ever. It was such a wild idea – the notion that she might be safe in such a dangerous job. Freddie had designs on a fat-cat job in the city and wanted them to move to London, but she couldn't leave the safety of Oxford. The more he tried to per-suade her, the more she dug her heels in. When he didn't get the jobs he applied for he blamed her for holding him back. So even then it never once occurred to her to confide in him.

Strange how the habit of mistrust grows until it pervades everything. A habit so ingrained she could never shake it off. Freddie was told nothing of her background. As far as he knew, she was born and bred in Oxford, adopted as a child by Nancy. Even from the start their relationship was a sham. She was a phantom. Of course he sensed

131

she was forever holding back and soon became convinced that she was living a double life. This was true, though not in the sense he understood.

Her emotions were stunted, blanketed by the all-pervasive urge to protect her from the nightmares of her past. Their relationship might have had a chance had she confided in her lover, but deep down she trusted no-one and therefore rarely connected on anything but the most superficial level. She had developed a rigid, almost Olympian faith in her own judgement; Freddie must accept her as she was. It didn't seem to occur to her that most new lovers shared their past, bonding with trivialities, details. What Juliet presented was an unfathomable blank. In a sense, without being in an institution she was emotionally institutionalized.

She did not realize that such unwavering self-protection would eventually stifle her character. And his. Perhaps one of the reasons she'd clung to Freddie was that he never felt he had to be nice to Juliet because *she had suffered*. How could he? He didn't know; she didn't tell him. But just because she kept her origins to herself, her pattern of mistrust didn't change, but, rather like a troublesome infection, she passed it on to Freddie. Stifling herself, she had stifled him, and thus removed all possibility of happiness together.

Initially she had latched on to Freddie as an escape from the terrible seriousness of her life. She was, quite simply, dazzled by his looks and his huge personality. The first time she saw him he was in the middle of a crowd, drunk and laughing.

Vibrant, sexy. She was immediately struck by how eagerly everyone jostled for his attention. How she longed to be part of that exclusive coterie around him. His light-heartedness was such a contrast to her own sobriety. Had she always been like that? Sometimes, when she allowed herself to look back, she had glimpses of a normal, rather bolshie, little girl, her arms spread out expansively, laughing.

Joining the police force was a perverse and quixotic idea. Looking back, that was when their troubles had begun and the honeymoon of their romance began to wear off. It was another six months before he got a job with a travel firm which was well-paid but which he considered beneath him. It certainly paid better than the police but, when she said as much, he accused her of patronizing him when all she'd wanted was to make him feel better about himself. She so desperately wanted them to be happy. But he was easily bored, and soon made it all too plain that she bored him. She should have told him then. Told him why the job and Oxford made her feel safe. Told him a lot of things. But she couldn't. Not then. And later? She didn't trust him. No matter how much she liked the sex, she couldn't rely on him to keep his mouth shut, specially in his cups.

They fell silent. Dallimore munched another few grapes. 'What d'you intend to do with yourself?'

'I plan to evaporate.' She raised her eyebrows ironically. 'Move away and not leave a forwarding address.' Her voice was bitter. 'And get a better-paying job.'

'Shouldn't be too difficult,' he snorted.

'Not sure about that, but we'll see.' She closed her eyes, her head was splitting.

Dallimore stood up and brushed a few random grape pips off the knees of his trousers.

'You've been a great help,' he said encouragingly, as if she had done him a favour. 'Julie? Er . . . anything else you can think of?'

'No, I don't think so.' She suddenly felt exhausted and fractious. She wished he would go and let her sleep. And stop being so damn paternal.

'Keep in touch and get well,' Dallimore said feebly, realizing he was no longer welcome. She didn't answer. 'I'll drop in over the weekend,' he said.

It hadn't escaped him that all through their talk, apart from just one reference to 'an accident', there was no mention of old men on pedestrian crossings – which instantly reminded him of his little grandson chanting 'green man, green man, green man,' whenever he was led across the street. He smiled at the thought and waited, in silence, to see if she would add anything, but she didn't and he was relieved. He assumed that it was as he, and especially Winter, had suspected, a ploy to distract them. Or more likely herself. A last-ditch stand to spare her the shame of confessing that she thought she'd been bludgeoned by her lout of a boyfriend.

A very, very complicated girl. It was one of the duty desk-sergeants who'd been the first to be sceptical of her breezy explanations for her various bruises. Dallimore eyed her uneasily, wondering how it was that he hadn't understood what was happening to her for so long. Perhaps it had something to do with her reserve? When he first met her he'd speculated as to what had made her join the force. And why she had, so assiduously, avoided the graduate fast track for which, he assumed, she was well qualified.

He had found the rather disturbing explanation quite by accident. A couple of years before, they'd been summoned to investigate an ugly incident in the vast Blackbird Leys housing estate on the outskirts of Oxford. A small child had been badly injured during a knife-fight between a couple of feuding drug dealers. When one of them insisted, '*It was a mistake, the kid just got in the way,*' Juliet had literally gone for his throat and would have been stabbed herself if Dallimore hadn't pulled her off. He hadn't reported it, but after they'd got back to the station he'd sat her down and hauled her over the coals, demanding an explanation. At first she adamantly refused to say anything but when news came in from the hospital that the child had died, she broke down completely. He would never forget her look of utter despair, nor the stark phrase she spat at him.

'That's how they wiped out my family. *By mistake*. They got the wrong car. The bomb was intended for someone else.'

Later, just once, when he tried to get her to explain, she had looked through him as if he were out of his mind. 'I don't know what you're talking about,' she said and turned on her heel.

But there are more ways than one to skin a cat,

and what Dallimore learned from other sources made him both circumspect and protective as far as Juliet Furbo was concerned. After all, it was his job.

CHAPTER THIRTEEN

Sometime after six on Friday morning, the nurse tiptoed into the room with a cup of milky tea sloshing into its saucer. Juliet, who was half-dressed and looking rather groggy, was sitting on the side of the bed, which was scattered with several copies of the *Oxford Mail*, the local evening paper.

The nurse, whom she hadn't encountered before, but whose name-tag identified her as Silvia, glared at her. 'And what do you think *you're* doing?' she asked crossly. She had a rather peculiar verbal tic of emphasizing every second or third word. 'And where on *earth* did all these come from? The *place* looks like a *bomb's* hit it.'

Juliet froze. 'Something I had to look up.' She squeezed out the words. 'I got them from the TV room.' As she had, an hour earlier. A whole week's supply. Even the previous Tuesday's edition had been in the pile on the floor beside the TV. But careful scanning had not revealed a single reference to the 'High Street incident' as she'd privately named it. Was Peter Dallimore right? Was it all in her imagination, after all?

'Finished with them, are we?'

'*We're* not sure,' Juliet countered, but was ignored.

Silvia pressed the cup and saucer into Juliet's

flaccid hands and held on until she felt the girl take the weight from her. 'Drink it while it's still hot, dearie,' she said bossily, and began to tidy the newspapers, with the obvious intention of dumping the lot into the waste-bin.

'Hang on. I said I wasn't . . .' Juliet began to protest but was cut off mid-sentence.

'I'll put them back in the TV room, where they belong. You can read them there.'

'Oh, for heaven's sake . . .' Juliet let out a pent-up puff of irritation and then caved in. She'd already gone through the papers several times trying to find again one vague reference which niggled at the back of her mind. A tiny paragraph she'd skimmed but which didn't really register at the time. Something to do with a hotel. If she could just think of the name, it might be easier to find.

'The doctors will be around shortly,' the nurse interrupted, and Juliet's train of thought instantly evaporated.

'Did you say something?'

'I said, why don't you lie down for a while? It's much too early to be up. Have your tea and I'll be back in a few minutes with your pills. You're looking peaky.' The nurse eyed her suspiciously. Juliet stared back, noticing, with some satisfaction, that Silvia's very shiny pink lipstick made her teeth look yellow.

'You're not thinking of leaving, are you?'

'Yes, I am.' Juliet roused herself. 'I've been lying around long enough.'

'I suppose you know what you're going to

wear,' Silvia sniffed and left the room in see-if-I-care mode, muttering, 'Some people . . .'

Fearing she'd gone to recruit the heavy gang, Juliet slipped on her uniform pants and tried to summon enough courage, or at least enough energy, to put on her shoes and go home. She was having a problem with the word *home*, even more so with the shoes whose laces her trembling fingers had got into a complete cat's cradle. She abandoned them to the floor and stared down at them. They seemed to embody everything she'd allowed herself to become: earnest, boring, stolid, melt-in-the-crowd. When what she most wanted to be was independent, lively, happy. The shoes looked alien: way too heavy, too serviceable, down-to-earth, competent. Not feeling any of those things, she kicked them irritably. How, she asked herself, could anyone wearing such shoes *not* be taken seriously? She felt as if her tenuous control of her life somehow rested with those workaday lace-ups. *Don't wear those horrible old clodhoppers, darling.*

She laid her aching head against the pillow to rest for a few minutes, then hauled the shoes from under the bed and sat with them on her lap. There was so much to sort out. She wished she could just leave everything, rush down the corridor to the lift and run out into the sunlight. And keep running. But there was no sunlight and little possibility of flight. The day was overcast and hazy, as if it couldn't make up its mind whether to rain or not. Yet the shoes, so suitable for the dingy morning, seemed more like an oppressive anchor than a means of escape. In her mind they had become a symbol of the hopelessness of her life, the mess she'd made of it. She dropped them heavily on the floor and, as she slipped her feet into them, was immediately overwhelmed with a sudden desire for something wonderful and giddy, like bright red dancing slippers. *Wear your new red coat, darling. For me.* She sat quite still, listening to the voices in her head, trying to catch the loving tone, the sounds of the past.

Was it the blow on her head which had awakened memory? She felt as though she were on a sort of mental see-saw, right in the centre, trying to balance the near against the far past. The illusion was that she had to keep the balance precisely in order to shut out both, and that the means of doing so was, for reasons she simply could not understand, the 'High Street incident'. Somewhere, someone was in trouble, or hurt, or in danger, and only she could help. And why? Because only she had seen it. What had she seen? Ah, she sighed, there was the rub. But something, whimsical, intangible, *important* was tugging at her memory, yet she couldn't grasp its meaning. If it had any meaning.

Frustrated, Juliet went to the wash-basin and splashed her face with cold water. A brand-new toothbrush and half-filled tube of toothpaste was sitting on the little glass shelf above it. She brushed her teeth vigorously and, feeling slightly more human, bundled her few possessions into her shoulder-bag which she found in her locker though she couldn't remember anyone bringing it into the hospital. Had Dallimore? Whoever it was had kindly slipped a crisp tenner into the otherwise empty purse. Plus her house keys. There was also an unopened letter addressed to her in Freddie's writing on the locker top which she couldn't remember having seen before, either. Juliet slipped it into her bag unread and, without so much as a by your leave, she slung the strap over her shoulder and walked resolutely out of the ward. She made the lift without being accosted.

A taxi was dropping a fare as she came through the entrance. Juliet grabbed it, climbed in, ignoring the driver's open-mouthed amazement at the state of her attire. The bedside locker had yielded only her neatly folded uniform slacks and bra but no underpants. Far from making her feel sexy, the rough serge chafed her bare skin. She wondered how many patients left hospital still wearing a hospital robe? Though she'd turned it back to front and tucked it tightly into her trousers to disguise the opening, it still was what it was: an over-washed calico shift with John Radcliffe Hospital stamped fore and aft. Juliet kept her hand on the strap of her bag to obscure as much of the mark as possible.

'Little Oxford, corner of Gypsy Lane and Old Road,' she instructed as nonchalantly as she could.

'I know where it is,' the driver said in a surly tone. 'Beside the Warneford,' he added more pointedly. Juliet ignored the reference to the local psychiatric hospital.

'I'll want you to wait outside while I collect

something. After that, you can drop me at the Café Noir in Headington.'

The meter read two pounds twenty by the time it pulled up outside the house. Juliet took her keys from her bag and, praying that Cindy Breckford was away on her school run, got out. It took considerably more effort of will for her to turn the key in the lock and push open the hall door against the clutter of envelopes on the mat. She gathered them clumsily and dumped them, with her bag, on the hall table. Her painful ribs made it difficult to breathe and every time she bent down the blood rushed to her head, making it throb. She leaned against the wall for a few moments to recover her equilibrium, and it was only the thought of the taxi-meter ticking away – not to mention Cindy's goggle-eyes – which propelled her into the kitchen.

The police, or someone, had made a stab at cleaning up what must have been a shocking mess. The smashed back window was boarded up, leaving the kitchen in merciful gloom. Bits of broken chairs were lying on the table and almost all the crockery was missing from the shelves. The walls had been sketchily washed, leaving great swooping dark streaks all over them. She peeped into the front room and saw that the sofa had been comprehensively slashed. She didn't stop to check for any more damage; the place stank like a urinal.

Her legs felt like jelly as she staggered upstairs. The main bedroom carpet had been removed, but the stink pervaded everywhere, making it hard to concentrate. She looked around for something to stand on and eventually, in one of the two back bedrooms, found what appeared to be the only remaining complete chair in the house – as far as she could tell. By now, her head felt as though it would burst open. Doing her best to ignore it, she hauled the chair out on the landing, climbed on it shakily and stretched up her hands. The ceiling trapdoor to the attic didn't appear to have been disturbed. She lowered it slowly, pulled down the attached ladder and, sobbing with pent-up anxiety, found what she was looking for. Underneath the fourth step from the bottom, below eye-level when the ladder was extended and completely obscured when it was folded, a plastic sandwich bag was neatly taped. Her 'running-away' money; safe and sound. Relief flooded over her. She tore away the Sellotape, pulled it free and slipped the little package into her trouser pocket. Then she clambered back up on the chair, folded the ladder and closed the hatch before returning the chair to the bedroom. She had intended picking up some shoes, clothes, make-up, anything she could find, but when she opened the wardrobe door the stench hit her in the face. Her clothes seemed to be impregnated with urine. She ran from the room empty-handed and down the stairs helter-skelter. On the way out, she grabbed her bag and an old tweed jacket from the coat-rack behind the hall door and slipped it on.

Ten minutes later she was nursing a huge cappuccino. The local branch of her bank was a convenient three- or four-minute walk away, and Masquerade, a favourite haunt, which she knew would have not the slightest difficulty in filling most of her clothing needs, was next door. But there was over an hour to wait before either bank or shop opened. She took Freddie's letter from her bag and tore it open: it was terse and to the point.

I've accepted the offer on the house. They want to complete next Tuesday. The estate agent is arranging for the place to be cleared and cleaned up on Monday. Take whatever you want, the rest will be dumped. Can you get to the solicitors in the Turl, at twelve sharp? Don't be late. I'm taking the train down and back and have barely an hour in Oxford. Old Barber says he can finalize everything in one fell swoop. When the debts are cleared there'll be about twenty thousand left. Then there's just the estate agent and the legal fees which can also be sorted at the same time. Sorry but there it is. I've arranged for half of what's left to be paid into your bank. If that's what you want.

Want? Bastard. The offer on the house was for one hundred and forty-five which should have cleared a good fifty thousand above the mortgage, including her deposit of ten thousand. Something in her snapped and she began to laugh, a dry bitter croak at first, barely audible, but within seconds she was gasping for breath. A curious face peeped around the bead curtain leading to the kitchen, but quickly withdrew.

She should have listened to her financial adviser. 'Why not go halves with your partner?' he'd urged. 'Ten thousand is too much. Leaves you vulnerable.' But, being in love, she'd been scornful of his mistrust. 'Oh, well,' he'd said. 'You should be all right. There's little as safe as houses. Unless, of course, negative equity rears its ugly head and we get a repeat of the Eighties.' But even then she hadn't listened.

Safe as houses? Five years' mortgage payments plus the down payment of ten thousand from her 'inheritance' wiped out. And Freddie waltzing off debt-free, without even saying thanks. Maybe, she thought sourly. Maybe one day he'll give me the benefit. Maybe one day he'll say *my* debts and not *the* debts. Half? That's a laugh. Maybe one day he'll realize I had a choice about whether to bail him out. Maybe one day . . . Oh, what the hell. None of it mattered any more. She was free of him. Free of the gut-wrenching guilt of it all. Free of the fear. Or that fear. There were others.

As the frail spurt of anger was overwhelmed by sadness and weariness, Juliet closed her eyes, leaned back and rested her head on the padded bench. She'd had a restless night. No, more than restless, frenzied. Her mind had gone over and over the events of the past days, weeks, months, years. Squirming, dodging, counting her omissions, evasions, stupidities. She tormented herself with guilt. Everything piled in on her, things said and not said. Sometime around four a.m., she admitted she'd made her irregular hours an excuse for gradually withdrawing from any active participation in either her partnership or her social life. When the sex began to fail Freddie accused her of all sorts including – oh fantasy, fantasy – fucking half of Oxford and the whole of the constabulary. She didn't see any point in trying to defend herself – all right, there had been one or two. She turned hot and cold when she thought of it – before she decided she wanted out. The only trouble was summoning the courage to admit defeat and go.

Was it her own constant demand for reassurance which made her resent the same need in Freddie? Yet who was she to talk of needs? What did she know? When it came right down to it, she couldn't shove all the blame on Freddie. In the end, she only knew how his behaviour affected her, not what drove him. How could she possibly begin to trust him when she never really trusted herself? Why had she refused to counter his accusations? To avoid confrontation? An argument? Was it her silence which had finally driven him over the edge to violence? 'What is wrong with you?' he'd shouted. 'Juliet, for God's sake, what is happening to us? TALK TO ME.' But all she could hear were the voices in her head: *Talk to no-one. Trust no-one. My name is Juliet Furbo. Say it, say it. Repeat it after me: my name is Juliet Furbo.*

It never occurred to him that his savage bitterness and compulsive carousing might have something to do with anything. Or their mounting debts. Two obsessives vying for sympathy. At the end she'd been so depressed, she even found talking an effort. She remembered watching him try to get through her silence, watching his frustration convert to violence, that terrifying first time. It happened precisely two weeks after the incident in Blackbird Leys had unleashed her demons. It was also about then that her confidence in herself as well as her ability to survive, so carefully garnered and cultivated, had evaporated – utterly and completely.

The truth was that Juliet had no close friends any more; she was too disengaged. That was one of the worst things. As the relationship collapsed, friendships seemed to collapse with it. It wasn't so much losing the man she loved – Freddie had ceased being that, the day he first struck her – there was something even more invidious and wounding about the way their friends marshalled, almost without exception, on Freddie's side. Freddie was fun, on for anything, popular. It quickly became clear that blame for the breakup was apportioned to her, which wasn't altogether surprising, since she'd never confided the true circumstances to anyone. How could she? It was too raw, too painful, too much of a loss of her fragile self-esteem. She might survive humiliation, but, as sure as hell, she couldn't begin to cope with pity.

Juliet pulled the wad of money from her right-hand pocket and counted it surreptitiously, under the table. It was all there. Four hundred and eighty-five pounds. She extracted a tenner before stashing the remainder in the inside pocket of her bag. It was still only twenty past nine. She ordered a second coffee, a black one this time, borrowed a sheet of paper and ball-point pen from the waitress and set about calculating her financial position while she planned her next move.

'You can't stay in that house alone. It's not safe.' Dallimore had said at some point the day before, insisting that she 'should have someone to look after you'.

'It's all arranged,' she'd lied. 'I'm going to stay with some friends. I won't be alone, I promise you.'

Her mouth twisted into a grim smile. Well, that at least was true. She would find a discreet guest-house and hole up there until she was ready to move on. Juliet began to compile a list.

CHAPTER FOURTEEN

By lunch-time Juliet, having completed her business with the bank, kitted herself out with the basics of a new and rather smart wardrobe, as different as she could make it from the dull and depressing black-blue of her uniform. After that, having decided on a course of action, she took the bus into the centre of Oxford, bought some underwear, then booked herself into the Miranda Lodge in Holywell Street, where she soon found that the relatively low charges did not quite outweigh the disadvantages of staying in a guest-house.

True, the room was well-aired and clean but, since it was not much bigger than a medium-sized bathroom, it was too tiny for twenty-four-hour occupation. This may have been one of the reasons why the landlady, Mrs Cowley, insisted that all rooms should be vacated between nine and one each morning. Juliet successfully sidestepped this for the weekend, though it was made clear that the usual order would be resumed on the Monday.

There were other disadvantages as well: the garrulousness of the landlady for one, the proximity of the other guests for another. Sharing a bathroom, however well-appointed, was not conducive to privacy. But then it could be argued that privacy, or at least solitude, was precisely what Juliet had fled. She told herself there was safety in numbers, anonymity in a crowd, and, for that, the Miranda Lodge did well. Within, it was bursting at its seams with tourists; outside, because it was halfway between New College and Wadham, the comings and goings of the undergraduates were apparent and audible at all times.

Juliet spent most of the weekend in her room, recuperating her strength and her spirits and making a noble effort to come to terms with her new situation. The weather remained warm and only the slightest breeze stirred the flimsy pink curtains. The hours took a muted, undemanding rhythm from the sounds of the passers-by in the street and from the adjacent houses. As she lay dozing in the half-gloom, music or little snatches of conversation floated through the open window which kept her mildly entertained while she succumbed to the peace and tranquillity. She half listened to a serial of courtship acted out by a girl in a window across the street playing Juliet to an aggressive-sounding Romeo boy on the pavement below. Each episode only lasted a few minutes but was replayed at regular intervals during both day and night. There was a curious consolation in being part, yet not part, of the human race. She didn't think about the future or make any but the most nebulous plans, contenting herself, as far as possible, with keeping her mind a safe, unthreatening blank. By Sunday night she realized that what she felt most was relief. The battles with Freddie were over, the pain had been endured; she was emerging on the other side. Glad to be alive. Literally battered but relatively unbowed.

Having eaten little since she left hospital on Friday, by Monday morning she was ravenous. She woke, naturally and without a headache, just after seven and made her leisurely way to the bathroom, only to find it occupied. As it was again at seven twenty, seven forty-five and five past eight. By then, need had turned to desperation. Cursing the entire American nation for their pre-occupation with cleanliness, she waited, poised to sprint, just inside her bedroom door. At eight twelve she beat off a vociferously surprised, blue-rinsed matron and locked herself firmly into the steamy and fetid bathroom. Central and safe though it was, she had already decided that the guest-house would not be sustainable for more than a few days.

Since the thought of joining the great over-showered in the dining-room below was enough to do her head in, she decided to stroll down to the covered market for breakfast and a rethink. She didn't quite manage to stroll, which implied something more relaxed and laid-back than the stiff-legged gait she achieved. Apart from the ugly multicoloured bruise on her forehead, she looked reasonably rested, though her muscles and joints screamed in protest at every step. By the time she crossed the road to the Broad, a mere hundred yards from the guest-house, she wondered how on earth she could possibly keep moving, and/or occupied, until the Miranda reopened its doors at one o'clock. She slowed down, painfully, aware of every step, and, as she staggered past the Sheldonian Theatre, realized she might have done better to exercise over the weekend, rather than hole up in her room.

A couple of hundred yards further down, at the corner of Turl Street, she rewarded herself by pausing by Blackwell's window, ostensibly to examine the new paperbacks but really to rest against it and draw breath. But, catching sight of herself in the plate-glass window, she was considerably cheered. She'd lost a little weight and the beige linen slacks and crisp white shirt looked good, specially since her old shoes weren't visible to spoil the effect. But her hair needed urgent attention, she decided, turning her head this way and that. Using her nail-scissors, she'd chopped a rough fringe to cover the head wound and scraped the rest of her shoulder-length hair back in a tight bunch which didn't suit her, but made her less recognizable. It was the only thing she was vain about. As an undergraduate she'd tried tinting it dark, but it made her look like death warmed-up. Blonde was even more of a disaster since it immediately turned into a bright yellow frizz and, after abortive remedial action, incandescent orange. She grinned at her reflection. It needed to be trimmed and conditioned. Or perhaps she might cut it short, find a good hairdresser. And a shoe shop. New shoes, new hair. 'Well, that's the morning sorted,' she murmured and continued her way, more cheerfully, down Turl Street.

Her initial target was Georgina's café inside the market, but, as she opened the door, the smell of coffee wafting out stirred something in her memory. The dim image of the two men on the

152

crossing, never far from her as she lay in bed all week, suddenly surfaced with such clarity she stopped short. Dallimore had clearly thought she'd made up the story to divert attention from her own plight. He'd almost convinced her. But not quite.

Though she'd allowed him to think otherwise, she'd resisted his obvious scepticism. She *had* witnessed something. Why it haunted her, seemed so important, she did not know, except that it had burrowed deep into her brain and continued to disturb her. Hardly an hour had passed without her speculating on the incident in some way. She dithered for only a moment before she turned on her heel and walked through the market towards the High, trying to sort the confusion in her head as she went along. At the arched gateway she paused and looked up and down the street, before she allowed her eyes to rest on the zebra crossing.

Were the figures becoming clearer? In reality or imagination? There was the rub. Could she possibly have invented those strange blind-looking blue eyes? She didn't think so; she could neither forget them, nor erase them from her mind. And now something she hadn't thought of, up to then, occurred to her: those eyes would be instantly recognizable.

What about the injured man? That was more difficult – it only now struck her as peculiar that she hadn't seen his face. She had an impression of scarce and untidy grey hair, dark clothes. It bothered her that the prostrate man didn't move. Also the way the blue-eyed man crouched over him, as if he were deliberately trying to shield him from her sight. Was he dead? Unlikely. After all, she'd scoured the newspapers, she hadn't found a report of the 'accident'. Nor mention of any disappearances. So where were her mystery men? Again, she had the briefest, fleeting impression of something missed. Where? How? She pulled and shoved her unwilling memory but nothing came as she pushed the newspapers out of her mind. For the time being at least.

Instead, she forced her thoughts back to the previous Tuesday morning. Not to what had happened at home, but to the point where she was cycling up the High Street. She hadn't seen anything until she was almost on top of them. She saw herself topple off the bike; look down at the two men. How strangely muffled the scene was. The traffic must have been roaring by, yet she had no memory of hearing anything. Silence. Then what happened? She must have left the bike somewhere. She was on the other side of the street. Running. Where? Where was she headed? As Juliet slowly revolved and looked up and down the High, it came back to her. *The Madeleine*. But why? There was only one way to find out. Juliet headed for the archway at the top of the street.

The Café Madeleine was crowded. The only available table was crushed up against the back wall and rather too close to the loo for comfort. Juliet stumbled over to it and sat down. Within seconds a cheerful-looking waiter took her order for a cappuccino and croissant. As she waited she looked around. The previous Tuesday morning apart, she'd only been in the Madeleine a few times, for a snack lunch, or a quick, daytime, cup of coffee. It had always been as it was now, buzzing, with customers bustling in and out.

Yet, strangely, the image she carried in her confused memory of that morning was quite different. Rather more surreal, like the bleak Edward Hopper poster she'd had in her college room. The one with a solitary woman in an American diner staring into space. But she'd never seen the Madeleine like that, had she? What about that morning? She dredged her memory. Maybe. There had been several customers scattered thinly through the large room, reading or staring at a TV above the bar. She checked. The TV was in place, the Kilroy show flickering silently. She'd come in to . . . she'd come in to . . . *Ambulance*, she thought triumphantly, this is where I came to call the ambulance. Odd what she suddenly remembered. She had a vivid memory of a curious stillness, as if the scattered clientele were poised, waiting for something to happen. Eyes everywhere. Were they watching her? Now, as the waiter plonked her order down on the table, Juliet bent forward and drew in the strong aroma of the excellent coffee. *Who was there that morning? Who had she talked to?*

A shout from the bar made her look up. A waiter, the head waiter by his authoritative air, was ordering one of the staff to hurry up. Jack, she thought with triumphant surprise. His name is Jack. He followed me out. 'My name is Jack,' he said, 'can you hear me? My name is Jack. You need help.' Or something like that. She half rose to go and accost him when he disappeared into the kitchen. There was another waiter. Where was he? Her eyes narrowed in thought. Smoking. He was smoking out in the courtyard as she ran past. What had he said? Something rude. He'd shouted something, made a rude gesture.

She looked around again. There was a phone sitting on the bar. Had she rung from there? No. No, no, there was someone using it. The barman pointed to . . . where? There, just along the wall behind where she was now sitting. Dallimore had said she'd called the station. It was a payphone, but that wouldn't have been a problem, since she habitually carried some loose change in her pocket against an emergency. Juliet stood up and, ignoring the couple at the table beside the phone, stretched her hand out to the receiver and, without knowing why, let it fall to the little slot which returned unused coins. She tilted the lid gently and felt around the aperture with her index finger. She was so lost in time that she didn't notice the couple staring at her.

'Excuse me,' an irritated voice said. 'Do you mind? We're sitting here.' Juliet went back to her table and, as she sat down, the memory clicked. She dropped her hands to her hips and patted her pockets. There had been something in the slot. She vividly remembered pulling out a screwed-up scrap of paper and stuffing it in her pocket. She tried to remember if she'd left the uniform pants behind her at the shop when she bought her new stuff, or if they were in the wardrobe at the Miranda.

Juliet paid her bill and hurried away. The stiffness of her joints forgotten, she half jogged, half sprinted for Holywell Street. Mrs Cowley was on the front step, polishing the brass door-knocker – a sight so old-fashioned that Juliet, for an instant, tumbled backwards to her childhood.

'You forget something?' Mrs Cowley asked and didn't demur when her guest muttered something about feeling ill and rushed past her into the house.

The bed had been made and her jumble of new clothes had been neatly hung in the small, plastic-looking built-in wardrobe. It took Juliet a few frantic minutes to locate her old uniform pants which had been placed on a lower shelf, obviously designed for storing shoes. The right-hand pocket was empty except for some change. Aha, she thought, letting the twenty-pence pieces slide though her fingers. At the very bottom of the left pocket, her fingers curled around a tight little ball of paper which she pulled out eagerly and smoothed open on the bedside table. It was an old betting slip, no more, no less.

She felt let-down, disappointed. It was neatly filled in under the columns provided: 3/6/97. 3.45. *Avenging Angel*. She turned it over idly and saw that there was something scrawled on the back, faintly, in pencil: another horse? A last-minute change of heart? *Remember 1-9-4-*. There was a final digit but it was too blurred to read. Because it was written on the betting slip, Juliet assumed the numbers must have something to do with odds.

Retrospective

CHAPTER FIFTEEN

Strange how little inkling I had of what was afoot. Had it something to do with the drowsy stillness of the day? The glaring sun, the low murmur of insects? It was like a protracted siesta-time. Dazed, yet with fascinated concentration, I watched the two soldiers come towards me, step by deliberate step. I was as dazzled as a hare in a headlight watching the approach of my own death. Yet what reality has death to a fifteen-year-old? I'd seen Angel felled before my eyes yet I refused to believe she was dead, then or later. I kept telling myself that as soon as the soldiers were off I would rush to her rescue. She would, had to, be all right. She must be alive.

On and on they came, remorselessly. Chatting as they might on a Sunday walk, a summer's day excursion. When I saw them stop to light their cigarettes I began to hope. For myself. I began to believe that they weren't looking for me – or indeed for any of us. But should we be foolish enough to present ourselves then . . . Oh, how smugly I reasoned. So smugly indeed that I soon convinced myself that Angel lay sleeping. For what possible reason had they for shooting her? It was just an hallucination brought on by the sun when I was still drowsy from my nap. I told myself triumphantly that I had imagined it.

The day is so torpid – or is it me? The only sound I hear – or is this also my imagination? – is the quiet rustle of the long grass as the soldiers pace the bank. I cannot even recall the sound of bird song in those hours. I watch the two soldiers stop and stand for a time by the water's edge. The taller of them relieves himself into the river, making a perfect steaming arc through which glitter, fugitively, the colours of the rainbow. As he buttons his fly, his companion points out the shade of a huge copper beech some twenty metres or so from the tree in which I hide. I dig my teeth into my trembling lips and pray that they will soon go off about their business, or, better still, fall asleep so that I might creep past them. But it is as if they are acting sentry between me and Angel. After a short rest they resume their search.

How long I cling to my lookout, there is no way of telling. Had I wanted to run for it, I could not, for my limbs have turned to jelly. I brace myself against the thick smooth trunk, ease myself into a sitting position and draw my legs up under me. The soldiers are nearer now, but slowing down. I can see they are talking to each other, one gesticulating angrily. The more agitated he becomes, the more the other, much taller soldier laughs. It is like watching a silent movie, with the noise of the tanks as a dim soundtrack. The soldiers are no more than ten metres from my tree when a half-truck comes by and stops. They run over to it and for a moment I pray that it will carry them away but, after chatting for a minute or two, the driver reverses, turns and heads back into the town. The two soldiers lean against a tree and again light their cigarettes, one from the other. The taller one pushes his helmet back off his eyes, the other throws his on the ground.

Each passing second seems like an hour. A red squirrel dashes past me, his tiny sharp claws tearing into my fingers. Startled, I draw back too violently and almost lose my hold, and, as the branch sways, the animal leaps for an upper branch and scampers along it. He repositions himself a safe metre or so above my head. I try to grab hold of him but he dances away furiously and, to my horror, drops to a lower branch where he sits chattering and scolding in full view of the soldiers, who point at him and laugh. The shorter one's hair is cut close to his skull, it glints red-blond in the sunshine. I see him clearly, therefore he must surely see me? Oh, oh. I hold my breath, waiting for him to shoot.

They rise languidly from their resting-place, stub out their cigarettes, replace their helmets. Then they cock their rifles and walk towards my tree. No dawdling now. This time it's clear they mean business. I am sure, then, that they know exactly where I am. On and on they come, leg on leg. The helmets are pulled down low over their foreheads. Being above them, I cannot see their faces. I wedge myself securely against the trunk and will myself not to fall.

I hold my breath and mentally count their last few paces to the base of my tree. The movements appear slow and dreamlike – five, four, three, two, one – halt. The tips of their boots are lined up below me. I hold my breath and pray the leaves still conceal me. Suddenly, there is movement and I see the squirrel chase another out of my tree. They scamper across the grass towards another further down the bank. One pair of boots spins around in pursuit. I slowly ease out my breath in relief.

Too soon. It is the taller of the two. He strides away and shoots. One dead squirrel falls, the soldier picks it up and holds it aloft. I hear a gun bolt slide and watch the barrel tip skywards. The remaining boots move forward a pace and now the shorter soldier is in my sights, surely I must be in his? I see him clear as day.

I try to melt into the tree trunk. He tilts his head backwards and searches the tree branch by branch. His helmet falls off. I stare down into his face. Not a man; a boy, no more than Roger's age. I keep my eyes firmly fixed on him, memorizing every detail: the way he walks, holds himself. The sound of his voice. The texture of his skin. It is pale but freckled. He has a couple of small patches of weeping acne or eczema between his eyes and on either cheek. His eyes are strange, large and unfocused, as if he needs glasses. And they are blue, blue like the butterflies. As blue as death. As my legs begin to tremble the leaves around me take up the rhythm. The sweat rolls down my face as I watch his finger creep around the trigger. Then, without warning, he suddenly lowers the rifle and runs off.

When I catch my breath, I squint through the leaves to the road where there is an army Jeep, with the driver standing up in it, gesticulating at the soldiers. They leap into the back and within a moment it is as if they've never been. I lower myself into a sitting position and begin to weep. My shorts are wet.

Oxford

June 1997

CHAPTER SIXTEEN

Half an hour or so later, Juliet was still in her room, standing by the window, contemplating her next move, when the door burst open and a vacuum roared in, closely followed by the chambermaid. She mouthed something at Juliet before turning off the machine. The silence was deafening.

'What?' Juliet shouted.

'I said, sorry. I thought the room was free. Guests are usually out at this time,' the maid added pointedly.

'Oh, haven't you finished already?' Juliet said mildly. 'Never mind, I'm just going.' She picked up her bag and made for the door. It was still only half-past ten but she'd already abandoned the idea of shopping for either shoes or hair-do until later. What she most needed was to get away from people and find somewhere quiet to think. She paused outside the front door, looked up and down the deserted street and took a few steps first one way then the other, uncertain about where to go or what to do. Making her mind up at last, she headed for the Pitt Rivers Natural History Museum which was about a ten-minute walk away. The day was warm and sunny and, it still being school term, she knew there was some chance of the museum being reasonably empty.

As it was. She wandered through the gothic doorway and found a stone bench against a wall in one of the side arcades which was shaded from the glass roof and, therefore, beautifully cool. She told herself sternly that the High Street incident was a waste of time, a diversion, and that she was, as usual when she was afraid to do something, dithering. Looking for excuses, putting off the evil day. But she knew she would have to leave that manufactured distraction and get on with her own plans. There were other things, beside phantom accidents, to consider. Her past and future for a start. For the moment, because it was the less painful option, she concentrated on the future. Laying the past to rest was an altogether more terrifying prospect.

On the credit side, her financial situation wasn't too bad. The bank manager had been unusually cheerful the day before. Perhaps, having taken stock of the speed with which Freddie had drained their joint assets, he'd decided she was a better bet single? It was only a guess, since she forbore to seek his approval, as she might once have done. Money-wise, at least, she was reasonably secure. She totted it up. There was still a sizeable sum invested, the insurance from the car, her remaining two month's salary and whatever superannuation she'd accumulated. Plus whatever was left from the house. Being pragmatic, she realized that Freddie would have seriously overestimated the residue. About twenty thousand, he'd said in his letter, but she knew they'd be lucky to be left with half of that. Specially when he realized the insurance company would be reluctant to pay. Mentioning the lack of contents to Dallimore had been a ploy to spike whatever scam Freddie might have set up – she was pretty certain that he was involved in some way – though she baulked at the idea that he had deliberately set her up. It was more likely that it had gone wrong when she turned up. Unexpectedly?

Juliet closed her mind against that evil fear. Surely Freddie would not have deliberately set her up? Refusing to consider that sordid implication, she had half a mind to tell him to take her share of the house and stuff the lot. Where she was headed, accommodation was rather cheaper than it was in Oxford. In any case, she had absolutely no intention of buying another house. This time, for once, she wanted to choose her own direction and, most particularly, how she lived: without responsibility and, definitely, without looking over her shoulder. She wanted to move around for a while, work when and where she took the fancy. Nothing serious or requiring much effort, nothing demanding. If fun became an option she would try that as well. Afterwards.

For the time being a nomadic life was what she planned, and she had the means. She mentally ticked off the list. Once the dreaded meeting with the solicitor was over, and the final confrontation with Freddie, there was really nothing to stop her, save only the formalities of tying up the loose ends of her life, collecting the insurance on the car, and replacing it with a cheaper, less flashy version. All that and getting her head together instead of wasting her time reconstructing an incident which might never have happened. Worse, it was dampening down her resolve to get out, get sorted, get even. Killing time, Juliet wandered around the rather moth-eaten collection of stuffed animals and skeletons. Dead as dodos, she murmured, and the voice in her head echoed back: *The little girl's alive and look . . . over there . . .*

She sat down abruptly on a nearby bench and, putting her face in her hands, wept. She had been given a second chance. Salvation had come when she least expected it and she hadn't recognized it. Now she *knew*, with deep certainty, that someone had cried for her help. Hers. She couldn't let go or it would haunt her for ever. What if she herself had been left? *Oh my God, my God, the little girl is moving . . . Help her someone, she's alive. The little girl's alive. Over there. Quick . . .*

It was some time before she recovered enough to find a cloakroom, where she dashed cold water on her face, swallowed a couple of painkillers and tidied her hair. At about twelve she left the museum, walked swiftly along Keble Road to Banbury Road where she crossed and cut through St Giles churchyard to Brown's restaurant on the other side of Woodstock Road.

She ordered, then could only finish a third of a huge Caesar salad and even less of a glass of Sauvignon blanc which seemed to react dramatically with the painkillers she'd taken at the museum. She sat in a semi-catatonic trance for about half an hour before she sobered up with a large black coffee. Then a second cup because the hiss of the espresso machine reminded her of the Madeleine which in turn stirred – not exactly a memory, more a vague disturbance at the edge of her memory. Something missed.

From the time she left the restaurant, the day developed into a series of cause-and-effect little incidents which led her inexorably back to the accident on the High Street. Because she was still feeling a little light-headed after lunch she sauntered down Little Clarendon Street, intending to have her hair done, but she was distracted by a pair of soft suede loafers in Hobbs window. She went in, bought them, discarded her heavy uniform shoes and put them on.

It was strange that now she'd shed the final item of her uniform she felt much safer, practically invisible. She realized how conspicuous it always made her feel, as if somehow the unsuitability of the uniform proclaimed her unsuitability for the job. She vowed that she would never again allow herself to be so watched, guarded, pampered, cocooned. She chuckled to herself while she kept a continuous eye out for any of her erstwhile colleagues. Dallimore, she decided, must be losing his grip. She was relieved but also mildly fazed at how easily she had escaped his over-watchful eye.

She crossed Clarendon Street and cut through Wellington Square down St John's Street with no clear idea of where to go or what to do for the remainder of the afternoon. But strolling in the sunshine was an altogether better option than holing up in a stuffy room, and besides, she found the more she walked, the looser her muscles became.

She wasn't sure where the old woman came from, or when. Juliet first became aware of her as she crossed Beaumont Street but it only dawned on her that they were keeping pace when they reached New Inn Hall Street with the woman still three or four yards ahead. It was her strange get-up which first attracted Juliet's attention. At least, strange for a warm summer's day. She was dressed in a heavy calf-length dingy brown raincoat, with a knitted maroon hat pulled low over her head. Her shoes were without laces and slipped up and down as she walked, making the backs of her heels raw from the abrasion. Her legs, Juliet noticed, were surprisingly clean. The old woman appeared to be carrying her worldly goods on her back, like a snail with his house. She held an over-stuffed black bin-liner over her shoulder and in her free hand carried two equally stuffed and rumpled plastic bags.

As a policewoman, Juliet had come across most of the city's derelicts, but this one was a stranger. Yet she seemed to know the town because she was headed straight for Bonn Square where the rest of the city's down-and-outs congregated. She wasn't moving very fast but she never faltered until Juliet stopped at the low wall outside St Peter's College to take a stone out of her shoe. When she looked up casually she was somewhat disconcerted to notice that the old woman was sitting a little further on, staring straight ahead, in a world of her own. Humming.

What's she up to? Juliet wondered, beginning to enjoy the old woman's little game. It was as good a way as any to pass the time; nonetheless she was becoming intrigued. She straightened up and walked past, pretending not to notice the old woman but still watching her out of the corner of her eye. Di diddle-di-di-di di dum. Di-diddle-di-di-di-di-dum, she hummed, still staring ahead. Juliet walked on a few steps, then glanced back. The woman was on her feet, rearranging her baggage. It now occurred to Juliet that there was something terribly familiar about her. Di diddle-di di-di-dum, she hummed as she raiked past, her head averted. Juliet stopped short and watched. Sure enough, though she didn't look around the old woman must have sensed this. She's waiting for me, Juliet thought in surprise. The bloody woman *is* playing games.

She began to feel uneasy. Where had she come from? Who was she? As if in answer, the old woman glanced over her shoulder. Juliet's heart began to pump. Something, something indefinable tugged at her memory. There for an instant, then gone. The old woman walked on, at a considerably increased pace. Juliet held back at a safe distance, keeping her in sight until she saw her turn into Pembroke Street. A few seconds later, when Juliet turned the corner, the woman had disappeared.

She looked around. There were only two places the bag lady could have gone, either the Museum of Modern Art or she might have used the back entrance of Marks & Spencer to cut through to Queen Street. Seeing this as the most likely option, Juliet ran up the steps into the back of the food department but couldn't see her. She walked swiftly through the shop looking to right and left but there was still no sign. It was only then that Juliet remembered there was a coffee shop under the museum next door. She retraced her steps.

The basement was crowded with everyone but the bag lady. Not stopping to wonder what she would say when she at last confronted her, Juliet checked the ladies' toilet, but again she drew a blank. From there, somewhat disheartened, she followed her will-o'-the-wisp upstairs and peeped into the bookshop but her quarry wasn't there either. In the unlikely event that she might be a secret art-lover Juliet went to the ticket office.

'Has an old lady come in, just now?' she asked.

'Depends on what you mean by old lady,' the assistant replied coyly. 'There are several inside, though I'm not sure they'd thank you for "old".' He laughed at Juliet's discomfort. 'What does she look like?'

'Down-and-out. A sort of bag lady.'

'Oh her? Yeah, she comes in all the time. Seems to have taken a fancy to our loo. She's a bit loopy.' He tapped the side of his head with his hand and grinned. 'But harmless.'

'Was she here today?' Juliet asked. 'A few minutes ago?'

'No. Don't think so and I've been around most of the time. Oh, hang about, I slipped into Marks to pick up a sandwich, she might have come in then, I suppose.'

Juliet took a fiver from her purse. 'I'll take a look.'

'You can do that without a ticket,' he said. 'But if you want to view the exhibition . . .?'

He launched into the hard sell. 'Great photographs. Local artist. You might enjoy it.'

Juliet shrugged. It was an altogether better alternative than haring around after a madwoman, specially so close to the central police station. She pushed her money across the desk and in return was handed a ticket and catalogue booklet.

'The exhibition is on both floors. Enjoy,' he called gaily after her.

CHAPTER SEVENTEEN

The photographs were stunningly beautiful. The exhibition was called, with accuracy if not originality, 'Blow-up' – probably with a nod to Antonioni – a point which went completely past Juliet, who was distracted and annoyed with herself for losing the old woman so easily. The exhibits were arranged in two sections, on two floors. The first gallery was devoted to looking, in extraordinary detail, at textures: of stone, cloth, hair, skin and so on. The second part, as yet unseen on the floor above, promised 'a look at the familiar from an unfamiliar viewpoint' according to the introduction to C.M. Bray in the short guide to the exhibition she'd picked up at the entrance. Juliet scanned it with about as much attention as she scanned the photographs, then stuffed it in her bag.

In truth, she was more interested in the people walking around, four men and three women, all elderly, though none, alas, her bag lady. There was also a small boy of about four or five, who was exorcizing his boredom by racing up and down the long white gallery. This may have been why a couple of the women left immediately after Juliet arrived.

'Hi.' The child pulled up in front of her. He had a strong American accent. 'What's your name?'

'Juliet,' she said distractedly. *My name is Juliet Furbo. Say it. Say it after me* . . . She shook her head and forced herself to focus on the child who was looking up at her expectantly. His bobbed hair, rather like her own, looked more chewed than cut, as though he had taken scissors to it himself. He had a slight but oddly attractive cast in one eye. 'You been here long?' she asked softly and looked about for a parent. Since none seemed young enough, she concluded the child was out for the day with a grandparent.

'Yeah,' he shouted. 'Hou-rs and hou-rs.' He pointed at a middle-aged grizzle-haired man who appeared to be totally absorbed in the exhibits. 'My da-ad just keeps looking and looking.' Oops, she thought, not Grandpa then. She should have guessed. The man in question strongly reminded her of one of the hairier of her college tutors who had, in his late forties, run off with an undergraduate contemporary, and whom she still saw occasionally, lumbering about the town pushing a double buggy, looking distinctly careworn and not at all the dashing 'older man' they'd all been half in love with.

The little boy was still staring up at her, marking time with his feet. 'I *needed* to go to the Disney Store,' he said petulantly, 'but my da-ad said we had to come here first.'

'What a pain,' she said sympathetically. She smiled down at him. 'Have you, by any chance, seen an old lady with a whole load of carrier bags?' The little boy looked up at her dubiously. 'And no stockings?' she added, hoping the child's-eye view might be from the knees down. The child beamed up at her, obviously enchanted by this show of confidence. 'Yeah, sure I did. I saw her. I heard her too,' he added, with widening eyes. 'She was singing. Wow.' He waggled his head from side to side. 'Cra-zy.'

'Can you tell me when you saw her?'

'Yep. When my dad was buying the tickets to come into this stoopid place. She came in and . . .' His voice trailed away as he squidged up his face in mock-thought.

'And?'

He hunched his shoulders and stretched out his arms theatrically. 'Gee, I don' know. I saw her legs though. Yuk, they were all red. All over and over.' No longer interested, he began to hop around on one foot. Hop, hop, hop, he went, then stopped and looked up to see if she approved. 'She your mu-ther?' he enquired conversationally.

'No, just an old friend,' Juliet lied, as disappointment welled up in her. The old woman became more intriguing with each passing minute. She was just about to walk away when the child began to hum. Juliet stopped dead. It was the same tune the old woman sang but this time she recognized it. The child had a good piping soprano. She remembered the little song from her infant school. The tune, but not the words.

'Hey, that's "Cadet Rousselle",' she said in surprise, wondering why the old woman was singing a French nursery rhyme.

'Yes ma'am,' he grinned cheekily.

'Know the words?' she asked casually.

'No way, it's French,' he shouted. She decided to not to try to get to the bottom of that particular prejudice.

'My name is Nugent,' he announced inconsequentially. She was clearly never going to get rid of him. She wondered what Papa would do if she told the little boy to get lost.

'First or last?'

'First of course.' Poor child, she thought and warmed to him. 'Nugent. That's nice. Do you like the pictures?'

'Uh-huh,' he started then suddenly took hold of her hand. 'There's some great ones upstairs,' he said precociously and pulled her towards the staircase. 'Would you like to see them?'

'Yes I would,' she said resignedly. 'But hadn't we better ask your dad?'

'Dad-dy, I'm going to show the lady the pictures upstairs. OK?' Nugent yelled. Everyone in the gallery said 'shuush' very loudly. The bearded man turned around tiredly and did his best to focus on his son. He looked as though he'd been on a bender or else up all night. Juliet suppressed a giggle at the thought that there might be an even smaller version of Nugent at home. Papa's eyes brightened a little when he saw her. 'We'll all go,' he said firmly. Somehow she didn't think it was fear for his son's safety which motivated him. Juliet chortled softly to herself.

The little boy plodded noisily up the staircase, followed by Juliet who saw at once that the child was quite right: the second part of the exhibition was altogether more exciting. The pictures were larger, more dramatic, and though they were obviously cityscapes it wasn't immediately clear which city. Certainly, Juliet didn't recognize it until his father began to quiz Nugent.

'Nugent, you know what that is?' The voice was rather pleasant, mellow and slow. Achieved, she had no doubt, with the help of a constant supply of covertly acquired, high-quality substances. He looked as though he had but lately rolled out of an energetic bed.

'Ye-es, Da-ad.'

'Tell the *nice* lady, then,' Nugent Père suggested. Pul-eese, thought Juliet. American or Canadian? she wondered.

'Carfax Tow-er,' came the triumphant cry.

'And this?' They were away. It was obviously an old routine, enjoyed by both.

'The Raw-cliffe Cam-er-ah!' Nugent shouted.

'Radcliffe, Newie. The Radcliffe Camera,' Papa drawled. Californian, she decided. So laid-back. So pedantic.

'Yes Da-ad.' The child edged over to Juliet and taking her hand again dragged her from one photograph to another. This is a bloody pain, she thought savagely and eased away her hand. Nugent senior was also crowding her. She stepped into the centre of the room both to get an overview of the exhibit and to distance herself from her admirers. That accomplished, she began to examine the photographs more closely and soon became so absorbed that the old woman temporarily slipped her mind. Her companions were a little more difficult to ignore, since the question-and-answer routine continued relentlessly.

She refused to step into the role of appreciative audience and had almost shut them out when Nugent minor yelled crossly: 'Ped-es-tri-an crossing, I said.' Startled, Juliet wheeled around. Father and son were standing before the centrepiece on the opposite wall. She walked back over to the picture in question which was such an odd composition that, at first, she could make neither head nor tail of it. But *'pedestrian crossing'* the child had said and after looking at it from every angle, that seemed to be exactly what it was. The image was wildly distorted, triangulated to the centre, rather like a striped tent, but if viewed from one particular angle it did indeed look remarkably like a street crossing. 'I wonder how . . .' she started.

'Probably two separate shots, cleverly joined,' Nugent major broke in. 'Perhaps several. See? There are people on one side.' He peered at it closely. 'Must have been taken from a considerable height. Carfax Tower maybe?'

'Oh? Where do you think it is? The crossing, I mean.'

'The High Street Oxford, it says here,' he said nonchalantly, running his finger down the list of exhibits. 'Number twenty-four: "*June morning on High*".' He looked up. 'Witty . . .'

'Huh? Did you say June? This year?' Juliet stood quite still and, with her eyes tightly scrooged the better to focus, stared in at the edge of the sharp black and white image. 'Say, look at that funny old bike.' Nugent's grubby little finger stabbed the air in front of her nose.

'Why, so there is,' cried his proud pa. And so there was. 'Oh well,' he sighed, 'time to go. Say goodbye, Nugent. Nicely now, say goodbye.' But Nugent wasn't interested in fond farewells. 'Can we go to MacDonald's now?'

Nugent senior rolled his eyes. 'Yes,' he said resignedly. 'We can go to MacDonald's, if you promise to sit quietly in the Bear while Daddy has a beer. First.'

'No way,' said the kid, a hard man. 'Second. MacDonald's first. The Bear, *yuk*, second.'

'Deal?'

'Deal.' The child put up his hand. 'Gimme a five,' he shouted. His professorial parent groaned.

'Bye Nugent.'

'Bye, Juliet,' Nugent threw back over his shoulder as he shot down the stairs, his elderly parent in game pursuit.

Juliet turned back to the photographs. Now that the little boy had taught her how to look, she translated her viewpoint and recognized several more views of Carfax and the High. Her excitement quickened as she went back over the photos one by one. There was certainly something that looked remarkably like an abandoned bicycle – *where is my bike?* – in at least two of them and, in one, she thought she made out a crouched figure on the crossing.

'Find her?' the man at the desk asked as she came downstairs. Juliet shook her head.

'I didn't think you would. She comes and goes. Strange creature.'

But Juliet was no longer interested in the old woman. 'When was that exhibition mounted?' she asked brusquely. He gave her a startled look.

'Why? Is there something wrong with it?'

'No, I'm sorry. Of course not. I just wondered, that's all. It's good. Very good. I'm glad I . . .' The assistant was grinning at her. The waffle died on her lips. 'I'm going on a bit,' she laughed, blushing a little.

'I didn't mean to be rude,' he said. 'It's just it was hung in such a hurry. That boy,' from the sound of his voice she reckoned he must fancy the photographer, 'that boy likes to do things at the very last minute.' He pushed his hair back from his forehead. 'Would you believe the last of those pictures was hung at two o'clock on Saturday morning? With the opening at five that afternoon. If I hadn't been here to help, God only knows when it would have been ready.' He waited for the applause and Juliet graciously obliged. 'It's fabulous. Really. Beautifully arranged. You must like the work.'

'Oh, I do. Catullus,' the name was lingered over sensually, 'is a sensational photographer. Really talented.'

'Catullus?' She tried vainly to keep a straight face. 'Catullus Bray? What's the M. for?'

'Matthew. C.M. Bray. He's usually called Cat.' By his friends, he managed to imply.

'Is he local?' she asked in as disinterested a tone as she could manage.

'Oh, yes. Very local. I'll tell him you liked the exhibition, shall I?' he asked eagerly.

'You could ask him if any of the pictures are for sale,' she replied diffidently.

'Not these. This lot is going on tour at the end of the month, but he may have others. Would you like me to ask him? I can do it now.' Juliet smiled as he tapped out a number on the phone pad. She watched his fingers and noted the number. 'Engaged,' he said sadly. She was relieved until he pressed the redial button. 'Answerphone,' he mouthed, and left a message to call Anthony a.s.a.p.

'Never mind, if he's local I could . . . em . . . drop by sometime?'

There was a moment's hesitation. 'I think perhaps it would be better to see him here,' he said and smiled sweetly.

Juliet said, 'Fine.' As she left the museum she found herself humming 'Cadet Rousselle' and trying to remember the words which she'd learned years ago at school.

Cadet Rousselle a trois enfants . . .
Diddle di dum, di dum, di dum . . .

But for the life of her she couldn't remember any more.

Retrospective

CHAPTER EIGHTEEN

How long I cling to my lookout, there is no way of telling. Had I wanted to run for it, I could not. Higher and higher I climb. Now there is so much noise coming from the town that I try and see what is happening but, even having gone as high as I dare, I cannot see beyond the blank wall of a tall barn which obscures my view. The air is filled with the noise of motors. It is deafening, perhaps because I am no longer used to the sound. The sight of a car, except for the occasional *gazogène*, is rare. But though I can hear a great clamour I can see nothing.

I turn my eyes from the town and look for the sight that I pray will not be there. But Angel has not moved. She lies like a crumpled rag doll. Should I go to her? How can I help her? I am too afraid. I can see several bodies by the bridge, or at least there are people lying on the ground on either side. Of Fanny and Marie-Eulalie there is no sign. Suddenly I am startled by a burst of gunshot from inside the walls. There is a great roar, then shouting, the sound of marching boots.

Do I imagine that was what I heard? I cannot tell any longer what I remember from what was later described, but it seemed as if those particular sounds were etched into the strange silence of the afternoon. A harsh shout, a child's cry, a woman

189

scolding. Every now and then a car or Jeep or some other vehicle roars out past the church and disappears to the south. After a few minutes I hear a mighty scream and four or five shots ring out with a muffled plop, plop. Then silence.

I begin to ease my way down out of the tree when I hear the first explosions. The tree trembles beneath me. I am poised to jump the last few feet when I am thrown backwards and almost lose my hold. My limbs turn to jelly as I hunch up against the trunk and cling on for dear life. Explosions come one after another then. The noise is deafening as great palls of acrid black smoke begin to rise from the village. Huge flames lick and spit upward. Bursts of gunfire come thick and fast but I can no longer see for the smoke which billows up and all around.

The day turns black. Suddenly there is an enormous explosion at the far end of the village by the church. I cover my ears to block out the sounds of screaming, shattering glass, children crying. The stink is terrible. Flames and showers of red-hot ashes shoot into the darkened sky, licking at the steeple. I can no longer hear, but oh the smell, the smell.

In my grandmother's house, there was almost always a great cauldron of soup simmering on the stove and a long-handled ladle hanging from a hook on the side of the chimney-breast beside it so that, at any time of day or night, those who were hungry could help themselves. The soup always lasted from Saturday to Wednesday getting better and better with each day that passed. By

Wednesday it was so thick the spoon almost stood up in it. On Thursday grandmother started the whole process again, so there was soup on neither that day nor the next. But then, for us, Friday was strictly a fish day.

The basis of the soup was a rich stock from either chicken or meat bones which were boiled for several hours together with a bouquet garni, an onion, celery and, if it was beef bones, a couple of tomatoes. The liquid was let stand overnight and the fat skimmed off the following day. The flavour of the actual soup varied, depending on which vegetable was most plentiful in her garden and according to season. In September and October Grandmother would wander off into the woods near our village and gather baskets of every conceivable variety of mushroom. That was my favourite of all: rich, brown and aromatic. The thing I remember best about the mushrooms was that Grandmother was very secretive about her source of supply and would never countenance any offer of help from me. 'There are vipers in the wood,' she'd say and laugh. And we both understood that collecting the *girolles* or the *cèpes* was her private pleasure and that she didn't trust me not to blab their whereabouts to my friends. Or worse, to the mothers of my friends.

My grandmother's way with food still lingers with me, and that look of quiet satisfaction on her face as she ladled out her soup, tipped a spoonful of cream or a tiny sprig of parsley on top and slid the blue-glazed bowl across the table to my waiting hands. Even a child could see that cooking, even the relentless everyday stuff, was a source of pleasure to her. She was a heavy woman but I always thought she produced her food daintily – a strange description, perhaps. Everything was just so and the kitchen always smelled delicious. Even after all these years I have only to close my eyes, sniff the air and the old, comforting perfume fills my senses – the taste, the smell, the memory, of my grandmother's cooking.

I thought of the kitchen that terrible afternoon as I clung to my perch in the tree, but for once it was not the usual memory which assailed me. I recalled, instead, one afternoon a couple of years before, when she had almost set the house on fire. It was a Thursday and she was boiling up some veal bones when something must have distracted her. Perhaps she was feeling unwell because she went upstairs to lie down and forgot all about the stock bubbling on the stove. The kitchen door was closed and there was no-one around to disturb her, so the stock boiled away and the bones began to burn. When I returned from school, a few hours later, there was smoke filtering under the door. I burst into the smoke-filled kitchen and the only thing I could make out was the red glow of the stove. The cauldron itself seemed to be on fire. The stench was disgusting: acrid, foul and sickly-sweet.

Now, as I cling to my perch, that remembered smell comes slithering towards me, borne in the billowing smoke which swirls all around, filling my nose, my mouth, my lungs with the putrid stink. At first I think that animals have been trapped by fire and wonder why they do not bellow. My deafened ears hear no sound except the staccato of explosions punctuating the eerie stillness. Yet even these are curiously muffled. Surely there must have been screams, cries for help? Yet now I can hear nothing, nothing. I dig my nails into the bark of the tree and cling on for my own dear life. The memory disgusts me.

At some point I pull myself upright and face the inferno. Sparks and flames shoot high in the air but the high barn walls shield me from the horror that is taking place. The silence and stillness increase as the filthy smoke blocks out the sky and drapes itself all around me like a pall, locking me in stillness. And blindness, as my eyes began to weep and weep. I don't know how long I hold on, impotent and terrified, trying to stop myself from choking as I gasp for breath. I can feel, rather than hear, myself retching and coughing but still no sound penetrates my head. No realization of what is going on inside the town. I think of Angel, lying injured on the path, but I am too cowardly to go and help her.

Why did I, could I, not climb down? In my recurrent nightmare I shin down the tree and tear along the bank to the spot where she fell. Yet though I run and run I never emerge from the deadly smoke which coils around me, bandaging my eyes and stopping my ears. But if in my dreams I try to reach her, that day I did not. I stayed aloft in my hideaway and saved my skin. I told myself that I was a witness, that I would tell what I had seen. Yet in the end the only thing I saw was the soldier shoot Angel. Did I think the soldiers would come back? For me? Is that what I was afraid of?

I do not know how long it takes me to gather enough courage to climb down. One of the lower branches breaks under my weight, I fall heavily and lie at the base of the tree until I recover enough breath to move. The smoke hovers a couple of feet above the ground, with particles of black ash suspended in it like confetti. But with my face at ground level, I can see a few feet ahead.

I crawl over to the water's edge, dip my filthy handkerchief in the water and tie it, cowboy style, over my nose and mouth. My eyes are still streaming but whether from the smoke or from weeping I cannot tell. Then, with my belly on the ground, I make my way, snakewise, to where Angel lies.

Oxford

June 1997

CHAPTER NINETEEN

'A gentleman left this for you. You've just missed him,' the landlady greeted Juliet, when she got back from the exhibition. She was standing in the hall holding a small padded envelope which she handed to Juliet, who looked at it suspiciously as she weighed it in her hand. It was quite heavy. As always when she was afraid, she froze. She swallowed hard, itching to fling it away. For the moment, Mrs Cowley didn't notice her guest's agitation. 'He said to be sure and tell you that Peter Dallimore left it for you. See, he left this as well.' She passed over a small white envelope. 'Said he'd call around', she glanced at her watch, 'again.' Juliet knew from her relaxed tone that Dallimore must have been in plain clothes; uniforms elicited an altogether more wary, even aggressive, response. She felt less sanguine at being tracked down so easily.

Her mouth went dry. 'Did he say when?'

'No. Just that he'd come back. You all right, dear?'

'Yes, thank you. I'm fine. By the way, Mrs Cowley, I'll be leaving tomorrow.'

She half expected the landlady to protest at the short notice and was therefore surprised when Mrs Cowley gave a relieved laugh. 'Whatever you like, dear. In fact that'll suit nicely. I have a group of

Japanese coming tomorrow, I didn't quite know where I was going to put them all. Just remember to leave your key when you pay your bill, will you? Feeling better now, are we? You're certainly looking a lot better than when you arrived,' she said, inviting her taciturn guest's confidence.

'Thank you, yes. You've made me very comfortable,' Juliet murmured with more politeness than accuracy and climbed the stairs. Inside she was seething. Why could they not just leave her alone? Bad enough that she had to face Freddie next day, but to have Dallimore shadowing her was more than she could cope with. He'd probably been on her tail all day, while she wandered around in the blithe belief that she was invisible. Ah well, as long as it wasn't Steve Winter.

This package arrived for you this morning. Don't be alarmed, it's perfectly safe to open, I checked it out, the note ran. *Please keep in touch. Even if you don't need help.*

Blast, she thought. Bugger. But her anger wasn't directed at Peter Dallimore personally, more that she was alarmed at how well he read her. Knew she'd jump to the conclusion that it was some sort of device to blow her up, or, more likely, to keep a tail on her. Cursing herself for an overactive imagination, she tore open the padded envelope. Inside was a neat mobile phone with an explanatory booklet. When she switched it on the screen lit up with the message icon flashing. Reluctantly she pressed yes and listened to two recorded messages. The first was an official welcome-to-our-network-spiel which, among other things, listed her new pin number. The second tersely advised her to keep in touch. She pressed the off button viciously and turned back to Dallimore's note. *Juliet, we've arrested three tearaways and need your help with charging them. Can you (a) either come to the station or (b) phone or (c) both.*

She stuffed the mobile back in the envelope and went to cool off in the shower. It was just after five past five by the time she was dressed. Then, in a perverse attempt at independence but also because she didn't want her calls monitored, she went downstairs to see if the pay phone she'd noticed in the hall was in working order. The local telephone directory was in a small cupboard below. There was only one C.M. Bray listed, at a Gloucester Green address. Having checked that the listed phone number tallied with her memory, she punched it in.

'Mr Bray?' she asked and was answered with a loud guffaw.

'Catullus, if you don't mind. Or Cat if you like. Are you the girl from MOMA? The one who liked the pics?' He spoke with a very slight drawl, which might have been American.

'That's me.'

'I'm surprised friend Anthony gave you my number.' There was an amused edge to the voice.

'He didn't.'

'Oh. Right. Only one C.M. Bray listed, huh?'

It was her turn to laugh, though in truth she didn't feel much like it. She felt trapped, watched, suffocated. Bloody predictable. 'Yeah. I wonder if I could call and see you? It would be a big favour.

I need to ask you a few questions,' she said, unconsciously going into police mode. 'About your work,' she added hurriedly.

'Need? That's a new one. But call, by all means. No cause for a song and dance. You don't want to buy any, then? Anthony was all excited about sales.' He sounded a little disappointed.

'That too. If you have what I want.'

'Need? Want?' he teased. 'As in desire?' He laughed again. 'It doesn't matter either way. When would you like to come?'

'Now? About twenty minutes?'

'Eager, eh? But that's fine. Say we meet in the bar at the Old Fire Station. How does that sound?'

'OK,' she replied dubiously. 'But how will I recognize you?'

'I'm a photographer,' he chortled. 'Guess.'

He rang off. Juliet dialled the station and asked when Inspector Dallimore would be on duty. When she was told that he was in the station, she cradled the phone, dialled a local cab company and asked for a car to be sent around. Then she ran back up to her room, parcelled up the mobile with a scribbled note of thanks-but-no-thanks and asked if he would kindly return the package to sender. That would give him pause for thought. To Dallimore himself, she added that she could be found at the Pitt Rivers – she couldn't think of anywhere else so private/public – at about two the following afternoon. If he wanted to talk to her she would be there until half-past, but he should know that she had absolutely no intention of pressing charges. She suggested that any further

action on the burglary was down to Freddie
Kimber. She wanted nothing whatsoever to do
with it. She knew she could rely on him to interpret the sub-text.

She waited at the hall door until the taxi rolled
up and directed it to Gloucester Green. On the
way she asked the driver to make a little diversion
past the police station in St Aldates. While he
dropped the package off, she waited in the cab,
slouched down to avoid being seen.

At the Old Fire Station, Catullus Bray watched
Juliet Furbo come into the bar and stand uncertainly at the door, looking around. He slid back
into his seat and pushed his cameras further under
the table while he studied her. Anthony, who knew
he was looking for faces for projected exhibition,
had been spot on. It was an interesting rather than
pretty face. Terrific structure, thought the photographer, and oh, that long Florentine nose. He
moved his head from side to side, setting up shots,
as he always did when he saw something or someone who excited him. Palely loitering, he thought
romantically. Well, he had read English. The eyes
in their deep sockets looked haunted. Except for a
badly-cut fringe, the hair was scraped back,
though curly tendrils had escaped and framed the
thin, high-boned face. The fringe was a disaster.
He wondered what her natural colouring was?
It looked darkish but in the poor light he couldn't
be sure. Average height and reasonable figure but
she held herself badly, slouched as if she were
trying to disappear into the background. Become
Miss Average. She was dressed neutrally, in

pale-coloured slacks – cream or beige, it was hard to tell – and a white shirt. He'd have chosen something more dramatic.

'Juliet Furbo?' A tall lean young man rose to his feet as he hailed her. The first thing she noticed about him was his hair, which was startling against his coffee-brown skin. It was cut close to his head, hardly more than a stubble, and was either white-blond or prematurely grey; indistinguishable in the subdued light. He had a rather sardonic, bony face, dark eyes, wide mouth. He looked – she searched for the word as she went towards him – confident, good-humoured, as if he found life amusing. Which, she was soon to discover, he did. He held out his hand and shook hers in a formal, rather old-fashioned way and, looking up, she saw that his hair wasn't dyed. He'd simply left it natural – a dramatic move. It had the curious effect of making him appear younger rather than the reverse. Close to she saw he wasn't as old as she first thought, mid-thirties perhaps. He was dressed, totally, in artistic black. Another dramatic touch. His nickname was spot on.

'Would you like a drink?' he asked. The voice was like coffee as well, rich and dark. The black and white theme was completed with a half-empty glass of Guinness on the table in front of him. She wondered if it was for taste or effect. Poseur, she thought savagely and, as it happened, wrongly.

'I'll have a small one of those,' she said, surprising herself. She usually stuck to wine but her lunch-time glass had been too acid, leaving her stomach slightly unsettled. She watched him amble like a dancer to the bar where he stood chatting to the waitress while he waited for the foam to settle. He was obviously well-known in the place. Seeing him at a distance, amiably passing the time of day, she changed her mind about him being posy. He cut an elegant figure all right, but seemed remarkably unselfconscious about it, laid-back. What rubbish, she thought, the man's a complete dish and knows it.

'When did you take those photographs on the High?' she asked abruptly when he returned to the table.

'You don't waste much time, do you?' he replied lightly, taking a deep slurp. He leaned back and wiped his lips. 'Mmm, nec-tar,' he said and grinned at her. His teeth, she was disgusted to notice, were also perfect. White, straight and pearly. 'Which?'

Juliet followed suit but more cautiously. The drink was surprisingly smooth and comforting. 'The ones of the zebra crossing,' she said abruptly.

'Last week, the week before. Over a period of a few days. They're not all just one shot, you know.'

Juliet was not to be deflected. 'What about last Tuesday?'

'Perhaps, I'm not really sure. I'd have to check. The contacts are dated. Why do you ask?'

She sat back and looked at him or rather through him, as if she were having difficulty sorting her thoughts, framing her questions. He waited patiently, now and then shifting his position so as to frame her against the light. He did this so unobtrusively that she was unaware of his scrutiny. Or,

203

if she was aware, she hid it well. He wondered vaguely when she'd get to the point, he'd arranged to meet a friend in an hour.

'It's a long story,' she said at last. 'I hardly know where to begin.' She pulled the exhibition catalogue from her bag and rifled through the pages. 'On one of those photos, number twenty-four, there's a bike, which looks as if it's floating above the ground . . .'

He laughed. 'I'm glad you liked that one, it's one of the best. The composition is an illusion. But the bicycle was there all right, leaning against the beacon.' He looked at her expectantly.

'Against the beacon?' she repeated seriously. 'Oh.' Pause. 'What else was there, on the crossing?' Her tone was urgent now and he became more interested. 'Please think.'

'It's important then?'

'To me, yes.' It's only important to me, she wanted to gush, but found it hard to explain to this godlike creature why the incident troubled her so much. She was still some way from realizing that *the way* the men were positioned on the crossing that morning, as well as being disturbing in its own right, had triggered, and continued to trigger, deep and bitter memories which troubled her profoundly. So far, all she could do was follow her instinct that it was important to do something to find out why. For whom? That was a good deal less clear.

'Can you remember? Was it last Tuesday?' she insisted.

Catullus Bray thought for a long moment, gave

a little grimace, then shrugged his shoulders. 'I'd have to look. Check through the contacts.' He glanced at his watch. 'Excuse me for a couple of minutes.' He went off again, hands stuck into the pockets of his jeans, through a door marked Telephones and Toilets. Juliet pushed away her half-finished glass and waited. The alcohol was a mistake. Her head was aching and she felt utterly drained again. She searched her bag for a couple of painkillers and washed them down with Guinness. Probably not a good idea, she realized, as a wave of depression hit her. She regretted her stroppy return of the mobile. Knew she should have faced Dallimore and, once and for all, come out with what really bothered her. The habit of lying low, causing no trouble and always apologizing for herself was going to take more courage to shake off than she could muster. 'No progress without pain,' she intoned to herself ironically.

'What?' Cat Bray was back, as silently and as easily as he'd departed, and was smiling down at her. 'Do you often talk to yourself?'

Juliet blushed. 'All the time,' she said. She looked up at him expectantly.

'Let's go,' he said casually. 'I've put back my . . . er . . . appointment, for a couple of hours.' He salvaged his cameras from under the table and sauntered to the door. Juliet followed.

'Do you mind?' she asked, when she caught up with him.

'Do I mind what? Showing off?' He raised his eyebrows at her. 'Or the fact that you want to see my work?'

'Whichever.'

'I'm flattered, Juliet Furbo. Don't you know that's what every artist wants? Needs? Constant and unquestioning admiration.' He laughed easily.

'Not just artists. Everyone,' she said. 'But only from time to time,' she added, in case he thought she was looking for sympathy – which she was, of course. But he didn't seem to notice, nor did he waste words of reassurance, as though he saw no need. This pleased her so much she almost gave a whoop of delight. She looked away and smiled a slow secret smile. Adult to adult. Person to person. She could feel the tension ease from her shoulders as they crossed the square towards his apartment block, on the other side of Gloucester Green.

CHAPTER TWENTY

The apartment was tiny. Or, more accurately, the part of it she first saw was tiny, since he ushered her straight into a small darkroom which was immediately inside the front door, off the entrance hall. The workroom, as meticulously neat as its owner, was no more than eight or nine foot square and, while she might have felt claustrophobic, she soon found that she did not. Catullus Bray was a spare and lithe mover who avoided contact, so that Juliet had no sense of being crowded in any way. It helped that his arm stretch was such that he had only to stand in the centre of the room to be fully in command of every inch of it. He switched on a CD player first thing. 'Hope you like Miles,' he said. She wondered how he'd react if she said she didn't. 'I prefer Wynton,' she said slyly, but he only laughed.

There was a workbench across one end of the room, with shelves above and two wire lines in front, on which were hung two or three proof pages. The shelves were entirely stacked with A4 spring-loaded file-holders, each neatly labelled. Catullus took one down, opened it and switched on a well-placed Anglepoise lamp and adjusted it to light up his working space. Juliet sat on a high stool beside him at the bench and watched silently as he stuck a jeweller's glass in his eye and flicked slowly through a thick sheaf of contacts. When he didn't find what he wanted, he took down another folder and repeated the process. And another, and another. He hardly spoke, evidently seeing no need to burden her with explanations of what he was trying to do or why.

Almost an hour had passed when Juliet surreptitiously glanced at her watch and wished her empty stomach would stop growling. But the photographer, now fully absorbed, didn't seem to notice. It was fully another fifteen minutes before he took a powerful magnifying glass from a drawer, passed it to her and, at the same time, slid a sheet of tiny contact prints across the bench.

Juliet pulled herself closer to the light and peered through the glass. There were eight rows of six contacts on the sheet. Under each was printed a date and a reference number. All were for the previous Tuesday. It took her a moment or two to realize that there was also a minuscule dial at the corner of each, which indicated an approximate time with, in this case, a handwritten a.m. beside it. The top of the page was marked in a bold hand: The High, Tuesday 3/06/97. A sidelong glance showed that the last shot, at the bottom right-hand corner, was recorded at five past six a.m.

'Find anything?' he asked.

'No, not yet.'

'Ah, later then?' For some reason he looked pleased.

'Yeah, I think so. Where did you take them from?' Juliet asked curiously. Catullus turned to her and chuckled softly. 'Guess?'

'St Mary's Tower?'

'Well done. Nearly, but not quite. I was up a crane on the other side of the street – between the High and Bear Lane. Brilliant, eh?' He looked dead pleased with himself; Juliet grinned back. 'Sways like hell, makes you kind of seasick,' he added.

'That why the angles are so peculiar?'

'I shouldn't be at all surprised. Look, try these.' The next three sheets brought the time to six forty-five when the zebra crossing began to feature, together with a slow build-up of traffic – actually more a series of minuscule blurs, impossible to identify as individual vehicles. 'You know, it would help if I knew what exactly you're looking for,' Catullus said. 'I take it it's not solely my amazing artistic flair?'

Juliet, not always sure when her leg was being pulled, looked at him solemnly. He wondered why she so often took on the look of someone who expected to be put down – rather like a stray cat. Once, as he unthinkingly moved too close, she had flinched. Curiouser and curiouser, he thought, and guessed she'd react badly to the idea of posing for him. No doubt she would assume, wrongly, that he meant nude, and take it as an insult. Was she shy or merely tiresome?

'That too,' she said, as if reading his thoughts.

'What?'

'Your amazing artistic flair', she answered patiently, 'made me want to buy a copy of the picture at the exhibition. But that's separate from this.' She indicated the contact sheets, then leaned forward on the bench and rested her chin on her hand. He noticed the bitten nails. The conflict raging within was so transparent that he wished he knew what had driven her to seek him out in the first place, since she patently found it difficult to trust him. While becoming even more intrigued, he saluted her courage, silently, but guessed she'd run a mile if he quizzed her. Odd girl, he thought, prickly, but she definitely had something. It amused him to bide his time. Against the odds he was beginning to rather like her. He certainly liked her looks.

'Last Tuesday morning,' she began after long internal debate, 'a kind of weird thing happened. That's what's bothering me – well, to be honest, it's bloody haunting me. I saw something on that crossing, I'm sure I did. An accident. At least I think so. Something odd about it, peculiar.' She puffed out her cheeks. 'There were two old guys. One was injured, lying on the crossing, the other was kneeling beside him, kind of shielding him.' She bit her lip. 'I went to call an ambulance, but when I got back they'd vanished.' She held up her hands, spread, palms outwards. 'Vamoosed.'

Catullus stood back from the bench and let his eyes fall, rather pointedly, on the dark bruising on her temple. Since the edges had begun to turn a livid yellow he guessed it to be some days old, and wondered if by any chance it might have happened on the day in question. He wanted to ask when she had been bashed up, since it might be relevant to her story, but somehow he couldn't quite bring himself to do so. 'Perhaps the old man wasn't really injured? Perhaps he just fell or something?' he said lightly.

Juliet looked rather defeated. 'Yeah, maybe,' she agreed reluctantly. 'That's what the other man said – the one looking after him – but he also said they needed an ambulance. I think.' She scowled. 'It was just so peculiar. Nobody else saw anything. They think I imagined it. But then . . .' She finished lamely without identifying 'they', he noticed. Perhaps the old man, always assuming there was an old man, had suggested an ambulance *for her*? It occurred to him, now, that she might be a nutter – having a nervous breakdown or something? Better humour her, he thought, feeling somewhat uneasy.

'But it matters?' he asked gently. Juliet nodded. 'Yes,' she said fervently. 'Yes, it matters like hell.' She went back into her shell. 'It's very good of you to take the trouble to do this,' she said politely.

'That's OK,' he said lightly and smiled. 'Right, then. You tell me the approximate time and we'll see if we can find your friends.'

'That's one of the problems. I'm not sure of the time.' Nor sure of anything, she might have added. Not sure how she got there or when she was dumped in the Radcliffe. Not even sure if she was sane. 'I think it may have been some time between seven and eight,' she said, taking a surprisingly accurate stab at it.

'That's quite a long time in terms of rolls of film.'

The phone rang several times, but was ignored, while he studied the next ten sheets, passing each

211

to her as he finished. He checked the recorded time while she desperately searched for her dramatis personae. Eventually, between them, they isolated about ten possible shots on three separate sheets which seemed to corroborate her story. And now, thoroughly involved, he slipped the first of these into an enlarger and, one at a time, moved them carefully into focus.

It was slow work. An hour became two. Eventually Catullus excused himself, leaving Juliet to continue alone. She hardly noticed his absence and became so absorbed that she quickly lost all track of time. Concentrating on one thing at a time had always been her way of keeping sane. She was hyper-careful in the way she worked through problems – personal worries excepted – slowly and sequentially. So, only now, it passed through her mind that she might have been better able to describe the accident had she not been (a) mugged and (b) so busy trying to protect Freddie. Not to mention herself. The police were, justifiably, suspicious of coincidence. Perhaps she was being hard on Dallimore and Winter? Would she have believed them had their roles been reversed? Now she admitted, reluctantly, that she would not.

When Catullus returned about twenty minutes later, he was bearing a couple of cans of lager and a *baguette jambon blanc* apiece. The girl at the Old Fire Station makes the best sandwiches,' he said when she thanked him. They bit hungrily into the crusty bread. He noticed that despite being in the stuffy little room for so long she looked a lot more relaxed and, for the first time, intelligence showed through. He was surprised at how much this pleased him and decided that Juliet Furbo – brilliant name – wasn't mad after all. Troubled perhaps, messed-up certainly, but probably not mad.

While they were eating Juliet could barely suppress her excitement. He waited for her to spill the beans and, because she didn't, he dawdled deliberately, teasing her. But then when he tried to draw her out she was polite but unyielding. He would have liked to find out more about her than he had from a quick phone call while he was buying the sandwiches. But at least he'd learned why she'd looked vaguely familiar.

'Good name, Furbo. Where's it from?'

'Catullus is better. I don't think I've ever met anyone called Catullus before.'

He shrugged. 'It's no big deal. Just another old classical name – like Horace or Alexander for that matter.' It sounded like a prepared patter. 'People call me Cat but I prefer Catullus – he was a good poet.'

'That who you were called after?' He noticed how much better she was at asking questions than answering them.

'In a way. I'm Catullus fifth. The name's passed from one generation to the next.' He grinned at her. 'My great-great-grandfather was a slave. They tended to get fanciful names. We were luckier than most.'

He waited for her to absorb that, then pounced. 'Where do you live?' he asked. Oh help, she thought. Only now she remembered she'd promised to move out of the guest-house next day. After the solicitor or before? Damn, damn, damn. 'Nowhere.' She gave a brittle little laugh. 'I've no fixed abode. At the moment,' she added in case he thought she was throwing herself at him.

'Come again?'

'My house was busted the other night, the whole place trashed, car burnt out. I'm staying with . . .' She was about to say 'friends' but for some reason found it difficult to fib to him. 'Here and there. For the moment. Till I get sorted.'

'When did it happen?' he asked, studiously avoiding her eyes. There was a brief pause.

'Well, if you must know, the morning this . . .' She waved her hand vaguely over the photographs. She smiled ruefully. 'I know what you're thinking. But I'm not out of my tree. I honestly believe that there was something very strange . . .' Her hand came to rest on the pile of photographs. 'Still, you may be right, I was concussed. Or something. But . . .' They looked at each other solemnly and she wondered what was going on in his mind. Her reaction to him amazed her. She, quite simply, wanted to be in his company.

'Well then, shall we just carry on?' He smiled encouragingly. He was beginning to like her particular brand of iron diffidence. 'By the way, do you want to . . .' he began.

'No, no,' she said hurriedly. 'I'll be OK. Fine.'

'You don't know what I was going to say,' he rebuked with mild exasperation, laying his long bony hands on the bench. Juliet curled her bitten nails into her palms.

'I think I do. Thank you, but I'm in a guest-house. For the moment. Anyway, you don't know me from Adam.'

'Oh, don't I? Juliet Furbo.' He narrowed his eyes. 'Weren't you at Drapier?' he asked, naming her old college. 'With old Sharman?'

'Yes,' she answered slowly. 'How do you know that?'

'I was there at the same time. Doing a D.Phil. in English – which I didn't finish,' he added, waiting for her reaction. There was none. 'I found Restoration theatre had limited appeal. I should have stuck to my guns and studied Caxton.' She continued staring at him but again said nothing. As a means of getting him to spill the beans it was very effective.

'Only thing I was ever really interested in. Not the man, the trade, craft, whatever. After I left Oxford I went to Reading and apprenticed myself to a printer. I took the traditional, old-fashioned route, first letterpress, in a local private press, then modern stuff in a more commercial outfit.'

'It's mostly photographic these days, isn't it? Computerized?'

'Yes. That's what eventually put me off, but by then I was more interested in this.' He waved a hand over his prints.

'Have you had many one-man shows?'

'No this is only my third. Bit of a gamble really. I've just given up the day job. Bit scary.'

'In printing?'

'In publishing. Designing books. The print, not the jackets.'

'So you were at Drapier,' she said, trying vainly to place him. There hadn't been all that many black students.

Catullus watched Juliet, trying to calculate how much he knew about her. She *had* a problem and he thought he knew why. She hadn't taken a degree. Was tipped for a first, then freaked out before finals. His friend said she mixed with a very fast crowd and couldn't keep up. Her tutor was desperately upset. There'd also been talk of a nervous breakdown, but Catullus thought it might have been more to do with the company she kept.

'Don't you remember me? I was junior dean for a while, during your time.'

She stared at him, her head sideways, as he picked up a sheet of black paper and draped it over his white hair. Juliet laughed. 'Yeah, I do now. Your hair wasn't white then, was it? But didn't you used to wear a little black embroidered cap?' He could see she was trying to divert attention from herself but refused to play.

'And didn't you used to hang about with that prat Freddie Kimber?' he fished.

'Yeah,' she drawled, giving nothing away. 'You remember Freddie?'

'How could I forget? Bundle of laughs, wasn't he? Pissed in the petrol tank of my nice, vintage MG and bloody nearly ruined the engine,' he said through clenched teeth suddenly getting heated.

'But didn't?' she asked. Their eyes met. 'No, I managed to retrieve the situation. I won't go into the details.' She raised her eyebrows. 'I may have gone over the top,' he admitted finally.

'We just split up,' she conceded. He wondered what she'd been doing with that lump of meat in the first place. Though he had to admit that Kimber had been extremely good-looking and athletic as a student. But a total hooray, always splashing money around. Liked his own way. He had a charming side, sober, but when drunk which was frequent – he was a loud-mouthed bully.

'Oh.' After another brief but awkward silence, he switched on the magnifier and held out his hand. Avoiding contact, she slid a couple of sheets across the bench and pointed out four separate shots, two on each. 'Could you interpret those for me?' She had become rather more businesslike, impersonal. Perversely, he was disappointed and wanted her to say his name.

'Catullus,' he finished, treading through the minefield of her sensibilities. She caught on quickly enough. 'Could you interpret them for me, *Catullus Bray*? Please?' She cocked her head to one side and grinned at him disarmingly. It was a brave effort. She looked exhausted.

'It'll be a pleasure, Juliet Furbo.' He adjusted the magnifier and fed the pictures through, one by one, commenting as he went: 'First, we have two figures at the crossing on the north, the market side of the street. Second: a solitary figure on the other side. Third: two figures wrestling – or locked together – on the crossing.' He turned his head to her. 'That right?' He sounded puzzled but Julie was preoccupied, miles away. Staring into space, her shoulders hunched. 'So where's the third guy got to? Fourth: somebody . . . Hey! You're right,

217

you know,' Catullus shouted triumphantly. 'That looks like somebody lying on the crossing and a – man? woman? – can't make it out crouched beside. And look, here's the bike against the beacon. Good heavens.' He stood back for a moment, then went through the process a second time. 'It's exactly as you say. How could I not have seen it?' He looked up at her thoughtfully.

'Sequence missing, I can't see any sign of the third guy,' he murmured as he went back over them more carefully. He straightened up and rubbed his hand over his hair. 'Well now, let's think . . .' He concentrated hard on imagining himself back up the crane that morning. He remembered looking down. Rain. There was a short burst of rain which blurred his lenses. One or two extraordinary shots that morning came through a screen of raindrops. He was back, back. The bicycle came hurtling out of nowhere. He'd leant over to see if it would crash into the people on the crossing. He'd laughed when he realized the cyclist was a policeman. Laughed so hard, he hadn't got a shot of the moment of impact. Something else had distracted him then. What? He trawled through several sheets before he remembered the rainbow. He'd followed it with the viewer until it lit up the front of All Souls. Those sheets were in another box; he hadn't used them for the exhibition.

'You know, these are just the shots I used for the High Street sequence in the exhibition,' he said quietly. 'I've got some more. Many more. One hell of a lot actually. Hang about a second.' He stacked the discarded sheets and reached up for yet another file.

'Would it be possible to work forward, minute by minute from the first print I isolated?' Juliet asked eagerly.

Catullus pursed his lips. 'It would, but it mightn't help all that much. That morning I was taking pictures over a range of three hundred and sixty degrees, so I was turning all the time. I got pretty dizzy, I can tell you. Still, there are plenty of discards, even some good shots I couldn't fit into the show, so we might be able to find some more pieces of the jigsaw.' He sounded quite excited at the prospect.

'Look, I should go. I've taken an awful lot of your time,' she said, unaccountably irritated that her problem was being taken over. Her vision was blurred and her head ached so badly she wished she could lie down and close her eyes. 'Didn't you say you were going out?'

'I've put it off. I'm enjoying this, honestly. It's very interesting.' He gave her a sidelong look. 'You're not a private detective by any chance?' he asked, half in earnest.

'No. Not a private detective,' she said pleasantly enough, yet somehow he didn't feel inclined to pursue the matter. There was something a little tyrannical about her moods, which were mercurial to say the least.

He went off to make a pot of coffee while Juliet found the bathroom, and raided his medicine cabinet for painkillers. They made desultory small talk while they drank the coffee and then quickly got back to their search. But somehow the brief spell of intimacy was lost and neither of them spoke while they concentrated on matching shot to shot. Eventually, having assembled about twenty photographs in time sequence, Catullus sought out their negatives, spliced them together and loaded them into the magnifier. By running the shots through quickly, they had what amounted to a short film. The enlarged images couldn't be easily sharpened and so were too blurred for specific identification of either vehicles or individuals. In taking the pictures, Catullus had been interested in the streetscape rather than the figures in it – yet, for all that, there was no mistaking the drama of what was rolling slowly before them, shot by shot. The revealed sequence was as follows:

1. Two figures, easily identifiable as men, on the north side of the crossing, another approaching the crossing on the opposite pavement.

2. Two men on the crossing.

3. Pan to south side where the (much more blurred) figures appear to be interlocked.

4. One blur (man?) crouched on the crossing – the other on the south pavement, running away? No sign of third man.

5. Man (A) lying on the ground, (B) crouching over him.

6. Bike at lamppost. Cyclist going towards A and B.

7. Huddled figures at open door of a car, impossible to distinguish who, how many, or what they are doing.

8. Third figure (policeman?) on crossing with

arms outstretched. Small figure on market steps.

When there was no reaction from Juliet, Catullus glanced up and saw that she was dead on her feet. He straightened up. 'Look, why don't I try to blow these up? And see if I can find any more. How would that be?'

'Now?' she asked politely. She looked defeated, bleary-eyed.

'Not tonight, if you don't mind,' Catullus laughed. 'I'm knackered as well. What about tomorrow afternoon or evening?' he asked.

Juliet smiled gratefully. 'If you don't mind? You've been very kind, Catullus, thank you.' She stood up and brushed down her crumpled slacks as Catullus began tidying the rest of the scattered photographs. 'It's like the outline of a murder mystery,' he said. 'Don't you think?'

She became completely still. 'Yes,' she whispered. 'That's what I'm afraid of . . .' Her voice died away. She bit her lower lip and stared into space and began to sway back and forth. *The little girl's alive . . . But look; look, the hand . . . It's moving . . .* Juliet, coming to herself, shuddered violently, afraid she'd cried out loud. But Catullus didn't seem to notice.

'Wonder what the policeman on the bike was up to?' he said, half to himself.

'Woman,' she corrected. 'Police*woman*.'

Catullus swivelled around. '*What?* That wasn't you, was it?' But Juliet didn't answer. She saw herself careering towards the crossing. The bicycle falling away from under her. Drowning in the shimmering blue eyes . . . *Look; look. Oh my God.*

Get the oxygen. Quick, quick . . .'

Catullus reached to steady her. 'Juliet? Juliet? What's the matter?' he asked but Juliet didn't answer. She stretched out her hand compulsively and scattered the photographs.

'*My name is Juliet Furbo,*' she mumbled. Her face was white as a sheet. A shiver ran down Catullus's spine. 'Oxygen,' she said, as if to herself. *If they wanted oxygen someone else must have been alive.*

Catullus Bray put his arm around her shoulders and led her gently from the room.

CHAPTER TWENTY-ONE

The room was stripped of furniture except for a large cushion in the middle of the empty carpet and a rolled-up futon under the window, which Catullus led her to. He left the room and returned almost immediately, carrying a couple of glasses of brandy. He pressed one into her hand.

'Drink it, you look all in. Sorry about the lack of furniture, I'm moving house.'

'Oh,' she replied listlessly and almost as an afterthought added, 'You too? When?'

'End of the week. But just up to the top floor, so I'm able to do it gradually. The flat's a lot smaller but I'll be on my own. It has better views and it's quieter. You want to kip here for a few days? I won't bother you,' he added hastily.

'You live alone?'

'I do now. I shared until recently. With the guy from the museum. He just moved out.'

'Oh.' She took a mouthful of brandy which burned a passage right to the depths of her stomach. She gagged.

'Try again. Sip, don't gulp. It'll revive you.' He sat opposite her on the second cushion and looked at her quizzically. 'And in answer to that unspoken question, Juliet Furbo, no.'

Juliet blushed. 'Not gay, you mean?' She looked slightly daunted at her own courage.

'That's right. What about you, Juliet Furbo?'

'I think, probably not.' She managed a grin. 'Where are you from?'

'Me or my colour?' God, he was confident. She smiled. 'Colour. You sound English. Well, almost. Bit of American somewhere, probably.'

'Excuse me, Afro-American, if you don't mind,' he said deepening his voice mockingly. 'Also Lebanese, Irish, French, American-Indian – or, er, native American – if you want to be PC, which I don't.' He counted his component parts on his long, slim fingers. 'Oh, and one small smidgen English. Good mix, eh?'

'Great mix, I'd say.' Pause. 'Er, can I ask you a question?'

'That depends. But fire away.'

'Something that has always puzzled me. Would you say you were more black than white? From what you say . . . I mean you seem to be a complete mix . . . yet you *say* you're black . . .' Her voice tailed off. She was on sticky ground but Catullus's expression hadn't changed, except perhaps that he might have been suppressing a grin as he waited for her to continue. Which she did after a fraught little pause. 'It's just that I notice mixed-race people nearly always define themselves as black, even when they're not obviously so.' She stopped short and bit her lip. Catullus burst out laughing.

'Well, that ain't my problem, as you see,' he said and stretched out his hand to her. 'Does it bother you?'

'Me? Why should it?' She flushed. 'Come on, it's

a simple enough question. If, say, one of your parents was white, would you define yourself as white?' This time he laughed so hard he toppled over. 'Hey, Juliet, look at me. I'm black. My mom *was* white as it happens. Well, whitish.'

She pulled her hand away, curling the bitten fingernails into her palms. Her face was scarlet. 'I'm sorry,' she muttered, 'I shouldn't have asked.'

'Of course you should. It's a simple enough question but I think you know the answer well enough; other people make their dispositions,' he said, then became more serious. 'I was born in London but I grew up in Washington – that's where my father's from. I lucked out to be born when I was, 1961. And lucky my dad was an *educated* black man. There weren't many of them about just then, the Civil Rights movement hadn't got going. But he managed it somehow – he's a very bright guy. He was an academic, but he got a job in the World Bank in Kennedy's time – he's only just retired. We did all right. Washington wasn't much fun for *poor* black guys, that I do know. It still ain't. But then being poor isn't much fun anywhere now, is it?' He straightened up. His back was to the window and against the evening light he was still and dark as an ebony sculpture. She was moved by his beauty, but more by his repose. How she envied his contentment, longed to catch it, as she might a cold.

'I like what I am. And who,' he said and Juliet wanted to stretch out her arms to him. 'I don't run out in the streets and shout about it,' he continued quietly. 'I'm comfortable with it. But I'm lucky. I like my work, live in a nice place, nobody bothers me.' He shrugged and smiled at her. 'Whoops, we're getting way too serious here. You know a lot about me, so tell me about you, Juliet Furbo? I love your name. What colour are you?'

She laughed then. 'I'm pink- ish. You should see me on cold days, when I go from blue to purple.'

'I hope I will.'

'What?'

'See you on cold days. See you again,' he said lightly.

'Oh.'

'Only oh? So tell me, where are you from? Where do you live?' He gave her the second option, guessing she'd choose it. She did. He was intrigued by her evasiveness, and surprised at how much he wanted to get to know her. Touch her, comfort the loneliness which veiled her.

'I told you. In a guest-house. In Holywell Street.'

'I see. That's nice and anonymous. Until when?' he asked, in a no-nonsense tone.

'Tomorrow, probably. I have to move – to another one. But it's only for a couple of weeks.'

'What then?' He was irritatingly persistent.

'I'm not sure.' She avoided looking at him and in the ensuing silence she acknowledged she was being a total pain. The man had given up a whole evening to helping her with her problems. For a moment longer she fought back the urge to confide in him. 'I'm sorry. Things are, er, a bit fluid just now.' She avoided looking at him. 'You've been a massive help,' she mumbled, 'but I'm still confused about what happened . . . that accident.'

Then in a rare burst of honesty she added, 'But it matters, I'm sure of it. It seems to be linked to . . . er . . . something else. Something more difficult to . . .'

'Why not try to talk about it? Get it out, whatever it is? I don't think blowing up the photographs will help much. I'll do it, but we'll never be able to see the faces properly, you know. I just didn't focus on the faces.' He was silent for a moment then he pounced. 'Tell me why did you say the word *oxygen*? And why did it upset you so much? You spoke it out loud, you know.'

'What?' Juliet jerked back her head. Her face drained. He held her gaze while he waited.

'I suddenly remembered hearing the word. If they needed oxygen then maybe one of the others was alive.'

'You've lost me. On the High Street, you mean?'

'No,' she said impatiently, 'not then. A long time ago. That's what I've been trying to say. That incident, your photographs, you, you've helped me remember the things I was supposed to forget.'

'You want to tell me?' he asked again, lightly, and somehow he managed to convince her it was a choice, up to her. In fact she was desperate to speak the things that were on her mind, and the kindness of a passing stranger seemed as good a repository as any. Since there was no vested interest there could be no come-back. He didn't insult her by promising to keep her confidence, but somehow she knew he would. She could speak or be silent, he would respect her either way. She

227

chose to speak. As she told her story, her voice altered, softened, even the pitch changed so that she lost her crisp Englishness and sounded – almost – Irish. She looked strange, *removed*, as if she were on another plane. Alone. Catullus was an irrelevance. She simply let the story flow out of her.

'When I was little,' she began shakily, 'I always longed for a *best* friend more than anything. But there was never time, because we kept changing our name and moving around.

'I don't know when I began to believe my father was a spy. Not any old spy, more the James Bond type, working under cover. Which I thought was the reason he kept disappearing. And why we kept ourselves to ourselves. We never had casual callers. Or friends. We were just us: a compact, sealed unit.

'At other times I imagined he was some kind of gangster. Very high-class, of course, that went without saying. The kind who'd always wear a hat and have a good-looking woman on his arm. A lithe, strong, mysterious cat burglar perhaps. Monte Carlo was my preferred scenario. I loved the name, so exotic and utterly unlike the places we lived. Casinos and jewels figured a lot in my fantasies. I watched too many old movies. Like my mother, I was addicted to them. At no stage did I equate "gangster" with "criminal" or anything squalid like that. Because the men who came to see my father were always so formally dressed. *The Suits*, my mother called them.

'Spy or gangster? Perhaps he was neither? I

don't know. I just don't know when the association with that idea began or even if it meant anything. All I know is that as reality replaced romance, it brought terror with it. Not just my private terror. The word had a very specific meaning during my childhood and it only now dawns on me that it was there all the time, stalking the edges of our lives. I have always felt afraid. I must have been picking up hints for years, tiny clues, meaningless in themselves but in the end adding detail to the image I must have been building in my mind. We must have been in hiding, though I didn't know it, my mother, my brother, and me. We never stayed long in any one place. First there was a series of cottages in the country, God knows where. Then we graduated to towns, finally cities. A year here, a year there, all the time my father came and went. Sometimes he was gone for a few days, often for weeks. The last time, it was months.

'When he came home that time he told my brother and me that he was writing a novel. Or maybe, if he was very lucky, a screenplay. Something that would make us a load of money. A man used to come and they would shut themselves in the front room for hours. Then one day the man was gone and my dad didn't say much, except that he had a bit of a writer's block. I looked at him closely that day, probably for the first time in my life, and I saw him from me – the way you do a stranger. From the lines on his face and the way his eyes kept flitting from side to side. I remember thinking, he's changed. After that all the excitement seemed to leak out of him. Not suddenly, just a little each day. He became more gloomy, more in on himself.

'Me too, when I tried to think what to say to my friends about the starring roles I'd promised them in my daddy's movie. I began to pray that we could move again, really soon, so I wouldn't have to. And, strangely, my prayers were answered. In spades. And I wished that I'd left the praying to someone better versed in the wily ways of the Lord. Someone who knew what to ask for. Someone who covered the options. But for a while things were OK. We packed our bags and before you could blink we were following the old furniture-removal van again.

'He took a job, just like all the other dads. In a school. It was such a let-down, specially since it was our school. I had to stop making up romantic stories about him. My brother, who must have been thirteen or so, was really mortified. Until my mother suggested – or did she insist? – that it would be easier if we pretended we weren't related. Maybe he was only there because he'd lost his nerve and wanted to keep a close eye on us, protect us, but when I asked him why he wanted to work at our school he muttered something about it being the only job available. He made a big thing of it, pretended he was dead excited. Neither my brother nor I bought it. We just thought he was making the best of it, for Mum's sake. At the time she was very twitchy, dead worried about us. Well, about everything really, but I only noticed because usually she was so quiet and calm. Strong.

'When I asked him why he wasn't going to be a writer any more, he explained that teaching was the job he knew and was good at. He'd leave the writing to those better equipped for it. Funny, I'd never thought of him as a teacher, it was the first time I heard him mention it as his real profession. Bit of a let-down, as I said. There were only three men on the staff and he was by far the best-looking. My handsome daddy. Tall, with a fringe of dark hair around his bald pate but with gorgeous sparkling, laughing eyes. And full of jokes. But, at the same time, not someone you'd mess with. I never heard anyone call him Baldy. They wouldn't dare.

'It's funny though, when I think of him I don't see him like that. As a little child, before his red hair darkened I used to love to tug at his long curls. Curly locks, I used to call him. Curly stuck. Or maybe that was what he was always called? Maybe I just happened on an old nickname? I don't know. He was funny about his hair; vain. Once I caught him in the bathroom and my mother with the electric shaver in her hand giving him the old medieval tonsure that they said made him look distinguished. They looked so . . . so private, the pair of them. As they shooed me away, I saw him take her in his arms.

'Then one day he was gone again. I had a friend by this time. I can't have been much more than eight. My mother wasn't fretting though. This time it was different. She told us he was going to a conference in Boston. I remember her words – he was giving a paper. Will he become famous, I asked? Will he be on the telly? She laughed. I remember when she threw back her head how the light shone on her hair. "No, darlin," she said. "No. Your daddy won't be on the telly."

'But he was. A few nights after he left there was a report of a bomb attack in Belfast. My mother was out collecting my brother from hockey practice. She said she was only going to be out for a few minutes, that I had to keep the door locked and not open it to anyone. I didn't take much notice, she always said that when she went out. The news flashed on to the screen while I was watching a film. They showed the front flying off a hotel. It was really dramatic. Kerpow, and the whole thing toppled over. But no-one was killed. That's what I remember the reporter saying and then something about "Intelligence thwarting terrorists' plans." That "the British government would never give in to violence." It was such bullshit, even a child could sense it. As the bland-faced, plummy-voiced politician uttered the phrase, I could tell something awful was going to happen.

'There were people milling about while he gave his interview. They didn't seem interested in what was going on behind them. A bunch of kids started making faces at the camera. The police shoved them back to make room for the hotel-owner. He wasn't bothered either. He had this broad smirk on his face as if he wasn't a bit upset to see his hotel go up in smoke. Maybe he already knew he'd get a huge compensation package. But, as he talked, there was a massive flash in the distance and the whole sky lit up behind him. He looked worried then, all right.

'I was just going to switch channels when I distinctly saw my father flit across the screen. It was only for a second and then he was gone. I told myself I was imagining things. But I turned off the telly, slowly, like a sleepwalker. I didn't want to think. It seemed all wrong, somehow. I did my homework until my mother came back. I don't know why I said nothing to her. Didn't mention the newsflash, didn't say a word about my dad. I must have hoped that if I said nothing that strange image would go away. My daddy wasn't in Belfast, he was at a conference in Boston. He was giving a paper. My mother said so and my mother wouldn't lie.

'He came home a few days later with a load of presents for me and my brother. He was all smiles but underneath he looked exhausted, the smiles didn't hide that. The stubble on the crown of his head had grown. Just enough to catch the light as he passed beneath it. He said he had a wonderful surprise, that he'd been offered this amazing job. I didn't ask where. I was much too disturbed by his strange piebald head.

'We had supper in silence and went to bed as usual. My mother woke me next morning. It was still dark. I know, because my bed was just beside the window. I stretched out my hand and twitched the curtain, there were stars in the black sky. My mother switched on the bedside lamp and in the dim light I saw that she was white as a sheet. But she had a fine smile slapped across her face. She said we were going Christmas shopping. Her desperate jollity terrified me.'

Juliet fell silent. Catullus sensed that she was just getting to the climax of her story, the truly disturbing part, and waited for her to continue. But she said nothing more. After some time she got slowly to her feet. 'I have to go,' she said. It took some persuasion to get her to accept a lift back to Holywell Street.

CHAPTER TWENTY-TWO

Neither spoke during the few minutes' ride back to the guest-house, though it was not an uncomfortable silence. It was more that Juliet was talked out and Catullus didn't feel like intruding. She was grateful that he left the images undisturbed since they felt so fragile that the slightest puff would blow them away. The pictures were not complete and she doubted that they could ever be so. Oddly the confrontation with the past had been less brutalizing than bottling it up. She had surprised herself with the coherence of her memory for, until she began to talk to Catullus, she thought she had no real picture of her childhood. Now she felt that if she didn't keep a tight control it would simply evaporate. Too many things were happening all at once, too many conflicting demands. Yet there was a certain excitement in knowing that by following her instinct about the High Street incident she had somehow begun to free herself. To understand. To mourn. To live.

All her life she'd teased the outer edges of her childhood tragedy, putting it out of her head, while struggling to leap-frog over it to her blanked-out life before it happened. This was how she'd been taught to deal with it, during those sleepless nights when she woke screaming and sweating to find Nancy sitting on the side of her bed, her large capable hands gently soothing her temples.

Catullus waited until she was admitted to the guest-house before driving off, so she didn't see him being flagged down and breathalyzed as he turned his car at Mansfield Road. The landlady, who opened the door, told Juliet that Inspector Dallimore had called. Again. She looked hard at Juliet and pointedly sniffed the brandy on her breath. With a few well-rehearsed sentences she implied that she was not keen on such attention from the police, however innocent it might be. Nor did she want anyone to regard her respectable home as some sort of refuge. One had to be careful of one's reputation, after all. Mrs Cowley was all set to prolong the diatribe but, since there was no response, she assumed the wretched girl was drunk or on drugs – or both – and gave silent thanks that she would be quitting her room the following day. She watched Juliet stagger upstairs and waited until she heard the bedroom door close before beetling back to the kitchen to regale her gentleman friend with her suspicions.

Upstairs in her room, Juliet, blessedly oblivious of the landlady's harsh judgement, undressed, slowly and deliberately. She folded her slacks and blouse over the back of a chair with careful precision, washed her underwear in the little bedroom sink and hung it on the cold radiator to dry. Each prolonged action was designed to calm her and help control her thoughts and emotions. Low-grade, mechanical activity to soothe the jangling nerves. She stood in the dark for a long time, leaning against the window, staring into the street below, thinking of that critical day in Blackbird Leys when her makeshift life began to descend, inexorably, into chaos. When she discovered that innocence and ignorance were first cousins, the one as lethal as the other. Selective amnesia kills.

My name is Juliet Furbo. Say it, darling; say it. My name is Juliet Furbo.

Indoctrination. There, she'd said it. It seemed so obvious all of a sudden. She had been indoctrinated. She must have mentioned seeing her father on the telly at some point during her long fight for survival. So they taught her what to remember and what to forget, so successfully that her memory as well as her origins were buried almost beyond recall. But not quite. Had she also made that other, more terrifying confession? Even before the mugging the previous Tuesday, tiny glimpses had begun to well up from deep in her subconscious, uninvited and unwelcome. Hers was not an upbringing overburdened with emotional curiosity. Teaching by rote was Nancy's preferred method. Adolescent curiosity had passed her by. She so desperately wanted to do the right thing by her beloved foster-parent. Was that why she had flipped so comprehensively a few months after Nancy suddenly died? The rot had set in almost immediately, though, for a time, Juliet continued to exist in the carefully invented vacuum and all was well until she began to ask herself very simple questions. Am I who I was? Where did I come from? Why do I keep blaming myself? And now and now . . . The worst questions of all had risen, unbidden and terrifying. *Was I to blame? Did I alone survive?* The fear she did not share. Nor could she. She asked herself harshly how on earth someone reasonably intelligent like her could have separated, so mindlessly, the processes of thought and remembrance; the personal from the general. L.P. Hartley got it in half a pithy sentence. *The past is a foreign country* . . .

More than ever now, she resolved to get away. To follow her head and make her own enquiries, take responsibility for her own life. For too long she had been separated from her past, pawned off with easy phrases uttered with terrifying certainty by strong men who – oh, how late she had woken up to it – had manipulated and moulded her life as well as her education and career. When had the idea of joining the police occurred to her? And where? It wasn't Freddie's, certainly. He had been utterly incredulous: 'How can you? What the hell have you in common with those yobs?' And a lot more about mixing with people socially beneath them – he meant himself, presumably. She hadn't absorbed, either, that he imagined his lousy degree had given him a natural advantage over her, which he relished. God, how he relished it. All through their undergraduate days she had been the one to whose intelligence people deferred. At the time, Freddie didn't seem to bother about being dismissed as a jock, but, deep down, he must have done. As soon as she became a police recruit he began to make sly, public reference to her failure. But sly soon became frequent, then, finally, almost continuous. And she'd quietly knuckled under. It was, after all, what she deserved. So she trotted meekly into the tender care of one Peter Dallimore. Ubiquitous, courteous, avuncular. *Her minder*. All the time, they wanted to know what she remembered. Juliet laughed harshly. When all the time she remembered nothing. Until now.

But that was too neat. Now that everything was coming under scrutiny, she would have to apply more rigorous criteria to her examination of the circumstances of her life as well as her own compliance. She remained at the window for a long time, marshalling her thoughts. Her energy gathered with the excitement of seeking explanations? Solutions? This was what she was good at, trained to do: examine the details; connect the clues; reach conclusions. Freddie wasn't responsible for every ill. It wasn't Freddie who had first suggested the police force; it was her college tutor after she'd failed to show up for her finals. Alexander Sharman – another kind, good man whom she trusted implicitly.

She gave a self-mocking laugh as she pictured the incident in her mind's eye. A warm sunny day, so warm indeed that he suggested the college garden for a chat. She'd been surprised by his kindness when she'd expected a bollocking. God, she was stupid. How could she not have realized how much he must have known about her? He was about to parcel her from one institution to another.

What an idiot she was. They were sitting on two very wobbly chairs in the shade of the magnificent chestnut in Swift Quad. 'You have excellent connective abilities. I can put you in touch with someone. Unless, of course, you would prefer to come back and sit your finals? You can do that any time, you know that, don't you? But perhaps a little time away, first?' Then he smiled encouragingly. 'I think you would be good at it, you know. You are addicted to *Morse*, I hear.'

At the time, she remembered, it seemed such a relief not to have to keep dithering about prospective careers. Or whether to repeat or bolt. But as usual she'd allowed herself to be led, insisted on it, letting others, it hardly mattered who, take the decisions. She convinced herself that they knew what was good for her, since she was always more certain of what she didn't want than of what she wanted. But then, having been brought up by a single woman, she had always been a sucker for strong views, pungently expressed, by strong men. Kind good men, even. She would be very, very careful not to succumb to Catullus Bray's certainties. For some reason she didn't find this very appealing.

As for Dallimore, decent though he always was to her, he could go to hell. She was through with taking orders or even well-intentioned help from anyone whose motives she didn't quite trust. The question was, did Dallimore believe her story about the Tuesday accident or not? If he didn't, she

240

could solve the mystery in her own way and in her own time. But if he suspected something had really happened, she would be whisked away at the first hint of danger. She had spent her years in the police force being shunted from one safe little niche to another. How could she *not* have noticed this?

'Connective abilities, my eye,' she murmured. 'When did I ever get an opportunity to connect anything?' *Now*, a small still voice told her, *now. You have the opportunity now.* She pushed aside the uncomfortable thought that she had accepted Dallimore's word that Freddie hadn't mugged her. Oh, and Freddie's own, of course. But then Freddie had always been a dab hand at persuasive letters. Blast and damn Freddie to hell. She wondered what he'd say when he discovered how neatly she'd spiked his little insurance scam. If there was a scam. She was going to look pretty damn silly if there wasn't.

Juliet wrapped a towel around her and slipped down the corridor to the loo. Afterwards she took a couple of codeine and got into bed. She felt curiously composed. At last she knew what she wanted to do and was determined that nothing would stop her. Personal danger didn't come into it any more. It meant nothing to her. What had she to lose? She was through with living a half-life. But she wasn't quite ready. The accident on the crossing wouldn't go away, nor the bag lady. She had a strong instinct that the old woman was both involved and pleading for *her* help. In the circumstances, the old woman was like a beacon of light; beckoning her towards salvation.

She could not turn away. So few people thought her capable; most thought she was a bit of a mess. Juliet desperately wanted to prove them wrong.

CHAPTER TWENTY-THREE

Juliet was woken at five thirty by rosy early-morning sunlight filtering onto her face through the flimsy curtains. She opened her eyes and, for the first time in a week, was instantly and totally alert. By some miracle she had slept soundly and dreamlessly, for a good five hours. She put her hand under the bedclothes and felt her ribs gingerly. The bruising was less sore to the touch and breathing not nearly so painful. She let out a long slow breath just to test her theory that she was on the mend, then rolled over onto her back and stretched luxuriously. Her palms stroked the night-smoothed skin of her flat stomach which produced, internally, much the same sensation as touching the surface of the external bruising, as if the flesh beneath the skin were slowly seeping blood.

She tested her feelings about the loss but found none she could trust. She still felt as though the stuffing had been knocked out of her, though not quite all the emotion. Perhaps, at last, she was beginning to grow a protective shell? Did she mourn the loss of the minuscule embryo? She could not think of it in any other, more sentimental term. It had happened the first night in hospital when she'd been heavily sedated. Another body punch – more, an assault on her very being. The nurse's whispered sentiments of regret meant nothing to her at the time, except as a reminder of how deeply into the quagmire she had sunk herself. She could not mourn the loss of something she didn't realize she had, could she? But she could and did blame herself, and during the following days she could not get it out of her mind. Whose issue it might have been was a trickier area to be explored later. If at all. It wasn't just Freddie who'd abused her, she'd made quite a good stab at it herself, at all times avoiding examination of how she'd allowed herself to become so debased, so self-destructive. Or why.

The cool order of the photographer's darkroom had jolted her into another reality, in a way more psychological constructs had not. It was so organized, clinical almost, and he too looked so neat and together, as well as being, most of the time, somewhat impersonal. Perhaps it was this last she found so calming. Enviable. The apparent order of his life contrasted sharply with the pathetic muddle of her own. But at least it was some consolation to reflect that she'd already begun, alone and however messily, to get to grips with it. She hoped she hadn't made a complete ass of herself.

She let the events of the previous day run slowly through her mind. Working backwards from the Museum of Modern Art and Catullus Bray's exhibition led her, inexorably, to the bag lady. For wasn't it she who had drawn Juliet there? Deliberately? The moment the thought was formulated, she was certain that the old woman had done precisely that. From there, she had led Juliet to the photographer. But if that was her intention, why had she disappeared? And where to? Or to turn it on its head, where had she appeared from? Juliet slumped against the headboard and shut her eyes tight, the better to conjure the moment when she first became aware of the woman.

She had been waiting for a break in the traffic to cross Beaumont Street when she first noticed her, clattering ahead of her, into Gloucester Street, her laceless shoes going flip-flop, flip-flop. All at once another vignette presented itself. Not the *pas de deux* of the day before but yet another incident which had, until now, completely slipped her mind: the weird little byplay outside the market on the morning of the accident when someone crashed into her. Hadn't one of the photographs shown something on the market steps? It wasn't much more than a smudge, yet Catullus had said it was – she remembered his words precisely – 'a small figure in the doorway'. Could it be? Surely it could? The same old woman? She had come out of nowhere – Juliet caught herself short at that lazy conclusion. She must have come from somewhere. 'The market!' she said aloud. 'Of course. The market.' In that case she was also, possibly, that little blur on one of the photographs. Juliet could still see, in her mind's eye, Cat's finger lingering on a shadowy figure in the market portal. Now she asked herself what time the market opened? Or had the woman been there all night? Sleeping rough. Because, if so, surely she would have seen the whole incident?

There was only one way to find out. Juliet

jumped out of bed but slowed down a little when she discovered that her recovery wasn't quite as miraculous as had first seemed. Her joints were still stiff and her aching ribs still caught her breath. But less, much less. The bathroom was free for once, and after she showered she dressed in the same, now slightly tired, slacks and shirt and threw a grey sweatshirt over her shoulders. More shopping was clearly called for as well as – damn, damn, damn – an alternative place to live. There was also the visit to the solicitor at twelve and Dallimore at two. She wrote a note for the landlady to say she'd be out for breakfast and would check out on her return.

As she left the room she picked up an envelope which must have been slipped under her door while she slept. This time Dallimore was more peremptory than usual. It was a terse little note reminding her of their meeting later that day. He'd obviously lost patience with her. Juliet swore silently and stuffed the note in her trouser pocket. It was six forty precisely when she left the Miranda guest-house and headed for the Café Madeleine. She only became aware she was being followed when she glanced at herself in Blackwell's window and patted her hair into place.

'Very tasty.' It was Steve Winter's voice. Juliet spun around. 'What the fuck are you doing?'

Winter grinned. 'Well that *would* be nice.'

It took a second. 'You . . . you . . .' she spluttered. 'Why can't you leave me alone? Go away. Get lost.' She could barely control the urge to fly at him and tear him apart. Like Freddie used to, she thought, aghast, when I wouldn't do what he wanted. She closed her eyes and leaned against the plate glass for support.

'Steve, you've no business following me, it's harassment,' she said wearily. 'I'm able to take care of myself. I don't need your help. Have you got that?'

'Yeah, I got it. You weren't so bloody high and mighty last week.'

'No. I wasn't. Thank you for your help but . . .'

He cut in. 'Nor at that party.' He stared at her, relishing the blush which started somewhere around her feet and travelled furiously upwards.

'No,' she said eventually. 'You're right. I'm sorry. It was a mistake. We both had too much to drink.'

'And that's it, is it?'

'I'm afraid so. I'm sorry.'

'Sorry? That all? Sorry?' His tone turned ugly. 'You know what you are, don't you? You're a tease, a tart.' They glared at each other. Eventually Steve Winter gave a little snort. 'Well, let me know the next time you want a quickie,' he said. 'You're pathetic, you know that? No wonder the guy does you over.' And with that little jab he strode off.

Juliet stayed where she was until she'd recovered her breath. Her self-esteem would take longer. She walked slowly down Turl Street, snivelling into a tissue, feeling very sorry for herself, and was still rather subdued when she got to the Madeleine courtyard. She stayed outside for a few minutes, taking deep breaths until she felt sufficiently in control of herself to go in.

The perfume of freshly-roasted coffee and newly-baked bread hit her as she pushed open the door. There were few people in the café. Disappointingly, there was no sign of the waiter who had been so kind to her. Juliet, after a quick glance around, settled herself, unconsciously imitating the Hopper painting, on a high stool at the counter, which was L-shaped with five seats on its long arm and two on the short. There was only one customer already seated – a large, heavy man who looked around at her approach, as if he were expecting someone. With his bushy eyebrows and darting eyes, he reminded her of Denis Healey. He nodded casually at Juliet before returning to his newspaper which she noticed, with a little ping of excitement, was open at the racing page. While she waited for service she looked around. The few customers having breakfast appeared to be regulars from the way the sole waiter managed to carry on a sort of general conversation, a word here, a word there, as he went on his rounds. When Juliet managed to catch his eye, he told her cheerfully, 'Jack serves the bar, he'll be with you in a moment or two.'

'Now then, what'll you have?' When she turned around, Jack was standing in front of her as if he'd been magicked in response to her request. Disappointingly, he didn't give any sign of recognition.

'The works,' she replied cogently. 'Orange juice, double espresso, bacon-filled croissant.'

'One or two?'

'One, for starters.'

He shouted her order through a hatch in the wall at the far end of the counter, opposite to where she was sitting. After a minute or two, a brawny hand shoved out a tall glass of orange juice which the waiter brought to her. It was cold, freshly-squeezed and utterly welcome. She drained it, and waited for her coffee. She noticed that while Jack was fiddling at the espresso machine, he glanced at her over his shoulder a couple of times with a perplexed expression on his face. As he came towards her with the coffee, Juliet casually flicked her over-long fringe back off her forehead.

'Ah,' he said. 'I thought I recognized you.'

She smiled. 'Are you feeling better now?' he enquired delicately and, without waiting for an answer, went off to collect her croissant.

'I wonder if,' Juliet began as soon as he returned, but was immediately interrupted by the other bar customer who asked if Jack might glance at the day's runners. Soon they were deep in discussion about the odds on some horse or other for that afternoon's racing. At first Juliet was too engrossed in her breakfast to lend more than half an ear to what they were saying, but gradually she tuned in and pricked up her ears. Betting? Betting slips. Was there – could there be a connection? But while she was trying to sort that out, they changed the subject.

'No Professor Forge again today, Dr Fibich?'

'No, poor chap is still feeling unwell. He thinks it may be hay fever.' The heavy man was obviously foreign. Middle European, she guessed, from his strangulated consonants.

'Oh. Unlike him, isn't it?' Jack sounded uninterested.

'Very. I've never known him ill. Poor chap's been working too hard. A little depressed too, I think.'

'You've seen him?' Jack at last caught Juliet's eye and in response to her proffered cup turned to the machine to make another coffee. 'Cappuccino, this time,' she called. 'Please.'

'No,' Fibich maundered on. 'I think I may have upset him. I phoned several times, but he says he's fine, he prefers to be alone.' The big man looked distinctly hurt. 'I tell him to get a doctor, but no, no, he will not listen to his old friend. I tell him to go to the hospital, to get someone to look after him.' He shook his large head from side to side. 'But he says he is content with his own company.' He shrugged his massive shoulders. 'I am at a loss.'

Jack brought Juliet her coffee and began sponging down the top of the bar. 'Old Madeleine must be ill, as well,' he said, after a few minutes.

'Oh,' came the uninterested reply. 'I don't believe I know any Madeleines.' Fibich shrugged and began to explore his teeth with a toothpick.

'Oh yes, of course you do,' contradicted Jack. 'The old woman who sits over there. Every single morning. You must have noticed her.' He pointed in the direction of the pay phone on the rear wall. A tingle ran down Juliet's spine. She swung around.

'Oh, is that so?' Not bothering to evince any interest, Dr Fibich lumbered off his stool. 'I'll be going away myself, in a week or two, to a conference in Prague. It will be good to be back in my own country again. Let us hope my old friend will be back to normal by the time I return.' He sounded quite soulful, lonely. In fact, Fibich was rather perturbed at the continuing absence of his friend, who had failed to turn up to a governing-body meeting, in college, the previous afternoon and, even more unusual, had failed to send in his excuses. Something that, as far as Fibich could remember, had never happened before.

He passed a fiver over the counter. Jack slipped it in the till then handed Fibich the change. 'By the way, how about Caledonian Spirit for the four twenty?'

'No more tips from you, my friend.' Fibich suddenly cheered up and gave the waiter a roguish smile. 'I have lost my shirt twice already last week, following your bad advice. Tut, tut.' Juliet, hardly believing her ears, looked from one to the other. Dr Fibich waggled his head and his plump finger in the waiter's face. 'I shall give it all up,' he laughed as he left the café while Juliet furiously searched her bag for the betting slip.

'And pigs might fly,' said Jack, *sotto voce*, as he waved his customer goodbye.

Seizing her opportunity, Juliet asked, 'Did a horse called Avenging Angel run last week? Or Remember,' she added more dubiously. As Jack swung around to face her she could almost see a rotafile flipping over in his eyes. But, disappointingly, he shook his head. 'Avenging Angel, yes. Blasted nag went into reverse on the second lap. Remember, no. That's a new one on me, love. What racetrack?'

Juliet shrugged and shook her head. 'Haven't a clue.'

'Neither have I. Remember, you say? Never heard of it, last week or at any time. Know who owns it?'

'Do you recognize this?' Juliet pushed the slip of paper across the counter. He looked at it and then at her. 'Yeah, it's a betting slip, from Ladbrokes,' he said with a shrug. 'There must be millions of them floating about.' He read the scribbled writing. 'Oh, I see. If you're asking if it's mine, I don't think so. But then they all look the same to me.' As he talked he casually turned the slip over. 'Hang about, no, it's not. Never seen it before. What makes you think that's the name of a horse?' he asked curiously.

'Seems obvious. Betting slip – horses?'

'*Back* of betting slip,' he corrected. 'Anyway, even if it was a horse, these are very peculiar odds. Looks more like a date to me,' he said, as he handed it back. Juliet looked at him thoughtfully. It was an interesting point but something to think about later. There was other information she wanted from the waiter.

'Do the same customers come in here every day?' Instead of answering Jack pointed to her empty plate. 'Want another?' And wishing to keep him near Juliet said, 'Just a plain one. Oh, and another cappuccino, no chocolate on top.'

It was now or never. The café was beginning to fill up and soon the waiter would have no time for idle chat. As soon as he brought the coffee Juliet took the bull by the horns.

'Do you remember last Tuesday morning?' she asked, looking him in the eye. He gave her a rather defensive half-smile.

'Do I remember *you*? Of course I do.'

'No. Not just me. Can you . . .' It was a long shot and she didn't quite know where she was headed. 'Can you remember who was here, in the café, early last Tuesday morning?' She glanced at the clock which read five to eight. 'Say, between six and, say, seven thirty?'

'We don't open till six thirty.' The wary look he gave her suddenly reminded her of how he'd treated her that morning. As if she were completely unhinged. Then it occurred to her that the man mightn't like gossiping or, more to the point, having it known, by a policewoman, of all people, that he was running some sort of illegal betting syndicate. She knew from her own experience that gamblers were shy and secretive creatures.

'Please? I think it's important. For me. It's nothing really to do with anything else.' There was another long pause while he busied himself polishing already well-polished glasses.

'The two professors come in almost every weekday,' he said at last. He waved the dishcloth in the direction of the door. 'You saw the old boy who was here, he's one of them. He usually comes with his pal. Then there are seven or eight other regulars, those three,' he nodded at a trio by the

253

window, 'the couple just leaving and the guy who left a few minutes ago. They all come in six days a week. Most of them work in the market. That any help?' He looked distinctly sceptical.

'You mentioned someone else to the professor.'

'Did I?' He was slightly more hostile now, as if he was irritated at being overheard.

'Look,' Juliet leaned towards him earnestly. 'This is not a police enquiry. I've left the force. This is for me. A private matter.'

'You were going on about some accident that morning,' he said suspiciously. 'And that bloody constable, sergeant, whatever he is, has been in and out all week. What's his name? Throws his weight about.'

'Winter?' she asked laconically. In your face, say-it-how-it-is Winter. It had to be. 'What did he want?'

'You, I shouldn't wonder,' said Jack, giving her a sideways glance. Juliet's heart sank. 'In his dreams.' She gave Jack a watery smile. 'Absolutely, no way.' The tension eased; he grinned back.

'So, can you tell me about the other customer? The one you mentioned to the, em, professor?'

'Old Madeleine? She's not what you might call a customer. She just drops in first thing every morning for a cappuccino and a croissant. Free. Funny old thing, never says a word. We just call her Madeleine – for obvious reasons. Completely gaga, but the boss is fond of her, to tell the truth I think he's a bit superstitious about her. Thinks she brings us luck.'

'And does she?' Juliet asked and Jack laughed.

'Well, I'm not sure about that. We haven't seen hide nor hair of her for the last few days and we seem to manage. I don't think we've ever been so busy.'

'Does she', Juliet asked circumspectly, 'sort of hum?'

'Yeah. She does. And drums the bloody table with her nails as well. Gets on my wick. D'you know her?'

'No. Well, yes. Not really. But I've seen her around,' Juliet babbled nervously and Jack raised his eyebrows. 'She's harmless, you know. You don't want to be bothering her,' he said defensively.

'I promise you, nothing like that. I told you, I'm not with the police any more. I just wondered if she was here last Tuesday, that's all.'

'When you came in? No. She leaves around seven. First in, first out. Usually. Excuse me,' he said as a couple of customers approached the bar. Juliet waited until he'd served them and then two others before she called for her bill.

'Can you tell me what she looks like?'

'Thin,' he said impatiently, 'straggly, vacant-looking. And dumb. I mean really dumb, she can't talk. Or doesn't. Always carries a bunch of old plastic bags.'

'Know where she lives?' Juliet asked quietly.

'Sorry. I know nothing else about her. Honest. Sleeps rough, I shouldn't wonder. Someone once told me he'd seen her wandering along the canal bank, near Jericho. Or was it Osney? Sorry. I have to go. Really.'

Juliet paid her bill then slid a ten-pound note across the counter and stood up. 'Don't tell the police I was in. Particularly Winter. You never saw me, right?' she said solemnly and allowed one eyelid to droop lasciviously. The waiter laughed outright, clearly diverted by the idea that one policeperson should be trying to protect herself from another. Sexy, Jack thought, as he watched her leave. No wonder that bumptious git was so hot after her.

CHAPTER TWENTY-FOUR

Coming to consciousness was like surfacing through opaque, stagnant water. The old man's eyelids were glued together with sleep so that on first wakening he thought he'd been blinded. Only by concentrating hard could he ease the lashes apart enough to give him a narrow view of a tall glass-fronted bookcase against a white wall. As far as he could make out he was lying on a rather lumpy, Biedermeier-type day-bed, propped up on an over-filled square pillow against the high padded backrest and swaddled in a white linen-covered down quilt. These latter comforts perplexed him, as did the tender, unseen hands which now ministered to his bodily needs but which had, so adroitly, felled him on the street. His sleep was punctuated by moments of semi-consciousness during which he felt warm liquids trickle into his parched mouth. But gratitude was quickly replaced by a prickle of terror at the back of his neck as he waited for the next attack. Waited and willed that it might happen without warning and swiftly. The pains in his chest travelled down his arms, his fingers pricked with pins and needles. He was too weak now to offer resistance. But, even had he been strong enough, he would not try to escape. He had wasted his life chasing a chimera.

The chink of china, as a tray was set down outside the room, alerted the patient to the coming intrusion. A couple of seconds later he heard a faint squeak as the foot of the door rubbed over the surface of the carpet. He sensed, rather than saw, his keeper enter the room. He didn't turn his head but noticed that the wall beyond the foot of the couch brightened with reflected light. Feigning sleep, he concentrated on keeping control of his fluttering heart, since he knew from experience that once it began to fibrillate the normal pallor of his skin would quickly become flushed. Not wishing to reveal he was awake, he did not stir as he waited for his gaoler to announce himself.

'Why?' the man asked in a tired voice as he did each time he entered the room. 'What have I ever done to you?'

The patient blanked out the sound and drifted back to sleep. When he came to, much later, both the man and the tea tray were gone. He couldn't remember if this time he'd allowed himself to accept the drink but, since the dryness of his throat had eased, he assumed he had. He realized he was getting better, more alert, and couldn't any longer seek refuge in the timeless, comforting vacuum which protected him from reality. He opened his eyes fully now and looked around, though not for the first time. There had been other brief moments of wakefulness during which he'd examined with as much interest as he could muster, the room in which he was – what? A guest? Held prisoner? Incarcerated? Or simply nursed?

As far as he could see he was in a study, which was small and rather cluttered. A heavy, old-fashioned roll-top desk was pushed against the window, partially blocking the light but, more sinisterly, making it impossible for him to see anything but the sky from where he lay. Other than the bookcase and a chair there was his daybed with an old-fashioned mahogany commode beside it. The walls were painted white, long enough ago to show discoloration where pictures or mirrors once hung, though there was nothing of that sort now. His only distraction was the music, played almost continuously at low volume, which he'd gradually recognized as the Beethoven late quartets. Those exquisite reminders of the fragility of life; the inevitability of death. Sublime, he told himself sourly, because of the promise of transfiguration. Not for him though, who had long since given up the expectation of salvation. Oblivion would suffice. As the music filled his senses he realized that, at some point in his incarceration, he had submitted to failure and now simply longed for peace.

He closed his eyes wearily and, for the umpteenth time, tried to work out what had happened to him. One moment he'd been on the crossing, determined on a final confrontation. The next, he was being bundled into a car. A cab of some sort, he thought, since he half heard the driver being reassured as he was given directions. He had no clear idea of the events immediately before, or after. Nor even how he'd come to be on the crossing in the first place. The only thing he was sure about was that it was early on Tuesday morning because, just as he was about to switch off the bedside radio before he left his hotel room, he'd heard the introduction to the news bulletin. The phrase had stuck: *This is the six o'clock news briefing, on Tuesday the third of June*. It was, more or less, the last really clear memory he had of that morning. He'd been unable to sleep after the débâcle of the previous day. Having wangled an invitation to the meeting, specifically to confront the enemy, he'd completely mismanaged the unprecedented opportunity it afforded. In the immediate aftermath he'd resolved to slink out of town and lick his wounds, assuring himself that when he recovered he would resume his campaign. From afar. No more eyeball to eyeball – it was against his nature. If he could not gain outright victory then at least he'd continue to whittle away at the professional reputation of his foe. That, after all, had already proved most effective.

How feeble it sounded. It was not at all what he'd originally set out to do. Oh, how those grand and brave schemes had dwindled as his energy dissipated with the tolling years. Once, he had intended killing the enemy, without quarter or mercy, ritually, with his bare hands or whatever presented itself at the material time. Then he had gone one better and purchased that clever little flick-knife. Right was on his side and the righteous are brave. How vague it all sounded now. There had never been a specific plan, it was simply that, for him, there was no other option. In his youth, an eye for an eye had a powerful appeal. But time had wrought many modifications, to this, as to so much else. His ideas, like his courage, had dwindled.

But the morning after the reception the fire in him stirred again as he slowly absorbed his humiliation. His heart was also playing up, even in repose he had severe angina, so that throughout the night he had overused his glyceryl trinitrate. As a consequence he had a blinding headache, which added to his sense of frustration and outrage. He couldn't remember what precisely drove him to seek out his quarry that morning, or how he intended to get his revenge. He'd left the hotel simply to take an early morning walk, clear his head before checking out. Then what? What had set him off? Something . . . Something had led him to that café. But what? Had he not gone there, he wouldn't have been reminded of the previous day's débâcle.

He had certainly had no set idea beyond a calming stroll when he emerged from his hotel. But he knew, from a week of shadowing him, where his enemy was to be found at that hour of morning. Was it the thought that his time was running out which had driven him to the café? It had certainly something to do with it. That and the terrible humiliation of the previous evening.

His shame still stung. His plan of public disgrace had failed dismally as the tables were neatly turned and he found himself under attack for unprofessional conduct, not just from the speaker but, more humiliatingly, from the floor. Recollection of those polite but damning rebukes set his heart pumping painfully. The very thing he had planned for his enemy had been visited on himself. He had lived inside his own head for so long, he imagined everyone in the world was party to his horror and revulsion and would applaud his search for justice. But it was no longer justice, was it? The chance for that had been missed or, worse, pitiably bungled, half a century before. By himself as well as everyone else.

Over the years, the past entangled him and sucked his life away. Revenge and retribution drove him until he thought that only blood-letting could release him from his agony. Now he knew that self-annihilation was what he'd been after all along. He should have killed himself but lacked the courage. But now, perhaps, help was at hand. The man he had stalked for a lifetime had him in his power and in his sights. He had already made one attempt, in broad daylight on a public highway. The only thing he could remember clearly was crashing to the ground. Had his strength failed or was his opponent too alert and nimble? The leg must have shot out and tripped him as he lunged forward with that pathetic little knife, which was taken from him like candy from a child. Was his opponent now biding his time, keeping him prisoner for a second attempt? 'Let him do it swiftly,' the patient murmured softly, but shied away from praying for what he really craved: the capacity to forgive. Himself as well as his enemy.

After all this time, life seemed utterly futile. He wished he had the ability to care whether he lived or died. One idea, and one only, had driven him since the moment Angel was killed. Not a day had gone by without her memory tugging at his conscience, urging him to seek out her slayer and destroy him in turn. But somewhere along the way the driving force had deserted him. He had failed her and failed his own youthful idea of himself. He was neither powerful nor idealistic. His motives, however they had started out, had been corrupted over the years as the emphasis of his life changed and his work gained ascendancy over his heart. He had grown desiccated and bitter. He did not deserve love. When it came he couldn't hold onto it. He had driven his second, as well as his first love, away. Or was it mere chance that he inexorably drifted into solitude and despair? He'd carved his own destruction from an impossible dream of lost love. A love which grew with each passing year, from the moment he'd watched Angel's lifeless, bloody body float away down river. He'd stood by, and let her die and not raised a finger to help her. He remained hidden *and safe* until her killer had fled, and only then had he come forth to seek salvation with brave talk of revenge. Tears of self-pity rolled slowly down the bloodless cheeks. His entire adult life had been blighted by self-loathing.

The tears softened his sticky eyelids and after a time he opened his eyes fully. He could see the sky through the half-drawn curtains. There was a vast yew tree immediately outside with a variety of birds flying in and out of its upper branches. He wondered how many days had passed since he'd been brought to this room? Five? Six? Earlier – he thought it might have been the day before – the pealing of a church bell had penetrated his drowsiness. In some hazy way he'd worked out that it must be Sunday. So now it was Monday? Late afternoon, by the light.

Something felt different. It was a moment or two before he realized that Herr Beethoven was being given a well-earned rest. Except for the chirruping of the birds, silence reigned until he gradually became aware of another sound, faint at first but becoming ever more insistent: a tap-tapping rhythm on the window. He tried to struggle upright but the searing pain across his chest threw him back violently against the pillow. The tapping stopped and then, through the rushing of his own blood, he heard a thin, eerie humming sound which he slowly recognized as an old nursery rhyme. It was repeated several times solo and finally accompanied by the insistent tapping. For three or four minutes it continued until the patient took up the refrain, hesitantly and creakily at first, then, summoning all his energy, he sang the little song as loudly as he could.

Outside, he heard a sudden roar: 'What are you doing there? Go away at once or I'll call the police.'

Shortly thereafter the patient heard the familiar sound of clinking china followed by the door being eased open. The smell of chicken soup filled the small room. The patient lay back against the pillow and closed his eyes.

Retrospective

CHAPTER TWENTY-FIVE

I cannot find Angel. It is harder than I thought to judge the distance so I cannot see her at first. I go back and forth past her, several times, before my searching hands find her. Do I imagine it, or is the air immediately around her clear? As though a protective dome or a bubble has been dropped over where she lies? It is almost as though we are protected by a little white tent. I kneel and put out my hand, but I am afraid to touch her. She lies face downward, oh so still, with her legs twisted grotesquely and her arms outstretched. I cannot see her dear face but her hair is bloody. I touch it with my trembling finger then lay my head on her back. I don't know what I am listening for, or even if I am listening at all, since no sound penetrates my ears. Shamefully, I am seeking comfort.

Another strange thing – I am on the ground but also in the air above, watching – I lean back on my heels and begin to sing to her. Such a silly thing to do.

She wears only one shoe. The white shirt covers only the upper part of her body, her legs and back-side are shamefully bare. I think that upsets me more than anything. I am ashamed to see her thus exposed for I know she would be mortified with shame. I cannot, I will not, let anyone see her humiliation. I pull her dress from my waistband, unroll it and lay it beside me on the grass.

Her legs are flaccid, as if her bones have crumbled beneath the skin, so that it is difficult to ease her drawers on. My heart is bursting with love and pity. I want to take Angel in my faithless arms and kiss her to life but I am afraid to turn her over. Her body feels as though it has no substance as I ease off the tattered shirt. Only the back of it is intact, the rest is in bloody shreds. Angel, lying face down with only her pink drawers on, looks as though she is sunbathing.

The dress has buttons up the front. She hadn't bothered to undo them when she took it off but now I open each one slowly, putting off the moment when I must turn her over. First, I drape the open dress over her back and gently insert her pliant arms into the short sleeves. And still I cannot bear to turn her. She looks so perfect as she lies there, with her pretty dress mantled around her.

I take off the shoe. The soles of her little bare feet are dirty. I lick my hand and rub them clean, singing, singing my love to her. It is as if we are the only two people left in all the world. Angel, oh my Angel. She is so silent, and oh, so very still.

I stand up and slowly dress myself in the remains of my father's shirt, whose tattered shreds are soaked with her blood, then I sink to my knees beside her and begin to pray: Help me, oh Jesu, help me.

On bended knees I move in close to her left side and, hardly breathing, gently ease her right shoulder against my thighs. I have to close my eyes, shut out the sight for, oh dear God, her body is a great open bloody mass and she has no face. The sound of piteous howling fills my head, and I find myself mouthing the words of the *Agnus Dei*. I do not know why.

I slowly struggle to my feet with Angel cradled in my arms and we are instantly shrouded in the foul smoke. I inch my way blindly, step by halting step, to the water's edge and slowly wade into the cold, cold river. Though the smoke is all around me the surface of the water is clear. When the level reaches my waist and begins to lap at her open dress, I lay my love, face downward, upon the water. Still holding on to her with one hand, I rearrange the folds of her dress modestly over her. I cannot let her go, I want her to surface from the river, as she did earlier, laughing. Oh foolish hope. Her blood slowly forms a halo around her as I push her gently into mid-stream. She floats away from me, and is quickly lost to my sight.

I sink down into the water until it covers me and washes me clean. I hold my breath as long as I can before striking out for the opposite bank, away from the town. When I pull myself out of the river, my hearing has returned.

All hell has broken loose. The bombardment is fearsome, overwhelming: explosion after explosion. Great rockets of light tear up into the sky, throwing off showers of burning rocks and debris. The din is indescribable, so tremendous I cannot understand why I had been unaware of it before. Bellowing cattle, howling cats and dogs. Through it all I hear the church bells toll wildly. And something else: the sound of wailing and lamentation fills my head. I cannot tell if it comes from me, or if I imagine it, but it is so heart-rending that I try to stop my ears.

Then suddenly through the smoke I see two little figures tumble over a garden wall and roll down the grass bank to the road. They limp away, one dragging the other, and disappear into the smoke. There is another huge explosion and the flaming church spire topples over. After that the bells fall silent as if they, like I, have given up hope that anyone can survive that concremation. But the dogs continue to yowl.

I stand for some moments until I hear, rather than see, the tanks roar into action. Then I take to my heels, the sound of the dogs ringing in my ears.

Oxford

June 1997

CHAPTER TWENTY-SIX

It was to be a day of global confrontation: with Freddie, the solicitor, Dallimore, Bray, and, if she could track her down, old Madeleine. There was also someone else she should contact, but that required a little more courage. Something she would have to work herself up to. But first, before anything else, she had to buy some clothes. She glanced at her watch and saw to her surprise that it was still only quarter-past eight. The shops, infuriatingly, didn't open until nine or half-past. She moved clothes to second on her mental list and shoved accommodation to the top.

She had to find somewhere more suitable, private and central to hole up for a week. She'd had it with guest-houses. She did a quick calculation, then full of resolve she hurried down the High Street to the Eastgate Hotel where she knew the manager who, more importantly, owed her a favour. Half an hour later she was shown into a small but adequate double room at a knock-down price, not just because the manager was in her debt but because it was tucked away on the top floor at the back with a clear, and indeed exclusive, view of the hotel car park. 'It's only for overspill,' she was told after they'd reached an accommodation on the rate – which was, as it turned out, precisely the same as the Miranda.

'We rarely use it. You stay as long as you like. Delighted to be able to help.'

'Thanks, Sue, it's very good of you. It's exactly what I want,' Juliet said, wishing she'd thought of it in the first place. 'But I only need it for a week.'

It was while she was arranging for her bag to be collected from the Miranda that the manager electrified her. 'By the way Juliet, you haven't heard anything about our missing guest, have you?'

Juliet's jaw dropped. *Now* she recalled that elusive little reference in the newspaper. She said, far more calmly than she felt, 'What missing guest?'

'Oh sorry, hadn't you heard?'

'I've been ill,' she said. 'I haven't been at work for a week. What happened?'

'Well, nothing much really. The guy booked in for five days but left, without saying anything, after four.'

'When was this?' Juliet asked.

'Early last week, he disappeared.'

'Disappeared?'

'Well, that's probably a bit dramatic since he packed his bag and everything. He may just have forgotten it. There was nothing in it but a couple of changes of clothes, shaving tackle, and some books. We had his credit-card number and all, so his bill's paid. But we reported it, just to be on the safe side.'

'So you know who he was?'

'Yeah, well, his name would be on the records . . .'

'What did he look like?' Juliet tried to keep the excitement out of her voice.

'I didn't see him myself, I wasn't here last week. Amanda, one of the receptionists, dealt with it. She described him as foreign and sort of elderly. But she's only nineteen so . . .' Sue laughed and rolled her eyes. 'Hopeless. He's probably about thirty-five. Quiet apparently. Up at the crack of dawn every morning, otherwise nobody saw much of him.'

'And you've heard nothing?'

'No. He probably just forgot the bag and went home. You'd be amazed at the stuff people leave behind.'

'And nobody contacted you about him, his wife? Family?'

Sue looked at her watch, regretting having mentioned the missing guest. In her experience he wasn't the first to go walkabout and probably wouldn't be the last. It was no big deal. The relief manager had passed the information to the police in case there was an accident or something, or, perhaps, more to cover himself. Herself, she'd have waited for a day or so, given him time to get home. Which presumably he had, since no-one had been ringing up looking for him.

'Amanda around?'

'No sorry. She won't be back until Thursday. Look, sorry Juliet, but I have to go.'

'You couldn't find out his name for me, could you?' Juliet asked, and, from the odd look Sue gave her, she realized that she'd overstepped the mark.

'I'm sorry, Juliet, I can't do that.' She raised her hands helplessly. 'Look, it's no big deal. Guys go missing all the time. Time off for bad behaviour? You should work in a hotel, kid. It's quite an education. If something had happened to him, we'd soon hear about it. He's probably at home right now, mowing his lawn. But if you're that worried surely you can get more information from your mates, at St Aldates?'

Maybe. But then maybe not. Maybe she'd tackle Amanda when she returned to work – but Thursday seemed a hell of a wait. Juliet had a hunch that she had found one of her men – but which one? Lost, found, lost again. She had to find Madeleine. Her head spinning, she took a bus back to Carfax. She spent the following hour flitting between the shops, kitting herself out with chinos, shirts and sweaters, shoes, underwear, and anything else that seemed essential. Then she hiked off to Jaeger and bought a navy blazer, having first bargained delivery of all her purchases to the hotel. By ten fifteen she was all set. She returned to the Miranda.

The ubiquitous Mrs Cowley was in the hall chatting to Catullus Bray when she arrived. He had a large envelope under his arm and a fixed smile on his face. He greeted Juliet with relief. 'I've got something to show you,' he said.

'Come upstairs,' Juliet answered. Mrs Cowley looked from one to the other and pursed her lips. 'Use the lounge,' she said quickly. 'It'll be more suitable.' She emphasized 'suitable' and ushered them into a large sitting-room which was a riot of bright orange sunbursts on carpet, walls and furniture. 'Psychedelic,' murmured Catullus, as soon as she'd gone. They both collapsed with laughter.

'Thank heavens you arrived when you did,' Catullus said. 'She doesn't stop talking, does she? She just went on and on. And so nosy. I thought I'd have to show her my passport.'

'She thinks I'm on drugs. Or booze.'

'And are you?' he asked lightly. It took a second or two for her to realize he was joking. 'Both,' she said. 'I'm totally depraved.' She grinned.

'At least you're beginning to take me less seriously,' he said. 'That's good.' He sat down on the sofa and patted the seat beside him. 'Come and see what I've got,' he said.

He spread a dozen enlargements on the floor in front of them. While the images were still out of focus, the background was not. A figure which looked remarkably like the woman she now knew as Madeleine was sitting on the steps of the market entrance, her hands clasped across her knees. Juliet picked it up and stared at it for a long time before she began to examine the other shots of the pedestrian crossing. In spite of being enlarged the figures in these were much less identifiable. Indeed it was almost impossible to tell if they were men or women. The one photograph which showed Juliet was equally ambiguous. She could just as easily have been a man. She turned to Catullus who seemed to be hugging something to himself, since there was a smug grin plastered across his face.

'When did you do these? You must have been up all night.'

'No, I woke around five. Didn't want to sleep

any more so I just got up and worked.'

'Isn't that funny? So did I.'

'So did you what?'

'Wake up at five,' she said and blushed. He touched the back of her hand with the tips of his fingers. 'I thought about you,' he said.

'Huh?'

He looked at her steadily. 'I said I thought about you, Juliet Furbo,' he said firmly. 'A lot. And when my thoughts got a bit dangerous, I thought about the photographs. So I did them.'

'I see,' she said slowly, though she wasn't at all sure she did. Sitting close to Catullus was deeply disturbing but she certainly didn't want to think about that. Nor move away, for that matter.

'They bring us no further, do they?' she said.

For answer he turned them over. Each was neatly dated and precisely timed. 'I believe two of them do,' he said softly. 'See what you think.'

Juliet began to check picture against time and was barely able to suppress her excitement as she quickly isolated the two he meant. One, of the crouched figures on the crossing, was timed at seven thirteen. The second, of the old woman, was taken at seven twelve. She looked up delightedly. 'You're brilliant, you know that? Really brilliant.'

'They help, then?'

'Yes. Yes. They must.' Doubt crept into her voice.

'Mind telling me how?'

'That, I'm less sure of,' she said slowly. 'But at least I now know that there was an accident and that the old woman witnessed it. So she might be able to identify the two men.' She wrinkled her nose. 'If I can get her to tell me, I can find out if they're all right,' she finished lamely and bit the inside of her lip. Was the pursuit always more exciting than the solution?

Catullus eyed her dubiously. 'I got the impression last night that the accident was connected to you, personally, in some way. Did you know the men?'

She shook her head. Her cheeks flamed. 'No, no. It's all mixed up. The whole thing reminds me of something else. I told you, didn't I?'

'I don't think so, Juliet. But you don't have to, you know.'

'But I did. I remember.'

'You told me a little about your family, that's all. A little about your childhood. Nothing more.'

'Not about the . . . not about them dying?'

Catullus shook his head. 'No, nothing about that. Are they dead?' He looked at her in horror. 'Your *entire* family? All of them? My God, that's terrible.' He reached out sympathetically to touch her arm, but she jumped up and began to dance nervously up and down like an impatient child. 'Don't you see,' she gave an anguished cry. 'Don't you see. That's just the point. That's what I just don't know.'

She broke down and wept then, sitting on the edge of the sofa with his arm lightly around her shoulder.

He was utterly baffled by what she'd said, but he didn't want to upset her by going back over it. In some way that he couldn't really understand, she appeared to be using the shock of the recent incident to face some terrible trauma of her own in the past. Hedging around her troubles like Mohammed Ali in the ring. Dancing around danger like a butterfly.

Did he pity her? Was pity driving his interest in her? He knew he desperately wanted to protect her, see her through whatever was distressing her, which was absurd. Twenty-four hours before, he hadn't even met her. Now he wanted to know everything about her. He had a strong urge to take her in his arms and kiss her. Make her remember her senses and not her fears. Strong men weren't supposed to fall in love at first sight, were they? Not cool cats like him.

After a few minutes Juliet wiped her eyes and stood up again. 'Sorry for that,' she said, gallantly trying to make little of it. 'Maybe it wasn't such a great idea getting up at five, huh?'

'Maybe it wasn't, at that.'

'Can I keep the photographs?'

'Of course, they're for you. Do you need any more?' he asked, suddenly aware that she was bringing the visit to an end and might, if he wasn't careful, manage to slip away.

'I was breathalyzed last night,' he said. 'Would you believe it?'

Her jaw dropped. 'Where?'

'Just outside. Corner of Mansfield Road as I was turning the car. Forgot to reset the headlights after I dropped you.'

'Youngish bloke, tall, receding hairline, sharp features?' she asked fiercely.

'Yeah, that's the guy.'

Winter. Just as well she was on the move. 'Git,' she spat. 'I'm really sorry about that.'

'No big deal. The damn thing didn't even turn orange.' He didn't mention that her weasel-faced pal had pumped him assiduously and in barely suppressed racialist terms about 'the girlfriend'. Hot on eugenics. Sadly, not all that unusual in Catullus's experience. But upsetting, always upsetting. 'I take it you don't share his racial views?'

'I damn well do not,' she said robustly. 'I'm sorry you should even ask.'

Catullus grinned. 'Well, in that case you won't mind having dinner with me this evening, will you?'

'That would be lovely. What time?'

'Pick you up here at seven?'

'Eastgate Hotel would be better,' she said. 'I'm moving there this afternoon.'

'I'll be there.'

'Me too.' She held out her hand impetuously. 'Thanks for everything, Catullus.'

'Oh, I think you can graduate to Cat, don't you?' He held onto her hand and eased her towards him. 'By the way, can you dance, Juliet Furbo?' But, without waiting for an answer, he quietly left the room.

Juliet gathered the photographs and put them back into the envelope marked C.M. Bray and slowly climbed the stairs. It didn't take long to assemble the few items she wanted to take with her which she packed into a plastic carrier with Catullus's photographs. The rest of her stuff, including the remaining items of her uniform, was dumped unceremoniously into the waste-basket. She brushed her hair and retied it – when was she ever going to get it done? – and splashed water on her reddened eyes. It was eleven fifteen, still three-quarters of an hour to her appointment with the solicitor. The walk there would take no more than fifteen minutes at the outside. Juliet went downstairs, settled her bill and bought a phonecard from Mrs Cowley. She waited until the landlady was safely back in her kitchen before she went to the phone in the hall and picked up the receiver.

'Hi, Uncle, it's me.'

'My dear? A moment.' As always, the line went silent as the phone was set down. Juliet followed the sounds as he went through his odd little ritual. While she waited she pictured his room which she had never actually seen. Bare floorboards, since she could hear the crisp sound of his footsteps: five, six. Today it was six. The squeak of a door closing. Then the returning footsteps to the round table where the phone lay. She didn't quite know why she thought the table must be round or why indeed there might even be a table. Since the sounds had a slight echo, there might be little or even no furniture at all. Today, she heard him speak a few words. To someone in the room? No, more like he was talking into another phone. When she heard the date it occurred to her that he might be about to record what she said. Did he always?

'Are you feeling better?' the quiet reassuring voice asked. She wondered for the umpteenth time what his name was, since she never addressed him as other than 'Uncle' which he certainly was not. He had only appeared on the scene after Nancy's untimely death. Though 'appear' hardly described the disembodied presence. The day of the funeral she had been told someone would contact her, and so he did, every few days ever since.

She had no idea where the calls came from, or where he hung out, since the dialling code didn't seem to apply to any specific area. She knew that because once, when she tried to check with the operator, she was told it didn't exist. She assumed he was from Special Branch but even that was sheer speculation. He might have been anyone, from anywhere. The voice was classless with no clue to its geographical origins. Sometimes she wondered if he lived close by, because he had an uncanny knack of contacting her just when she most needed to talk. Talking was as much as she would do since she could never bring herself to ask for help. There was something unnerving about his instinctive timing, which made her feel that she was less a consenting adult than an insignificant wind-up toy which only operated with a starting push.

Of late, in her thoughts she referred to him as the Mind-bender and increasingly resented his soft and concerned enquiries. He was like a well-intentioned but infuriatingly manipulative parent.

'I'm leaving Oxford,' she said tersely, knowing that he wouldn't like her mention of the name. Names were strictly avoided in their strange surreal conversations, names, places, exact times and dates. She wondered if the day might come when verbs or nouns or even prepositions might be arbitrarily, and for reasons of security, deleted.

'I see.' The reply was terse, almost angry.

'Look. I want you to get this straight. I'm dealing with my life myself from now on. It has nothing to do with—' She was about to say security but he cut her off.

'You sure?'

'Yes, I'm sure. Thanks for the mobile, but I wish you hadn't. It was from you, wasn't it?'

'Yes, I was anxious about your health, that's all.' For him it was a long sentence. An expression had crept into his voice that she'd never heard before. Might it be respect?

Juliet paused a moment before replying. 'I've made my decisions. I know what I'm going to do. I've got it sussed. I . . .'

In your dreams, she thought, self-mockingly, knowing she was far from having anything sussed. But it was true, at least, that she knew what she wanted. She would leave Oxford and go, go, go. Away from her mistakes, away from Freddie and away from these weird phone calls. She was a little taken aback when he offered no argument.

'Yes, I think you probably have. I'm glad.'

'Right. Well, thanks,' she said lamely. 'Does that mean we won't talk again?' A tiny note of anxiety crept into her voice. Strangely, now that the props were being removed, she felt vulnerable.

There was a soft and surprising chortle from the other end of the line. 'Well, now. We can always talk. Shall we say that I'll keep in touch until you sign off? How would that be?'

'Fine. Providing . . .' She didn't quite know what made her say it and having half formed the thought she wondered if it might not seem, well, a bit stupid. Flirtatious, almost.

'Providing?'

'I would like to meet you. Just once. I would like to see what "my uncle" looks like.' She drew in a deep breath. 'I would like to thank you, in person, for all those years of . . . well . . .'

'We'll see what can be done.' There was a moment's silence.

'It'll have to be soon.'

'We'll see what can be done about that as well,' he said lightly and cut the connection.

CHAPTER TWENTY-SEVEN

Peter Dallimore was waiting outside the Pitt Rivers when Juliet turned up. As they went inside she linked her arm in his. It was such an uncharacteristic gesture that it took him completely by surprise, but then Juliet was still feeling elated after the confrontation with Freddie and the solicitor. She had put everything else out of her mind and arrived well-psyched, and a little early for the meeting. But when she was shown into Kenneth Barber's office, she found them already in cahoots. She was thrown for a moment, but quickly recovered.

Kenneth was some sort of cousin of Freddie's, whom she'd only met a few times, and disliked. This feeling appeared to be entirely mutual. His manner towards her was arrogant and dismissive, as it was perhaps towards everyone. He certainly treated his secretary with lofty disdain, she noticed. For once Freddie was fairly muted and, it quickly transpired, was working up to cajoling the majority of the residual estate out of her. 'The debts were, er, somewhat larger than I'd anticipated,' he said. And growing, she had no doubt.

Anger sustained her, controlled and smouldering beneath the surface. But had Freddie, even once, referred to the debts as *his*, or made the slightest attempt at taking responsibility or, at the least, apologized to her, she would not have gone for the jugular.

'Do you mind, Kenneth? I'd like a word with Freddie,' she flashed after a five-minute waffle. 'In private.' And without waiting for a reply had stormed out of the room, Freddie following limply in her wake.

That was when she dropped the bomb about the insurance. 'It won't wash, Freddie. I don't know how you ever imagined it would. I've told the police the contents of the house were already sold.'

'What'd you do that for?' His eyes were out on stalks, an ugly flush spreading up from his neck. 'You know, you're a complete bitch.'

'Well Freddie, the way it is, I reckon you set the bloody thing up,' she said quietly and waited while he shuffled, hemmed and hawed.

'I never meant them to injure you,' he muttered eventually. 'I wouldn't do that. You know that. But I was desperate. You could have bailed me out.'

'I have. Many times. But you always need more, don't you? Your lovely pals damn near killed me. You're bloody lucky I didn't shop you.'

'You didn't? You won't, will you?' he pleaded and she wondered where the golden youth she'd fallen for had gone. Why she'd stood him for so long.

'I won't, but there's a price.'

'What? Anything. I promise, Jools.'

'Fuck off, Freddie.'

'I promise. Whatever you want,' he repeated.

'That's what I want,' she said and watched the light dawn. 'Just get out of my life.'

He looked crestfallen. 'I'm sorry,' he said at last. 'I never wanted it to happen. You know I never meant to hurt you. Jools?'

'But you did, Freddie. You always did.' She'd almost broken down then. However you looked at it, the end of a relationship was failure. For everybody.

'How much will there be left?' She glared at him. 'After *your* debts are paid?' She held up her hand. 'No bullshit, Freddie. Just cut the bullshit. Just say it. Spit it out.'

He avoided her eye, took in a deep breath. 'All up, six five.'

She gasped. 'But we should have cleared forty thousand. Fifty, if you count the deposit.'

He swallowed. 'Yeah, well . . .'

She didn't trust herself to say another word. She marched back into Kenneth Barber's office, a rather crestfallen Freddie at her heels.

'I hear you've cleared the slate, Ken. Ten thousand of that belonged to me, you know. What are you going to do about it?'

After that, there was a great deal of fast footwork, but Juliet took no part until they had rounded themselves well and truly into a corner. Then she named her terms.

'Why don't you both shut up?' she said loudly. 'I'm out of here in five minutes, so you better listen. My terms are these: I want you, Kenneth, to draw up a binding agreement that Freddie Kimber will never, ever come near me again. OK?' She turned to Freddie. 'And when you sign it, I want a copy, and my ten thousand. You're going to have to cough up, Fred. I mean it. And if you ever come near me again, I'll sue you for twenty k. And have you locked up. You know I can, don't you?'

Juliet smiled sweetly at them both. 'Now Freddie, why don't you just tell cousin Kenneth precisely what you've been up to? Get him to write it down, have it witnessed and send me a copy and deposit the ten thousand in my bank, I'll send you the details. Take it or leave it. There's always the alternative. You better believe it, I'm not joking.'

She almost burst out laughing at the way Kenneth's head swivelled from one to the other of them, with ever-increasing speed. She wouldn't have been in the least surprised had it fallen straight off, plop, onto the desk. Good ole cousin Freddie as abuser had clearly never occurred to him. To do him justice, he looked profoundly shocked. Disgusted even. There was no longer any question that he took her seriously. With that, she picked her way daintily out of the room. She was still shaking by the time she'd walked the couple of miles to the Pitt Rivers. Shaking but high.

Peter Dallimore was waiting for her on the steps outside, looking anxious. When he saw her he waved and it was like seeing him properly for the first time. As she came towards him, she realized how fond of him she really was, and grateful. He had always been there for her. After years of resenting him she suddenly knew she would miss him. He was wearing plain clothes: a rather dashing natural linen suit with a blue open-necked polo shirt. She felt quite shabby beside him.

They went inside and strolled around the museum trying to avoid a classful of seven-year-olds, hell-bent on taking the place apart. One child was screaming for a proper dinosaur. 'It's got no skin,' he kept yelling, clearly neither convinced by nor contented with mere skeletons.

'I've never been here before,' Dallimore confessed and laughed. 'And probably won't again. I thought you said it was quiet?'

'Private. I said it was private,' Juliet argued. 'But it is usually also very quiet. Sorry about that.'

'Doesn't matter. I'm glad to see you looking better. Not changed your mind about coming back to work?' She shook her head.

'What about Steve?'

'What about him?'

'He's fond of you. Keeps asking for you. He's not a bad bloke, you know.'

'No,' she replied. For a moment she contemplated telling him about her most recent encounter with Winter. But found she could hardly bear think of it, much less discuss that horrible, demeaning incident. He would think her incapable of inspiring anything but violence. Another private terror. She said, trying to keep all emotion from her voice, 'You can make a fool of yourself once, if you're drunk. You don't have to compound the felony. When I'm smashed I tend to get amorous.' She blinked. 'Or worse. It was a mistake. He probably deserves better. But not from me.'

Dallimore looked down at her, his head to one

side. 'You've come a long way in a week. One of these days you'll find a good man. There are some, you know.' He waited but she didn't reply. 'How did the meeting with the solicitor go?' he asked.

'Is there anything about me you don't know?' she asked crossly, but after a moment climbed down. 'It went well, very well as a matter of fact. I'm shot of Freddie, I hope. I think I found a way. And don't ask, I won't bring charges either against him or those thugs who beat me up.'

'Am I to guess why?'

'As you wish, Peter.' She smiled at him shyly. 'Look there's something I want to say. I know I've been a bit prickly with you and don't always seem to appreciate the way you've, er . . .'

'Kept an eye on you?'

'Yes. Just one thing. Were you, er, was it official?'

'What makes you ask?'

'I didn't tell anyone where I was staying, so you must have been tailing me. And the mobile, of course.'

'Not official. Well, let's say semi. I found out quite a lot after Blackbird Leys. I was asked to keep an eye, but I would have done anyway. Did I ever tell you you remind me of my daughter?'

'Several times.' She smiled.

'Yes. Very like her. Same smile, same stroppy way of going on.' He became more heated. 'If what happened to you, happened to her I'd make damn sure everyone in sight felt responsible for looking after her.'

'But don't you see, Peter? There's been too much

of that. I want to have a crack at looking after myself.'

He glanced at his watch. 'Are you ready then?' he asked, the corners of his mouth twitching. Juliet looked at him in surprise. 'For what?'

'I promised your "uncle" I'd take you to visit,' he said quietly. 'He's waiting.'

'Where?' God, what next? Hadn't he been listening?

'Not far,' he teased.

'Here? In Oxford?' She swallowed. 'Is there anything you don't know?' she said bleakly.

'About you? Not a lot. As I said, I was asked to keep an eye on you.' He clasped his hand on hers and led her to the door. 'After the Blackbird Leys incident, I started asking questions about you. Your "uncle" came to see me. He was worried about you. Worried that you'd do something foolish.'

'Like what? Kill myself? Shoot my mouth off? Who is this bastard who runs my life?'

'To tell you the truth, I haven't a clue.' She gave him a sharp look. It might have been the truth.

A black taxi-cab, with darkened windows, rolled up to the entrance as they came out.

Peter Dallimore opened the door for Juliet, handed her in and climbed in beside her. The driver pulled away without waiting for instructions. Juliet nudged Dallimore.

'Where are we going?'

'You'll see,' he replied enigmatically. He tapped the driver's window. 'You can drop me at the Broad,' he said and turned to Juliet. 'I'll say goodbye, Julie, sorry, Juliet,' he grinned. 'For the moment anyway. I'm off on holiday tomorrow. Keep in touch. I'll miss you. I meant what I said in the hospital, you know.'

'What was that?' He'd said so much. Contrarily, now that he was going, she felt her spirits droop.

'That you have great qualities. You've done the right thing, dumping that bastard. But be careful, he'll probably try to worm his way back. Don't let him near you. Promise?'

'Promise. I'll miss you, sir. You've been . . .' She stopped, embarrassed. 'You've been like a, well, like a father.'

'And as irritating,' he laughed. 'I'm always here for you. Remember that.' Before she had time to reply, the cab stopped at the lights outside the King's Arms and Dallimore stepped out. He gave a little wave and rapped the door twice. As the driver pulled away she tried to ask where they were going, but the dividing window was shut, and, short of shouting, she would not be heard. When the cab cut, illegally, through Turl Street and turned left on the High, she assumed they were headed for London. She lay back in the seat and closed her eyes. Three or four minutes later they swept through the entrance of Tradescant College, through the first quad into a second and pulled up outside a doorway through which a stone staircase idiosyncratically disappeared upwards.

The driver opened the cab door. 'Set three, first floor right, Miss.' He waved his hand at the stairs. 'I'm to wait.'

She climbed the stairs slowly. Door three had

J.M. Boyce in the name-slot. She stood outside, with her heart pounding for a good three or four minutes until she summoned enough courage to raise her hand to knock. But before she did so the door swung open to reveal a middle-aged man waiting just inside the room. Juliet stood back and looked him up and down. She'd waited years to meet him and whatever she expected it was not this ordinary, anonymous-seeming man. He was about five foot ten and appeared to be in his mid-fifties. He was pleasant – rather than good-looking, with rather blunt features, fresh complexion, grey eyes, abundant dark hair. He wore a pinstripe navy blue suit, white shirt and striped – regimental? – tie. *A suit*, she thought. He's one of the suits. And I've seen him before. Several times. Dining with my old tutor in Drapier. Keeping an eye?

'Juliet, come in.' The voice was low and beautifully modulated, but even in the flesh hard to identify its origins. He stood back courteously to let her pass. Like many college rooms this had double doors, heavy oak outer and the baize-covered inner. Her host closed both and turned the key in the second. 'We won't be disturbed,' he said. 'Will you have a glass of wine? I have a nice chilled bottle of Sancerre.'

'I think I need it.' She didn't know where to begin. She found it utterly confusing to be with a man who was familiar, yet not familiar. To be back in a college which was the twin of her tutor's and therefore also familiar, yet not. The ancient book-lined room was beautiful and extremely light, with two oriel windows looking over the quad. There was a blue and red oriental carpet in the centre of the room surrounded by well-polished elm floorboards. She crossed and stood awkwardly by one of the windows, with her back to him, looking out. The quad below was deserted except for the waiting taxi, whose driver was nowhere in sight. It all looked so normal, so reminiscent of the many times she had come to a room very like this for tutorials. Anger boiled and bubbled to the surface. Still with her back to him she said quietly, 'Can you tell the driver not to wait for me. I shall walk to my hotel.' She was answered by a low chuckle. She stood still, listening to him cross the floor, then open the door to the second room of the set. His footsteps drummed on bare boards. The sound of a telephone being lifted, dialled. He waited a moment before speaking. She closed her eyes, the better to listen. 'Stevenson? You can go. Pick me up as arranged at ten. Thank you.'

Most people have telephone voices, he was no exception. He was the man she'd been speaking to for years, all right. She watched Stevenson climb into the cab and drive away, then swung around to face him as he re-entered the room.

'I've seen you in Drapier, several times, haven't I? Dining with my tutor.'

'Yes, Alex Sharman is an old friend. As is John Boyce, whose room this is.'

'I noticed. Why the subterfuge? I don't know where on earth I am with you.'

'For my protection, not yours. Well, possibly

yours too. Please, won't you sit down?'

'So you can give me a tutorial? Tell me what to think? How to behave?'

He sat in a high-winged armchair a little to the side of her and began to talk in his quiet, mesmeric voice, about the weather, a concert he'd been to the previous evening, the delights of Oxford. At first she couldn't listen for the questions that were bombarding her skull but eventually she sat down meekly and sipped the wine.

'It wasn't a mistake, was it?' she asked abruptly and without preamble. 'They intended to blow us up? It wasn't a mistake.'

'Is it ever?'

'I don't know. You tell me,' she said coldly.

'Yes, we believe it was intentional.'

Her jaw dropped. 'They meant to kill all of us? Michael and I were only children.' He nodded.

'Why?' she asked. She was overwhelmed with sorrow.

'Reprisal. It's always reprisal. First one side, then the other. Tit for tat. Your father was working for us. He may have also been working for them. Both sides against the middle. He was a clever man.'

'But not clever enough'. She took a deep breath. 'An informer then?'

He shrugged. 'An ugly word, specially in Ireland. Why not say he was a spy? That's what you thought, as a child. Isn't it?'

Juliet froze, remembering the night before. Was there no-one she could trust? 'Who told you that?'

'Nancy Furbo.'

'God. I don't suppose it's any use asking who the hell you are?' Silence.

'Or what is your function in my life?'

'To care for you.'

'What do I call you? Don't say uncle or I'll scream.'

'Most people call me Malcolm,' he replied ambiguously.

'Smith, I suppose?'

He chuckled amiably. 'Well, yes, as it happens. Pathetic isn't it? But with a y, if you don't mind.' She could see he was enjoying himself. Juliet remained stony-faced.

'Smyth. Cross my heart.' She noticed that though his eyes twinkled, they never left her face. She did her best to keep her reactions to a minimum.

'Nancy was working for you as well?'

Malcolm Smyth with a y sat up. 'No, Juliet. Nancy was working for you. You were dreadfully ill. She loved you enough to give up her career to care for you. To protect you,' he said earnestly and she knew what he was holding back.

'Did you think they'd come after me?' she asked. He gave a slight nod of the head. The room was still. He watched her without blinking.

'Where did it happen?' she asked. He thought for a while before answering.

'A quiet street in a suburb of Dublin . . . Clontarf.' He spoke reluctantly, his face closed, the eyes expressionless. The room went deadly still.

'Ah.' Her mother had said they were going to Bewley's, which triggered Grafton Street. Which in

297

turn had triggered Dublin. Clontarf meant nothing to her, she would have to look it up on a map later. She hesitated, then asked quietly: 'When did he die?' Smyth sat up, obviously shocked, but to his credit he didn't miss a beat.

'Six weeks later. He never regained consciousness.'

'And me? When did I recover?' The following silence seemed interminable. He was not to know that a week ago all of this had been a blank.

'Physically? About four months. But your speech was gone and, of course, you'd lost your memory.'

'No. Not lost, unfortunately, just misplaced.'

They were like cat and mouse, the one watching the other, warily, mistrustful.

He sighed. 'You remember?'

'Some? Most of it? How can I tell how much I remember?'

'That is difficult.'

After some thought she told him the story she told Catullus. Smyth understood every nuance. He listened intently and, when she'd finished, replenished her glass. She guessed which question he would ask first, and he did.

'When did you recall seeing him on the television?'

'I don't know. A week ago maybe. After the mugging. It just gradually became clear.'

She looked at him steadily and told him the thing that haunted her.

'I told someone in my class. I didn't tell my mother. I told my best friend. I thought I had a best friend, but she betrayed me. She was the only one I told.'

'We wondered if . . . Can you remember her name?' he asked gently. He looked appalled. Juliet tried, then slowly shook her head.

'If you ever do, tell me. Please. It would confirm what we know.' Would, she thought, would, not might. The implications of that tiny, vital link were not lost on her. Confirmation was still important? After almost twenty years? Would it never end?

'It was my fault.'

'No.' He barked the word. 'No, no, no. That bloody conflict has been going on for thirty years, a hundred, three hundred, six hundred. Who knows any more? Your family was killed because people remember too much, hate for too long. They posture. Take up untenable positions. It has become as confused as a plate of spaghetti, impossible to unravel right from wrong. Listen to the politicians talk, for God's sake, they don't even understand each other and when they do they move the goalposts. Too many resentments, too much emotion, too much living in the past. Too many vested interests.' He stopped short, embarrassed by his own outburst, and for a whole minute they both remained silent.

'You were not to blame,' he said emphatically. 'You were not to blame. Your father was being watched.'

'I saw him on the television. I told her, I told that friend.'

'And you're afraid she inadvertently passed it on to her elders?'

'Yes, I'm afraid of that. Is that why Nancy brought me here?'

'Yes. She was originally from Oxford, as you know. She'd only lived in Dublin a few years.'

'She was a diplomat, wasn't she? She worked in the embassy.'

'A secretary,' he said, tight-lipped.

'You sure she wasn't one of your people?'

He held her gaze steadily. 'Absolutely not,' he protested. She didn't believe him.

'There was a family set-up and she was anxious to take care of you. She was the first to notice you were alive, first on the scene, and she never left your side. You would certainly have died without her help. She wasn't security, she was your neighbour. You do believe that, don't you?'

'She never said. But it wouldn't have mattered either way. Nancy was good, I loved her.' She drew in her breath. 'Would it have happened had I not told my schoolfriend?'

He shrugged. 'Who can tell? I guess they would have got him eventually. You weren't responsible. You were little. How could you know you couldn't trust another child? Tell me that?' He flushed and his voice became harder. 'He shouldn't have been allowed to expose his family like that. Don't be angry with yourself, my dear, save your anger for those who didn't take the threats seriously. Spying is a dangerous game. Seductive too.'

She could think of nothing in answer to that. Eventually she asked, 'Which side are you on?'

'Yours.' He sighed, closed his eyes wearily.

'Why?'

'I told you. Protection. You were whisked away. Nobody realized you'd survived. They thought you were dead. That was what was announced, that the entire family died that day.'

'And you've been my . . . er . . . minder ever since?'

'Yes,' he inclined his head. 'I am happy to have been of service.'

'Thank you. Not my uncle then? Not related.' It was a feeble attempt at levity and didn't work. For either of them.

'Not really, except by nationality.' He gave a bleak smile.

'Oh? I thought . . . You sound English,' she said bluntly.

'So do you, almost. I've been in London since I was eighteen. A long time.' Silence fell between them. They both looked grief-stricken, but separately. Into the silence through the open window came the song of birdsong and Juliet thought about choices and how seldom they are what is expected. How one decision can involve the entire lifetime of other people. What was a child's careless word to a schoolfellow compared to playing romantic roles in a vicious grown-up world?

'He played one side against the other, didn't he?'

Smyth hesitated. 'Probably. He always liked excitement.' He didn't hide the dislike in his voice.

'Did my mother know what he was doing?'

'I think she must have.' He looked stricken, and for the first time she fully comprehended that he was locked into that violence as much as she.

Ruled by it. Looking after someone else's child – maybe many children. Praying that when and if she remembered vital clues she wouldn't shout them to the wrong people and plunge them all back into the morass. She was overwhelmed with gratitude to him. And relief. He is trapped, she thought, but I can start again.

As if he'd been reading her mind, Smyth said, 'Dallimore tells me you have resigned. What are you going to do now?'

Juliet thought for a long time, then she went to him and awkwardly took his hand in hers. 'I'm going to Italy to learn to cook,' she said. 'I'm through with thinking. And the past.' She gave him a cracked smile. He stood up, and still holding her hand walked her to the door.

'I'll keep in touch,' she promised.

'Good. I would be grateful. Ours is a lifetime relationship,' he said as lightly as he could manage.

'Perhaps we could meet from time to time?'

'Perhaps,' he said, as he showed her out. 'Meantime, there's always the phone. We both seem to be, er, easier with that. For the time being, at least. Don't you think?'

She ran down the stairs into the sunshine, and crossed the quad to the lodge, half wishing that she hadn't ordered the car away. It was well after five and Cat was due to pick her up at seven. The interview had exhausted her and she was regretting that the ten-minute walk to the hotel was going to make heavy inroads into the time available for a long soak in a bath, when something happened to wipe all thoughts of Mr Smyth with a y clean out of her head. As she was hurrying through the gateway she collided with an elderly man coming in from the street.

'Oh, I'm sorry,' she apologized and had a fleeting impression of anxious blue eyes. But her momentum was such that she was already a few yards down Merton Street by the time it hit her. Those strange swimming blue eyes. 'Oh crumbs,' she cried, and sprinted back to the lodge, which of course was deserted. She hurriedly looked around both quads but there was nobody about. Had she dreamt him?

'Can you tell me who the man was who came in just now?' she asked the porter, who was watching her over the lodge desk. 'Elderly, blue eyes, with glasses. I think.'

'Sounds like Professor Forge,' he said.

'Could I go and see him?'

'I'll ask.' The porter picked up the phone. He held it to his ear for almost a full minute before he shrugged and put down the receiver. 'Sorry, he doesn't seem to be in his room.'

'Do you know where else I might find him?'

'Sorry Miss, the college is a big place. He could be anywhere. He hasn't been well, you know,' he added conversationally. 'Why not try tomorrow? Meantime if I see him, I'll tell him you were asking for him, shall I? What was the name?'

'*Is*,' she corrected absently. 'My name is Juliet Furbo. Will you tell him I'll call tomorrow?'

CHAPTER TWENTY-EIGHT

The curtains at the hotel bedroom windows were an altogether different variety from those in the guest-house. Being heavy they did not let in the light and so, next morning, it was well past eight when Juliet slowly surfaced to consciousness. She lay quietly for a few minutes trying to remember where she was or how she'd got there.

The dinner with Catullus had been a muted affair, and probably something of a mistake. Both of them were tired and neither would admit that five hours' sleep in twenty-four was not enough. After some deliberation they'd plumped for a Thai restaurant about five minutes from the hotel. The Chiang Mai Kitchen was situated down a narrow alley off the High, close to the crossing – from which, reflected Juliet, she seemed destined never to escape. This proximity to the crossing threw a sort of blight over the evening; the previous Tuesday's incident became almost their sole topic of conversation.

It had been one hell of a day and Juliet was in low spirits. She could hardly keep awake, not only because she was tired, but because she kept thinking of her earlier encounter – indeed both encounters – at Tradescant College. She couldn't quite get over the series of coincidences which had dogged her so persistently over the past week, as if the massacre of her family and the incident on the High were interwoven in some way. It had been only a week, yet there were moments when it seemed like eternity.

She debated so long as to whether to tell Catullus about the meeting with Smyth that she ended up not mentioning it at all. She found it hard to sort out her feelings about Smyth in her mind, or come to terms with the knowledge he had confirmed. She knew that she could only deal with it a little at a time, in her own way. To make sense of the tragedy for anyone else, she would have to clarify her own reactions and her part in it. But she found she could not do that, at least not in one fell swoop.

It was enough that she could begin to think of Smyth as a benign presence. She wondered what his name really was, but then decided that his way was right, better not to know. Smyth with a y he would remain. She couldn't help noticing how little she had asked him, getting him to confirm only those things she already knew or had worked out for herself. What really surprised her – and perhaps him? – was that she hadn't asked her own name, her birth name. Another blank. Someone had done quite a handy job on her personal documentation. He obviously assumed she remembered it, but the strange fact was, she didn't. *My name is Juliet Furbo. Born Oxford April 1969. Parent, Ann-Sophie Furbo etc etc.* What had Catullus said? Juliet Furbo is a brilliant name. It was. She had grasped that identity, and she had absolutely no intention of letting it go.

She had lied to Smyth about one thing. She wondered if he'd noticed? Italy had popped out as a spontaneous replacement for Ireland when he asked her plans. Was that because she knew he would try to dissuade her? Or that he had carried with him an almost tangible and unattractive image of her homeland? A poignant reminder of the violence, and, with it, her own secret fears. He was a subtle man, he didn't have to say a word. And, of course, once she said Italy she knew it was where she'd wanted to go all along but somehow couldn't give herself permission. Italy. Twenty years of *angst* was enough.

She laughed out loud. 'Do you know the Italian meaning of my name?' she asked.

Catullus looked startled but gamely played along. 'Juliet, you mean?'

'No, I mean Furbo.'

'You're Italian now, are you?' He looked sceptical but amused.

'No. Nor is the name as far as I know. Just it happens to have an Italian meaning. Not a very nice meaning either. Want to know what it is?'

'Can't wait.'

'Cunning. Sharp.'

Catullus looked at her dubiously. 'You trying to tell me something?'

'Not really, just that I've decided to go to Italy, in a couple of weeks.'

Catullus put down his fork. 'Come again?'

'I said I was going to Italy in a couple of weeks,' she repeated ponderously. 'When I get one or two things cleared up.'

306

'Oh? What have you to clear up?' he asked. So then, at last, she told him about sighting and identifying Professor Forge.

'He's a fellow of Tradescant, he may be resident there. I tried to find his home address in the phone book but he's not listed. So the college it will have to be. I thought I'd track him down tomorrow then maybe I can forget about all this.'

Cat hadn't said too much after that, except that he'd been offered an exhibition in Edinburgh, during the festival, in August. They left the restaurant around ten and strolled back to the hotel. 'We could try again tomorrow evening, if you like?' he asked, rather glumly, as they were saying goodnight. Her heart lifted. 'Yes,' she said. 'I *would* like that. Very much. I'm sorry I've been such a wet.'

'You look exhausted, Juliet, I shouldn't have dragged you out. Right then.' He sounded more cheerful. 'Have a long sleep and I'll see you tomorrow evening. Seven – seven thirty, at the hotel?'

She watched him saunter across the car park and then suddenly spin on his heel and come back to her.

'You have me confused. Is your name really Italian? I thought, after what you said last night, I thought you might be . . .'

'Irish?' She looked at him steadily but her heart was pounding. 'Yes, I am.' She swallowed. 'How did you know?'

'The girl in the bar at the Old Fire Station is from Dublin, you sound a little bit like her

307

from time to time. On some words.'

'Oh?' She looked terrified. Catullus took hold of her arm. 'Juliet? Juliet, it was only once, last night when you . . . when you were upset. It's OK, you can trust me. I promise.'

He held her close until she stopped shaking. 'Juliet? I have to ask you something. This is probably not the time or place but, are you free? I mean are you with anyone?'

Juliet stood back and ran her hand over her eyes. She gave him a weak smile. 'No, I told you. I just split up.'

'So you're not going to Italy with anyone?'

'No. What is all this?'

He stood facing her and held up his hand to stop her interrupting what he had to say. 'I'm not with anyone either. I just want you to know that. I have been, several times. But not for the past couple of years. My last relationship broke up then. We were together five years. Not married, no kids, so no commitments. I don't want you to go away without knowing that, Juliet. I don't know how to say this, but I think something important is happening . . .'

She stood on tiptoes and touched his face with hers. His skin felt cool and soothing.

'Cat, my life has been a total muddle for years. I think I need a bit of time on my own but I would miss you . . .'

'Would? Not will?' He gave her a broad smile. 'I'll work on that, Juliet. See you tomorrow.'

'Catullus,' she called. 'Thank you.'

'For what?'

'For . . . being? Goodnight.' *Goodnight sweet prince.*

Juliet watched him get into his car before she turned into the hotel and went upstairs. She couldn't even remember falling into bed, but had slept soundly. When she awoke it took a few minutes for her head to clear before she reached for the phone, ordered breakfast in her room and planned her day. The chance sighting of Forge the day before, and Sue's mention of the missing guest, had rekindled her sense of urgency about finding him and his companions. She knew, from the momentary glimpse of those harried, anxious eyes, that it wasn't only her own overexcited imagination that was at work. She was uneasy too that the bag lady hadn't reappeared.

The obvious place to look for her was the café, but since it was almost nine o'clock it was way too late to go in search of her there. First in first out at seven, every morning, Jack had said. Of course, now that she knew the whereabouts of her main protagonist, the old lady wasn't all that vital. Or was she? Juliet felt she was missing something until it struck her that Forge was also the name Jack had mentioned when he was talking to – what was he called? Fibich. They sounded like a music-hall act: Fibich and Forge. The porter had identified the man she'd seen as Professor Forge. So all three went to that café every morning. And could have been there together this very morning, while she slept. There was nothing for it but to seek him out and confront him. Not that it was going to be all that easy to bang on Forge's door and ask what he'd done with the guy lying on the road. She bit her lip and wondered if she should try to find the old woman and quiz her first.

About what? Juliet changed her mind and rechanged it several times while she dawdled over breakfast but, in the end, she decided to go first to Tradescant and see if Forge was to be found. If he wasn't there, she'd try to track the old woman. The waiter had mentioned that she was sometimes seen by the canal in Jericho or Osney.

It didn't occur to her that old Madeleine might pre-empt her, but that was precisely what happened. Juliet was just leaving the hotel when a tourist coach pulled up outside and disgorged fifty camera-laden Japanese tourists onto the pavement. Juliet was immediately engulfed and tempted to shout, 'Oi, you lot are supposed to be at the Miranda,' when, out of the corner of her eye, she caught a glimpse of the old bag lady slithering past *en route* to Magdalen Bridge. 'Excuse me,' Juliet called, trying to flag her down over a sea of bobbing heads. 'Excuse me. Wait.' But the woman continued unperturbed. She moved astonishingly quickly for one so elderly. By the time Juliet had struggled free and returned a few dozen apologetic bows to the sublimely polite Japanese, Madeleine was a couple of hundred yards down the street.

Here we go again, Juliet thought, and set off in pursuit. The chase went precisely as it had done on Monday. The woman first steamed ahead, then looked back, paused for Juliet to gain on her, then toddled away again. After the first delay it would have been very easy for Juliet to catch her up but she quickly divined that was not what that strange woman wanted. For someone without speech she made herself surprisingly clear. Follow me, but not too close, she seemed to say. Juliet obligingly slowed down and allowed herself to be led, and, like a child of Hamelin, followed her personal pied piper out of town.

At the Plain, Madeleine took the left-hand fork along St Clements and from there past London Place as far as Headington Hill where she entered the park. When they emerged at the top end, she went from one back lane to another, all the way up to the Radcliffe Hospital grounds, which they crossed. They eventually emerged on Osler Road in Old Headington, where Madeleine zigzagged across into a narrow alley leading to the Croft, an enclosed warren of rather rural lanes and alleyways off the main drag.

It was then that Juliet noticed a change come over the old woman. For the first time she stopped when she turned to check that Juliet was still with her. Juliet halted and remained standing a little way away, waiting for the woman to indicate what she wanted. But Madeleine just stood in silence, staring at her, as if she were straining to convey something. Strangely, for once, she didn't hum. She made no sound at all. They stood motionless about fifteen yards apart and Juliet saw that the woman's face was white, and rather beautiful. Then, with some surprise, she also saw that Madeleine wasn't nearly so old as she'd first thought. She was reminded of photographs of Virginia Woolf in middle age. The long grey woollen coat she wore was buttoned right up to the neck and there were beads of sweat on her forehead. 'What is it?' Juliet asked. 'I won't harm you, I promise. I just want to ask you a few questions.' The woman didn't answer.

The lane was deserted. On either side there was a high brick wall over which a profusion of shrubs formed a dense archway. As Juliet watched, Madeleine reached up and snapped off a long branch from which she pulled most of the leaves. She laid it on the ground and, with great deliberation, slowly unbuttoned the coat, took it off and dropped it on the ground at her feet. Underneath she was wearing a pale blue cotton dress, crisp, clean and in stark contrast to her tattered old laceless shoes.

Juliet was gobsmacked. 'But you *were* in the museum on Monday,' she gasped in amazement. 'You were walking around, but I didn't recognize you. And the little boy didn't either. Did you change in the loo?' she asked, but Madeleine just gave her a distant and fleeting smile and, with her eyes still holding Juliet's, slowly bent down and picked up the branch.

She straightened and, in slow motion, turned away. She held the long twig aloft in her right hand, and began to sing, wordlessly, la, la, la. As she walked forward, she raised her left and beckoned Juliet to follow.

Every few yards she looked back, smiling gaily, her gait no longer slatternly but young, almost sprightly. Childlike. At the end of the lane they took a right turn and, after a little while, came to the garden of a small detached house which looked as though it had been converted from an old chapel or barn. Madeleine stopped so suddenly that Juliet almost crashed into her. She stepped back hurriedly. Madeleine ceased her crazy la la-ing, reached out, grabbed Juliet's hand and shoved a piece of paper into it.

It was another of the pink betting slips. On one side was written *Félix*. Juliet turned it over to read what was written on the other side. This time it was unambiguous: Angel Remember ✝ June 1944.

She could talk. For now the woman began to sing the old French nursery rhyme which Juliet had learned at school. Different words, though. She repeated the lines over and over:

> *Cadet Rousselle ne mourra pas . . .*
> *ne mourra pas . . .*
> *Car avant de sauter le pas . . .*

Juliet strained to understand but couldn't make head nor tail of it. Cadet Rousselle cannot . . . will not die, that was easy enough. But *sauter le pas*? Cannot jump? Cannot *pass* over? No, it didn't make sense, must be an idiom. Leap? Jump? Jump for it . . . no, not quite. *Going for it. Making a decision*. To die? Could that be right? The words, along with the sentiments, seemed morbid for a child's rhyme, but then nursery rhymes often were pretty bloodthirsty. She turned her attention back to her companion, who kept singing as she pushed Juliet ahead of her through the gate and pointed at the front door. Then she stood still and stopped singing. She repeated this action several times: stopping and starting, then stopping to listen, her head cocked. Each time the singing became more strident, frantic, until to Juliet's horror they heard a dim echo of the song coming from inside the house.

A couple of seconds later Professor Forge opened the front door. He didn't seem in the very least surprised to see either of them. His face was grey and resigned.

'You'd better come in,' he said and stood back to let them pass.

CHAPTER TWENTY-NINE

A week can be eternity. For a week, Professor Paul Forge had been entertaining Nemesis – he couldn't quite think of a male version of the Goddess of Retribution. Though entertaining was hardly the word to describe the constant care necessitated by the frail health of his reluctant house guest.

At first, while feeling irritated by the imposition, Forge could not help being pleased with himself for so neatly turning the tables. The irony of the intended assassin – if only of Forge's professional reputation – being still *hors de combat* after a week was not lost on him. His guest appeared to be as inept at attempted murder as he was at character assassination.

This time there was no point in lying doggo. Even without opening his eyes Felix Hiller knew his host meant business. Paul Forge stalked into the room, dumped the tray on the end of the bed and practically threw a balloon glass at his patient.

'Drink that. You look half dead, it'll do you good,' he said gruffly. 'It's reasonable Scotch but I've put ice in it. Come on, sit up. I know perfectly well you're awake.' He waited until Hiller had struggled into a sitting position and opened his weeping eyes. The two men looked at each other, properly, for the first time. Forge was the first to break the silence.

'Well, you don't look much like a murderer, do you?' He waited, but Hiller said nothing. 'Come on. You owe me an explanation, I think.'

'What does a murderer look like?' Hiller's accent was overlaid with American, the consonants slurred. 'Vell?' he added ironically.

Forge shrugged but didn't answer. In the long minute's silence that followed a chill began to travel up through his body. He took a sip and held the fiery drink in his mouth, then let it trickle slowly down his throat.

'Rather like you, Professor Forge.' The voice was soft but Hiller's eyes were hard and unyielding.

'I don't know what you're talking about,' Forge said firmly enough but the ice tinkled against the glass in his shaking hand.

'Oh, I think you do.' There was no triumphalism, just resignation in the tired voice.

The atmosphere in the room became electric. The condemned man swallowed but said nothing as he played for time. So it had come to this, had it? After over fifty years of exemplary living, he was cornered in his own house? He'd heard correctly then, at the party. It wasn't the work that was at issue, but that ancient murder. Hiller was indeed his nemesis.

His colleagues and students had been outraged that the man should attack him during the presentation of the festschrift – the culmination of his life's work. Of course the students knew exactly who Felix Hiller was because he'd been spiking their guns for years, had, almost single-handedly, caused the near-closure of the research unit. They understood Hiller had some sort of grudge but didn't know what it was or at whom it was specifically directed.

Now they did. They mightn't fully understand for the moment, but eventually the penny would drop and then he, their admired professor, would be ostracized. War criminals elicited little sympathy.

The only saving grace was that Hiller's incoherence hadn't helped his case – he'd sounded and behaved like a madman – so it had been easy for Forge to shrug his shoulders and claim not to understand his accusations. But he had, of course, he'd made the great mistake of humiliating him publicly, by pointing out in front of everyone, fluently and coherently, chapter and verse, Hiller's transgressions against him personally and against his students.

Then amazingly, out of nowhere, Mowbray had suddenly popped up and taken a hand. He had surprisingly little trouble shutting Hiller up, specially when Hiller started using the glyceryl puffer. This meant he was suffering badly with angina, Forge knew, since he was troubled with cardio-vascular problems himself. He kept on talking until Hiller was forced, by his palpitating heart, or by Mowbray, to sit down before he keeled over. But the incident had been deeply upsetting and utterly destroyed the occasion for everyone else as well as Forge.

Then the surprise of Mowbray turning up in the café next morning. That series of strange little episodes had been unnerving. That damned woman tapping out her eternal Morse code, or whatever it was, had been more obstreperous than usual. Then suddenly Hiller was standing at the door, talking to Mowbray. Finally, as they came out of the café, Fibich, who had also been at the meeting the evening before, weighed in. Fortunately, he hadn't grasped the wartime connection which, considering his own history, was strange. He offered to go with Forge and confront Hiller about the plagiarism of his work. Forge closed his eyes with horror at the thought of what that survivor of the massacre of Lidice in 1942 would make of Hiller's story. The whole thing was horrendous.

Hiller drawing the knife had amazed him. He knew he was dangerously mad then. He should have walked away, left the bastard to rot when he cracked his head against the paving. At first he had done so but he'd looked back and seen Hiller move, and panicked. What if he talked? What if someone believed him? That bumbling policewoman couldn't have appeared at a worse moment. Forge knew there was little Hiller could do after so long, but oh, the public humiliation. The degradation of having that ghastly tale retold for public titillation. The squalor of watching his painfully constructed life crumble away. Surely he had suffered enough?

But something else troubled Paul Forge. He could not bring himself to think of it. But it wouldn't go away. It had haunted him for fifty-three long years before Hiller referred to it. Threw it in his face. That collective act of brutality and revenge. How much responsibility did he, not eighteen and one of the youngest of the perpetrators, actually bear? How could anyone connect him, a law-abiding, distinguished scholar, with a group of lumpen soldiers obeying orders? How could any one act be pinned on one individual? They'd been forced to round those people up. Was it too easy to say, 'There was no option but to obey'?

Forge sat down heavily at the end of the bed and looked at Hiller, who seemed to have grown in stature. For a long time they just sat, occupied with their own thoughts, until Forge said, 'I could have left you to die.'

'Yes, indeed you could.'

'Dr Hiller, will you please tell me what it is you think I did?'

'Murder. You committed murder. During the war. June . . . You killed a young girl. Angel.'

Forge closed his eyes and slowly expelled his breath. Was this the moment he had been waiting for, all his life? The moment of truth? 'So you were the boy up the tree,' he said, his expression a mixture of horror and disbelief. 'Dr Felix Hiller. Strange we should have ended up in the same discipline.' The rheumy, half-blind eyes stared into time. 'And all this while I thought you were only a professional rival. And a mean-minded, unscrupulous one at that. How stupid I am. How stupid we both are.'

'You knew I was there?' It was as if the present had completely faded from Hiller's mind. Only

319

that single day counted – for them both.

'Yes. We watched you for a long time. The squirrel gave you away. It would have been easy to shoot you. My companion wanted to bring you down. "Ping", he said. "I could get the little beggar with one little ping." I stopped him killing you.' He leaned forward earnestly. 'Hiller, believe me, the girl haunts me as well. She comes floating through my dreams in her billowing shirt. I thought at first she was a man, a boy, you see, because of her shirt.'

Felix Hiller cried out. 'No, oh no, don't say it! Don't say that. It was I who made her wear the shirt after she fell in the river. My father's shirt killed her.' Tears trickled down his parchment skin.

'No. I killed her. There had been so much killing the days before and the days after on the way north. We were still reeling from the blood bath at Tulle. I deserted a few days later, before we got to Falaise.' He leaned forward earnestly. 'My life has also been haunted by that terrible day. I am not a bad man. I was a youth, barely out of school when I was conscripted. Terrified, utterly terrified that if I didn't follow orders . . .'

'Not when you shot Angel. You were showing off then.'

'Hiller, I didn't kill the others, you know.'

'What others?'

'The two little girls. She was standing in the long grass with her back to us, shouting at them. They ran back across the bridge. I diverted my companion's attention to what I thought was the man – the boy – in the white shirt, while the children got away. Only it wasn't a man, was it? But she saved the younger children, if that's any consolation.'

'Fanny and Marie-Eulalie, Angel's little sister – she was so young, no more than seven or eight. A sweet little child. She sang that day.' Hiller closed his eyes and was silent.

'I thought I heard that song again,' Hiller said after a time. 'After all these years trying to remember it, and failing. I'd forgotten what it was and then I heard it while I slept, yesterday or the day before. "Cadet Rousselle." Such a silly little song.'

'Rousselle the redhead? I was a redhead in my youth.'

'Yes, I remember.'

'You know what date it was yesterday?' Paul whispered. Felix shook his head. 'I have lost all track of time, lying here.'

'It was June 10.' There was silence. Hiller opened his eyes. A tear trickled down his cheek. 'Fifty-three years,' he sighed, sounding amazed. 'For all that time, I used to think . . . I don't know what I used to think . . . War is a terrible thing. We were corrupted by violence. Both sides.' He gave a bitter little laugh. 'We have lived poisoned lives. I don't know what I feel any more. Don't even know who I am.'

'Nor I,' said Forge after a long silence. 'I've lived my life *en masquerade* so long I sometimes think I've forgotten. Like you, Hiller, but we're not alone. Ours is not the only war.'

'There's an Irishman in my college with whom I have a strange unspoken, underlying sympathy.

Strange, because he knows nothing of my true origins. Unspoken because even now, in my old age, I have not grown into the habit of trust. He is from Northern Ireland, though he calls it Ulster. No, he is not a die-hard. That would make his position much less interesting, more understandable. He is an intelligent cultured man to whom all discussion of religion is abhorrent. Once, in the midst of some brutal episode of the present troubles in his benighted country, one of our newer colleagues, trying to get a fix on his political position, foolishly asked his religion. Those of us less brave, who had speculated on this question for years, waited with some curiosity for his reply. He took his time, I recall, before turning to his interlocutor with his usual courtesy but with a distinctly wintry smile. "Do you know," he said, "that I have never once, in this college, heard any other Fellow asked that question."

'He tried but couldn't hide his repugnance. What he said then, intrigued me. Instead of admitting to his religion, he simply said his name and waited for a reaction. The other Fellow looked mystified but I shall never forget Boyce's reply. "Had I spoken my name in my home town, my inquisitor would know, or think he would know, not just my religion, had I one, but also my income, the part of town I lived in and precisely what attitudes I would strike on the twelfth of July. And he would be, quite possibly, wrong on every count. So I would ask you to contemplate a scenario where the most important political statement you can make is to tell your neighbour your

322

name." There was a moment of edgy silence, then Boyce added, "The answer is I have no religion."

'I think he actually meant he had many religions, for I've frequently seen him slip into Christ Church or New College chapel at evensong. Once I saw him scurry out of Blackfriars after Sunday mass. We share much, my troubled Irishman and I. Or rather, we have much in common did he but know it. I know his religion has not, in spite of what he says, determined his politics. In some ways he is lucky, he can choose. In Alsace, during the war, it simply hinged on my age. Had I been born a year or two later . . . I sometimes long to come clean. Talk to him. Explain myself.

'Oxford colleges are strange places in many ways, anachronistic in an age where institutions are not valued or, worse, looked upon with suspicion. We are all individuals these days, or else pretend to be. Mine, Tradescant, is a distinguished old place with a reputation, centuries old, for tolerance and free thinking. I use free rather than liberal because that word, these days, has a specific, and therefore a narrower, meaning. Too wishy-washy for my tastes. Not all the Fellows could be said to be tolerant, some are downright reactionary, but, sometimes, even those whose thinking you find unsympathetic can educate you out of complacency. There are scholars of many nationalities; it could be a microcosm of society.' He paused.

'You've been in Oxford all this time?' Hiller asked.

'Yes, forty-five years. It's a good place for displaced persons, you know. There are so many incomers, you don't stand out so easily. Maybe that's why I feel comfortable, I don't stand out. Sometimes it is easy to talk, to strike poses, to dazzle verbally while obfuscating. Never giving the slightest hint of the self. I am a chameleon, but I am not the only one. I switch my talk to suit those I sit next to and since, apart from the Master and the Senior Fellow, we have no fixed places, I can parade my meaningless conversational gymnastics according to my whim, or where I allow myself to be led by whomsoever is at either side. Strange how easy it is to be private, so publicly. One can conceal and almost forget, at least for long periods of time, shameful memories and pain.

'But there have been times when, under unusual stress, I have wanted to burst through the barriers of collusive silence. Once or twice, adrift in a pleasant miasma from too much excellent wine, I have toyed with the idea of standing up, beating the long board with my glass and commanding silence. I have dreamed of reaching my hand to those other *refusés* sitting around me. "*Achtung!*" I want to shout. "Listen, and I will tell you my story."

'So we live our lives in close proximity and share nothing. Just like you and I, Felix Hiller. We are both Alsatians, are we not? Born by fate to different sides in that terrible war. How old were you?'

'Almost sixteen.'

'Barely two years apart. You were lucky. So much in common, so little communion. When I hear those with no direct experience or knowledge or even feeling for things as they truly were, pontificate at length on matters that any one of us could elucidate, then I despair. Not of them but of us, who know the pain and the shame of violence at first hand. Know that war is not a glorious adventure. That its corruption takes hold and destroys not just the past but the future. Perhaps history teaches so few lessons because we, both as perpetrator and victim, will not explain that it does not end with an armistice, but continues to wriggle, like a cancerous worm, into the mind and the body for a lifetime.

'I'm not talking of mammoth evils, the self-evident ones, like the Holocaust. I think of forgotten atrocities which happened all around, in every town and every village. Scores being settled, horrid underhand little deals being done. Lidice, Tulle, Oradour. Enniskillen, My Lai, Srebrenica, Rwanda. My poor friend, Anton Fibich, saw his entire family massacred in Lidice. But the list is endless. Reprisal, repression, revenge, sectarian violence, punishment beatings, ethnic cleansing. It all comes down to the same thing in the end: small men forced to follow, and make possible, grandiose, evil, stupid ideas.'

Hiller had long since fallen asleep. Forge took the glass from his hand and went out to his lovely garden to think. He had just returned to the room when he heard the demented humming. The old woman was back. His blood ran cold. Now he knew the significance of the song, if not the singer. Hiller was sitting up in bed, gasping for breath.

'Who is she? Let her in,' he begged. 'Please, Paul, let her in.' It was the first time Hiller had used his name.

Paul Forge opened the door and stood aside to let the girl in. He recognized her immediately as the policewoman. She was on the High Street the previous week and was still on his trail the day before. For surely she was the girl with whom he'd collided on the way into college?

The woman followed hesitantly, eyes averted, all the time humming her dreadful, skittish dirge. Forge led them to his study. All three stood around the end of the couch, where Hiller lay quietly, watching.

'Who are you?' he asked softly.

The woman shuffled forward and knelt down beside the bed. She clasped his thin hand in both of hers and laid her head sideways on the bed-clothes, looking into his face. Then in a faint, high-pitched, childlike voice she said:

'Je m'appelle Marie-Eulalie.'

CHAPTER THIRTY

'So you needn't have worried?' Catullus asked.

'Probably not. Although Forge said there was a moment when he might have plunged the knife into Hiller's side. Perhaps he might? He says he certainly meant to, but it seems my intervention stopped him. I blundered in at the critical moment.' Juliet shrugged, as if she couldn't quite believe it was so. 'The knife was actually Hiller's, you know. Pathetic really, he hasn't the strength of a baby. Forge got it off him easily when Hiller lunged. Forge ran off but then panicked and went back to find Hiller unconscious. He managed to get rid of the first person who stopped to help. He had a pocket cell-phone and called a taxi but then I arrived. So whatever might have happened, didn't. That's something, isn't it? Poor old Hiller would have been very easy to kill, his heart was bad and he was already knocked out by the fall. But I'd seen Forge, I was in uniform and he was afraid I could identify him, so he couldn't do it.'

'But would he, do you think, had you not turned up?'

'I honestly don't think so. Not a chance. They're unlikely killers, either of them, poor old sods. And poor Marie-Eulalie. All three, destroyed by the same terrible event. They've been walking backwards most of their lives. Chasing their past.'

'No wonder you had sympathy with them. They were lucky it was you, Juliet.'

'I think we were all lucky, somehow. They helped me more than they know.'

'You mean this afternoon? In what way?'

Juliet considered a moment before she replied. 'No not just this afternoon. The incident itself – coming upon it like that triggered a whole plethora of memories, I don't quite know why. Maybe it was the combination of that and the blow on my head?' She fell silent. Catullus waited while she gathered her thoughts; a lifetime of concealment was hard to slough off.

'Something about the way Forge was crouching over Hiller. And the scent – one of them was wearing eau-de-Cologne, the real stuff. It has a very distinctive smell. I found that very disturbing. It took me a while to remember why. It's strange, isn't it, how things work out? I feel I've finally broken out of a strait-jacket.'

'In what way?' he asked.

'I couldn't have said so before, but today I saw what living in the past does to you. This week has been very extraordinary for me.'

'And for me. I wouldn't have met you,' he said softly. 'So I owe them as well, you can work me into the equation. I intend to hang around, you know. And come visit you in Italy, if you like?'

'I'd like. And I'll come back for Edinburgh, if *you* like.' They grinned at each other. Like idiots. She thought: I can't stop smiling at this heavenly man.

They were in the new, as yet unfurnished flat,

sitting on the floor, which was scattered with a couple of empty pizza cartons and one empty wine bottle. Catullus had just opened a second. Juliet could feel a soft glow of contentment radiating through her.

'Mmmm.' She sipped the wine. 'This is delicious. Where's it from?'

'It's a Rioja, Ardanza. I found it in Barcelona last year and brought a few bottles back with me – a couple of cases, to be exact. Good, isn't it? I meant to take you out to dinner, though. Not slum it here.'

'I prefer this.' And she did. It had been well past seven when she finally got back to the hotel. She'd phoned Catullus from Paul Forge's house before she left and had only just caught him as he set out to meet her. Initially, she suggested postponing their date until the following night, but had quickly fallen in with his suggestion that while she took a nap, he'd organize a takeaway. In fact she was too wound-up to sleep, so had settled for a long, drowsy soak in the bath. It was nearly nine when she dressed in a short blue cotton shift and sandals. She went downstairs to find Catullus sitting patiently in the lobby.

It was another warm evening. They strolled, arm in arm, through the town to his new flat. It was still unfurnished but he had set the picnic on a linen cloth in the middle of the living-room floor. Through the open windows they could hear the workmen clearing the stalls from the day's open market in the square below. Inside Miles was doing his stuff with occasional help from John

Coltrane. It seemed to Juliet as if her whole life, and more particularly the events of the past week, had led her step by step to that moment. A half-line from Wordsworth ran though her mind: *Bliss was it . . . to be alive . . .*

The day had been so strange. After she and Marie-Eulalie invaded Forge's house the professor excused himself and said he needed to call a friend. About fifty minutes afterwards Anton Fibich arrived like Red Riding Hood, with a basket of goodies covered by a sparkling white linen tea towel, and announced lunch. He was an extraordinarily kind man whose concern was, first and foremost, for his friend but quickly encompassed them all. His expansive nature was irresistible. He was also extremely practical. Felix – under Anton's influence, formality didn't stand a chance – was quizzed about his medication. Anton would take no nonsense about letting nature take its course, which had evidently become Felix's preference. It turned out that the pills in question and a glyceryl trinitrate puffer – apparently a life-saver – were all the time in Hiller's suit pocket. Once they'd been decanted into the unwilling patient, they let him sleep, with Marie-Eulalie sitting quietly in a chair beside him. She held on to his hand as if his life, and maybe her own, were dependent on it – or as if she could transmit her strength to live, by force of will.

The others went to the kitchen to eat. And to listen while the whole sad story poured out of Paul Forge. Juliet was amazed at how tolerant the two men were of her presence and how quickly they included her in their confidence. Paul Forge told them everything. The attempted murder of Hiller. Felix Hiller's accusation. Then he confessed to the ancient murder with more stoicism than emotion, and finally explained how poor demented Marie-Eulalie fitted into the story. When he'd finished, he turned to Juliet and held his arms out together in front of him, as if he expected her to snap handcuffs on his wrists. At first Juliet didn't quite understand, since she wasn't sure he'd recognized her as the policewoman from that morning. But he had, of course.

'You've come to arrest me, haven't you?'

'No, I have not.'

'Why not?'

'Well, for one thing, I'm not in the police force any more. But even if I were, I couldn't. Wouldn't.' She had her hand over his, and held on. She couldn't think of anything else to say. There was no need, Fibich said plenty in defence of his friend. They had, he told Juliet, much in common. He waggled his head like a perplexed lion and talked about the similarities of his experiences, as a child, in Lidice in 1942 when he had seen his father and uncles gratuitously mown down. 'We never talk about the war, my friend and I,' he told Juliet. 'But, my dear, we do not need. We have seen what we have seen. We understand, even if no-one else does. I was a child. Paul was a poor frightened boy.'

When Felix woke up, he was slightly better, though still weak. Anton took over again, coaxed him to eat before he talked, which was clearly the only thing he wanted to do. That and keep Marie-Eulalie close by his side. Sometime after three, the college bursar, Mowbray, showed up in response to a call from Anton, and it was he who finally persuaded Hiller to agree to go into hospital and have his heart checked. There was a further delay while all three men, speaking French, finally prevailed on Marie-Eulalie to go home. Surprisingly, the omniscient Mowbray knew where she lived and left with her and Hiller in the ambulance, promising to take her home later. By seven, Anton and Paul were alone in the house and Juliet was on her way back to the hotel.

'And that's about it,' Juliet finished.

'Not quite. How on earth did they all come to be in the café that morning?' Catullus asked. 'What was the connection?'

'Mowbray was the connection.'

'How come?'

'Another long story, I'm afraid. Have you time?'

'All the time there is, Juliet Furbo.'

'Both Paul and Felix were born in Alsace. Felix was evacuated to his grandparents in Vichy France for the war years, but seventeen-year-old Paul was conscripted early in 1944. They just happened to coincide in that one place on that one dreadful day. The village was razed. Felix thought all his companions were dead. But they weren't. Marie-Eulalie and Fanny survived and so did Roger, though he was killed in a skirmish a few weeks later. Fanny died a year later of pneumonia. Marie-Eulalie was sent to live with relatives in the Landes district, well away from the fighting, and to all intents and purposes dropped out of the picture.

'Felix ran away and met up with Roger whose Resistance pals protected him for the remainder of the war. Amongst them was the Englishman, Mowbray, then about twenty, who'd been parachuted into France in the run-up to D-Day.' She paused. 'They were all so incredibly young, weren't they?' she said thoughtfully.

'It was not until the Eighties that Felix Hiller happened to recognize Paul Forge as the soldier who had killed Angel. The odd thing was that they were both involved in medical research, though until about ten years ago in different fields, but still near enough to give Hiller a way into Paul's life. He became obsessed with the man. Stalked him, found out everything he could about him, then sidetracked his own career into Paul's precise field, the better to do him down. Paul didn't cop on for years. But when he did he was absolutely livid and, in turn, set out to undermine Felix's credibility. It all happened quite slowly, over a period of time. Forge, who had no idea of the wartime connection, simply thought that Hiller was a jealous, mean-minded sod. Out to do him down. For professional rather than personal reasons. The groves of Academe can be fairly cutthroat, as no doubt you know.

'When they finally met up in Oxford last week, Paul still thought that Hiller was solely motivated by professional jealousy, until the celebration of the festchrift when the light finally dawned and he realized that Felix Hiller really could destroy his life as well as his professional reputation.

'Meantime, other forces had come into play and were converging. Marie-Eulalie was equally marked by her sister's death. She, too, had been beavering away trying to find Angel's killer. She devoted her life to it, never married. She'd become a rather high-powered civil servant in Bordeaux and spent her spare time researching the survivors of the division which razed her village that day. And during her search she met Mowbray, who was still with British Intelligence at the time. She fell in love, or perhaps made him fall in love with her. Either way, they had an affair.

'Mowbray was married with a family in London, but he spent a lot of time in France, and more and more with her. Through him, she found out that Felix had survived the war though, critically, *not that he was still alive.* But it was he who led her directly to Forge. I can't imagine what convolutions brought Mowbray to the same college. Maybe someone had voiced disquiet about Forge's past? Wondered if he was quite what he seemed? Who knows? What is clear is that Mowbray inadvertently mentioned his name to Marie-Eulalie who had an encyclopedic knowledge of that whole army division. The name had been ticked off as deserted, presumed dead.

'When Mowbray became bursar of Tradescant, Marie-Eulalie threw up her job and followed him to Oxford where she got a part-time job teaching French at one of the crammers. He was not entirely overjoyed, it seems. But the affair continued spasmodically, and meantime she kept an eye on Forge. It's not at all clear what, if anything, she intended. However much of an instinct she had about the event, there was simply no way she could link him to Angel's murder. In desperation, it seems, she began to stalk him. Maybe it was her intention to drive him round the bend?

'Instead it was she who began to go dotty. If she did. Maybe it was a bit of an act? Mowbray says she was always quite eccentric – whatever that means. But that may be because he chucked her a year or so after she arrived in Oxford. He was annoyed with the way she hung around, specially as she became more strange – which he assumed was because of him. He didn't want the responsibility, it would have been more convenient for him if she'd disappeared back where she belonged. But Marie-Eulalie just ignored him and went her own way. He had ceased to be on her agenda.

'She was bloody amazing. As far as I can work out, she was a perfectly respectable teacher, living in a little terrace house in Osney and at the same time wandering around as part-time bag lady, using the Museum of Modern Art loo as her changing-room. She was very, very clever. Anthony obviously had no idea either and of course, when you think of it, it is the complete disguise, isn't it? Nobody ever really looks a mad person in the eye. And a bag lady is, to all intents and purposes, completely crazy.' She shook her head in disbelief. 'Amazing woman, she never let Forge far from her sight.'

'So what about the café then?'

'That morning, Mowbray's main concern was keeping the two men apart. After the débâcle the evening before, Mowbray got Hiller back to his hotel, the Eastgate by the way, another coincidence. Unfortunately, Mowbray had to go to an all-day meeting in London on Tuesday, but he dropped into the hotel on the way to the station to check that Hiller was OK and found he was out. Mowbray knew, it wasn't a secret, that Paul and Anton would be at the Madeleine for breakfast, and was afraid that Hiller might go there as well. So off he went to check it out. And for ten minutes or so everything was just as normal. Mowbray had his breakfast while Forge pretended nothing was wrong. They chatted for a bit, then Mowbray announced he was off to the station. That's when things began to go haywire.

'On the way out of the loo he looked down and saw his erstwhile lover playing mad and just when he was about to upbraid her, looked up and saw Hiller at the door. He thinks he may even have said his name in her hearing. Something like – "Oh hell, Felix Hiller – what's he up to?" So of course she saw, and recognized Felix. And saw the effect the sight of him had on Forge.

'Mowbray dashed over and headed Hiller off, persuaded him to go back to his hotel by promising to set up and referee a meeting between the two men next day. Meantime Marie-Eulalie legged it out of the café only to find Hiller had disappeared. So she took up her usual position on the market steps and waited for Forge to emerge so she could follow him.

Halfway down the High Street, Felix got angrier and angrier and eventually turned back to confront Paul. And meantime Paul was describing the confrontation of the previous evening to Anton – careful to avoid the wartime connection – and working himself into a fine old sweat. Felix and Paul fetched up at the crossing at the same time, facing each other on either side of the street and raring for a fight. And Fibich, by dashing off, gave them the opportunity. Silly old men. The rest you know.'

They were silent for a reflective moment.

'What's going to happen now?' Catullus asked. 'Who'll take care of Marie-Eulalie?'

Juliet laughed. 'I'm not sure it's a question of taking care. She was strange, but she was mostly *acting* daft. She's determined to stick by Hiller, won't leave his side. But the poor fellow probably won't survive long, he's really ill. So my bet would be on Forge. He seems a good man. He'll look after them.'

'You liked him best, didn't you?'

'Yes, I believe I did. There's something about him.' She thought for a moment. 'So sad, but I felt, somehow, he's accepted what he is, what he's done. It sounds trite, but he . . . I don't know, I can't explain . . . he does his best, I think. He's a good man.'

'Even though he is . . . was a murderer?'

'Even so. I'm not in a position to judge,' she said softly. Catullus cocked his head to one side, inviting an explanation.

'Tomorrow. I'll tell you all about myself tomorrow.' She smiled. 'And, if you'll let me, tomorrow and tomorrow and tomorrow . . .'

'Suits me,' he said, and laughed. After a moment he held out his hand to her. '. . . *let us live and love, My Juliet And care not for old men . . .*'

Juliet raised her eyebrows. 'Catullus?'

He grinned. 'The first – or minus first, if my great-great-grand-daddy was the first.'

The noise outside in the market square had long since stopped. The sky had darkened and the moon was coming up. Catullus cleared the floor and changed the CD. Piaf's raucous, plaintive voice filled the room, as always, singing of happiness in adversity. Juliet stood by the window and looked at the stars. An insect fluttered around her and landed softly on her face. Catullus stretched out and caught it in his cupped hands. 'What is it?' she asked. He peeped between his fingers, smiled up at her and slowly opened his hands. A beautiful blue moth lay on the palm of his hand, its wings spread. Juliet stretched out her finger to touch the open wings. 'Like velvet,' she said. Catullus quickly flicked over his hand and let the moth rest on the back of it, palest blue against the smooth brown skin. 'It matches your dress,' he said. He held his arm out of the window and they watched the moth flutter away. 'Will you dance with me, Juliet Furbo?' he asked. 'Yes,' she answered quietly. 'I will.'

Retrospective

CHAPTER THIRTY-ONE

In my dreams I walk through the village, as it was in my childhood. The people have not changed but, strangely, I am no longer a boy. I do not exactly see myself, I just know that I am grown-up because my eyes are at the same level as theirs. They are not talking to me as to a child but as an equal. I strain to hear what they say. They nod and smile and I pass on.

I hear the sound of the tramcar clattering past, the blacksmith hammering his anvil, the clip-clop of horses' hooves, the lowing of cattle from the open barns. There are bales of cloth stacked outside the haberdasher and tables outside the café by the church. A child walks home nibbling the crust of a new loaf he has just bought from the bakery. Behind him the baker stands at the door of his shop, a floury cap perched on his bald head, his hands in the pocket of his apron. The priest hurries past. Upstairs over one of the shops, a woman shakes her bedclothes out of the window. She wears a pink satin slip with cream-coloured lace at the hem and over her bosom.

There is a small queue outside the butcher. The men all wear hats – cloth caps, or berets. Some of the women are bare-headed, others have scarves tied under the chin in the fashion of the time and now only worn by the Queen of England. A young mother pushes a high, swaying baby carriage from which a child with a pink knitted bonnet peers out. A small boy walks alongside the carriage, beating a hoop with a stick. It is not really a hoop, but the bare wheel of a bicycle without a tyre or inner tube. The chrome spokes gleam in the sunshine as he rattles it along.

There is water rushing along the gutters by the side of the road, not from rain but from what is left over after the pavement, in front of the houses and shops, has been washed down by ardent housewives. An old woman is scrubbing her front doorstep. On the high double steps in front of the undertakers three or four children are playing. They march up either side of the triangulated stairway, meet at the top, clap their hands one against the other and then solemnly march down the opposite side. The door opens and a moustachioed face looks out; the children scatter. They skip down the path to the sweetshop and stand with their noses pressed against the window until they are shooed away from there as well. A beautiful young woman passes, the schoolteacher. She smiles at the children and throws them a couple of centimes. They stretch up their little hands to catch the coins which gleam in the sunshine. I think of butterflies.

A couple of dogs mating in the middle of the road are almost run down by the doctor's car. A milk cart and horse jingles past and a herd of cows are driven from a barn down towards the meadow on the far side of the church. There are people in every house, busy, smiling, chatting as they go about their business. The scene is timeless, unchanging. I move among them smiling too, here making a friendly remark, there passing the time of day, until it gradually bears in on me that they do not see me. I pass through them as if it were I, not they, who is the ghost.

✝

I went back, but only once. Or twice, if you count my pilgrimage to the cemetery, but that was many, many years later when I had learned to live with my memories. Then, I followed the distraught survivors as they slowly crossed the bridge and processed past the church. I spoke to no-one and kept my distance well behind the cortège, as it turned right into the straight avenue which led up to the graveyard gates. I always pictured the place in sunshine, but it was raining hard that day and it looked quite different. It was perhaps as well that the weather provided me with a safety-valve, for I could not have borne that melancholy place in sunlight.

I was there for the burial of a contemporary of my aunt who, alone of her friends, had survived to old age. My motive was unclear, even to myself. I suppose it was to pay respect to the woman who had remained within the shadow of that ruined place for fifty years, when I, a mere bystander, could not bear it for even a day. Her quiet courage was awesome, impossible to contemplate without humility.

It rained that day; serious cold, harsh rain. The force of the deluge mocked the flimsy, inadequate umbrellas, soaking those who held them aloft. It suddenly struck me that the mourners didn't care. Wet or dry, dead or alive, what did any of it matter? Their minds, like mine, were full of images of the past, of pain, of guilt, of innocence betrayed: their own and those they had lost. Perhaps they, and I too, hoped that the cold, abrasive rain would wash the memory away and soothe the pain. *Absolvo te.*

✝

My first, penitential, visit was much earlier, four or five years after the war ended. I was on my way north, to start my studies. Having avoided the place for so long I did not want to go, yet desperately wanted to lay my ghosts to rest and obliterate my turbulent memories. I did not succeed.

I arrived at dusk and alone. Then, there were no gates to keep nocturnal visitors away. There was no need; few ventured into that terrible place by dark. But I could not go by day. I did not want to share my grief, or face anyone who might ask me why I ran away. I came by stealth, carrying only a small bunch of bluebells and rosemary.

I approached the village indirectly, slowly, gathering my courage with each hesitant step. But at the last minute I funked and, rather than enter, I remained outside the boundaries and followed the low perimeter wall which encircled the village. I trailed my hand over the lichen-covered capping stones, marvelling that the wall alone had survived unscathed. It was exactly as I remembered and, as

I shut my eyes to the looming shadows of the ruined buildings behind, I made believe that I was back to more carefree days. Only then could I retrace our journey along the river-bank.

It was early in the summer and the river was in spate, the cold, pellucid water tumbling and rushing over the submerged rocks by the mill. I sat under an old apple tree and watched the bats swooping wildly overhead, until it grew dark. Though it was the same time of year, June, the air was chilly and my clothes too light. I pulled my jacket collar up around my chin and thrust my hands into my pockets. My flimsy shoes quickly let in the damp from the dewy grass, adding to my discomfort. This seemed right, somehow. Even then, I had begun to observe in myself a growing addiction to such penitential arrangements which, though ostensibly unconscious, ensured that enjoyment was always kept at bay. I was already set in a mood of joylessness. I pursued anonymity like my own, private, Holy Grail.

I came and went like a ghost. There was no-one left who knew me, even in the surrounding hamlets. My grandparents were dead, my aunt had moved to her invalid husband's family in Albi. War leaves victims in many guises.

I eventually cut away from the boundary wall and crossed the deserted lane to the river. When I found the lime tree, vestiges of the rope still clung to the branch from which it had once hung. I sat beneath it for a long time, gazing across the water, and time, while I tried to conjure my friends from the gloom. They were clearly in my mind but I could not restore them to my sight. Yet strangely, when I laid my head on the dewy grass and held my ear to the ground, I fancied I could hear their dancing footsteps. I closed my eyes and began to hum, trying then, as I've tried so often since, to recall the song that Marie-Eulalie sang that day. But it would not come.

As it grew darker, I retraced the girls' journey to the iron bridge, as I should have done that day. When I tried to find the old tobacco field where I'd seen the little ones hide, I could not recognize it in the darkness. The little embankment leading up to the bridge was muddy from recent rain and I found it difficult to keep my balance. I leaned against the iron balustrade at the centre of the bridge until I had enough courage to go on.

Each detail of that walk is etched in my memory. The disused tram tracks were still embedded in the dusty roadway. I would not have been surprised had a ghost tram come clattering by. I listened to the water rushing past the derelict mill until I could force my heavy feet, step by weary step, across the bridge.

I had planned to turn right and walk the other bank but after a moment's hesitation I changed my mind and took the road which sweeps around the ruined church and, at last, entered the deserted village. Strange to say, it looked larger than I remembered, the skeleton buildings seeming peculiarly majestic. The air was so still that the soft plod of my light shoes was plainly audible. There was no birdsong, no sound of any kind.

The silence wrapped itself around me like a shroud.

✝

My hair stands on end. I keep to the centre of the street but, even so, I am disturbed by the shadows cast by the dim moonlight on the blank windows. Some of the shops' signs are still legible. I hold my gaze upwards, until I muster enough courage to lower my eyes, inch by inch, down to the empty doorways. Behind those ruined walls I can sense – there are no words to describe what I feel – a profound presence of other lives continuing unobserved all around me. I am seized with terror that I may disturb those restless spirits. No, it is stranger than that, I fear somehow my memory of that calamitous day will condemn them to live through it all again. And die.

And die. I sink down on the dusty road and weep. Then I take off my shoes and socks and walk slowly on, my bare feet searching out those other, smaller footprints, as if – oh futile hope – I might quicken their steps once more.

I hadn't expected the artefacts: a rusted bicycle frame soldered to a wall; contorted iron bedsteads, the overhead cables still waiting for the tram; the burnt-out car at the corner of the market square. I come upon it so suddenly that I hear myself cry out, *forgive me*, as though I had crashed into the owner rather than the car. It must have been the doctor's car; most of the others had been hidden or stored for want of petrol during the war years. It is the car, more than anything, which wrenches the images from my mind and brings back my dream.

The terror and panic is all around me. I can almost smell it, feel the tension clutch my heart. I want to beat my breast and cry out: *mea culpa, mea culpa*. I close my eyes and see the village as it had been that Saturday morning, bustling with life. The eternal little boy flitting past, beating his old bicycle wheel along the pavement; the little girls on the triangular steps; the mother with her baby carriage. I see the carpenter, the innkeeper, the draper and all the other ghosts glide up and down, in and out of the shops and houses. It does not seem possible that they are no longer there when I open my eyes. But they have all gone. The town is silent as a tomb.

I turn away and stumble back the way I've come. I leave the church behind and make my way slowly to the spot where I last saw Angel. I could have found it in my sleep. I scatter the wilted flowers on the damp grass and lie down beside them. Deep in the earth I hear Marie-Eulalie sing, the childish treble turning the childish phrases into a dirge.

Cadet Rousselle ne mourra pas
Car avant de sauter le pas
On dit qu'il apprend l'ortographe,
Pour fair'lui-mêm' son épitaphe.

How strangely apt that I should recall those singular words now – Cadet Rousselle must learn to spell, in order to write his own epitaph. Was it a sign? For me? Is it that I must learn to forgive myself before my Angel can rest in peace?

Ah! ah! ah! Oui vraiment,
Cadet Rousselle est bon enfant.

I begin to hope, yet, when I get up to walk away, my ghosts come with me. They are with me still.

THE END

Acknowledgements

I would have found writing this book more difficult and a great deal less enjoyable without the courteous and generous companionship of my husband, John O'Connor, who shared this and many pilgrimages and on whom I relied for technical advice. Any mistakes I've made should be laid at my door, not his. I would also like to thank WPC Kathy West of the Thames Valley Police, Jean-Claude Faudot who searched out an appropriate version of *Cadet Rousselle*; my editor Francesca Liversidge and Gwen and Arthur Tanner for finding the cover illustration.

Finally, I have taken a few (necessary) liberties with the detailed geography of the High Street, Oxford which those familiar with the town will recognize. And though I mention a crane on the Lincoln College site, it was well gone by the time this book opens.